# AWAKENED

## THE POWER TRILOGY
## BOOK 1

A WORLD OF DREJON NOVEL

# DOT CAFFREY

*Awakened : The Power Trilogy Book 1*
Copyright © 2014 Dot Caffrey

This novel is an updated edition of Awakening Powers: The Trilogy of Power Book 1
Copyright © 2014 by Dot Caffrey

This story is a work of fiction. References to real people, events, establishments, organizations, or locales are intended only to provide a sense of authenticity and are used fictiously. All other characters, and all incidents and dialogue are drawn from the author's imagination and are not to be construed as real.

Cover design by eBook Launch
https://ebooklaunch.com

ISBN-13: 978-1-947392-32-8
First Printing: 2018

## Dedication

This book is dedicated to all my friends who endured reading the many rewrites of this novel and still wanted more – Linda Keim, Diane Wagner, Rhonda Morgan, Kristi Fojtik, Janet O'Neil, Amber Rosen and Zarra Van De Kreeke – and to the other friends and family who always encouraged me to get it done. And my sincerest gratitude goes out to my editors, Julianna Feher and Laura Taylor, whose help and encouragement has meant the world to me.

And, a big thanks to the staff and attendees of the SCWC (Southern California Writers Conference) for their unstoppable willingness to inform, educate and support upcoming writers. Thanks for adopting me into the family.

This novel would not be without all of you. Thank you.

# CHAPTER ONE

REGNARYN SHIVERED at the unexpected chill in the air. The brightness of the room told her it was much later than Mama normally let her sleep.

She quickly dressed, wondering if she should take the time to braid her long red hair. This was one of those moments when she wished she was not the only human in Reissem Grove. The others never needed to worry about such things.

Halfway down the sweeping staircase, the silence of the house assailed her. She ran through each room, calling out. No response. The house looked right, neat and tidy, just the way Mama liked it. But no one was there. She mindcalled to them, but heard only silence in response.

She ran outside. Still, no one there. Where could they be?

The Square!

Regnaryn raced down the trail and through the dense wood.

The sound of familiar voices as she neared the clearing made her so glad, she barely noticed the oddity of their presence.

She called to her mother.

No response.

She called to the rest of the family, then to the others.
How could they not hear nor see her?
She called again, raising her voice. Still, no one reacted.
Regnaryn mindspoke to everyone.
Nothing.

"At last, you are here," a strange voice boomed. "I have been waiting. Now, it can begin."

She looked around but did not see the owner of the strange voice.

Regnaryn heard a crackle and saw a flicker of flame. She watched in horror as it flared and spread toward the oblivious crowd.

She cried out. They did not respond. Only when the fire engulfed them did they react; not to her, but to the flames.

Their shrieks filled her ears. The stench of burning flesh, fur and feathers permeated the air. Her feet felt rooted like an old tree, and she could not move to help them. Regnaryn knew it would be just a matter of minutes before the fire consumed her, too.

Yet, as everyone around her was ablaze, she alone stood untouched.

*:You have caused this,:* the unknown voice said as it invaded her mind. *:If it were not for you, they would not be suffering. You are the cause of their pain and the horrific end they face.:*

Regnaryn stared, aghast, as the others burned. Tears streamed down her cheeks. Helpless, she closed her eyes.

"You horrible little thing, closing your eyes will not remove the sight from your mind. You say you are not at fault, yet, you alone stand unscathed. Explain how that is possible?"

She shook her head and sobbed, "I do not know. But how could I cause this? Why?"

"Because you are evil."

"I would never do this!" she screamed.

"Yet you have, but I can help you," the now velvety smooth voice said. "Give yourself, your power, to me. Allow me to purge you of this evil."

Regnaryn almost yielded, but something deep within stopped her. She fell to her knees.

"No!" she screamed over and over until the words no longer made a sound.

### 

"Regnaryn," a familiar voice said as a gentle hand stroked the teenager's shoulder. "Child, wake up, you are having a bad dream."

Regnaryn opened her eyes to see Trebeh's face, her large amber eyes and silky white mane untouched by the flames. Regnaryn bolted upright and threw her arms around the yekcal's neck. On any other occasion, Regnaryn, so close to adulthood, would not cling like a child to her mother. But after the horrific nightmare, she welcomed the comfort and safety of her mother's arms.

"Oh, Mama, it was horrible. The flames. Everyone was burning and... and..."

Regnaryn sobbed until she could no longer speak. Still, she held fast to the cat-like yekcal.

"There, there, child," Trebeh said.

"It was horrible, Mama. There was fire everywhere. Everyone was screaming. I tried to warn you, but no one heard me. And, that voice... that vicious voice saying I was to blame. Saying I was evil."

The girl looked into Trebeh's eyes. "Mama, it is not true, is it? I could never do such a horrible thing. Could I?"

"Dear one, you would never do anything to hurt anyone. It was a dream, just a bad dream," Trebeh purred softly, trying to calm Regnaryn's fear.

"But Mama, it was so real. I could feel the heat."

"Dreams are like that."

Trebeh continued to stroke Regnaryn's hair until the youngster calmed. Trebeh rose, walked across the room, picked up Regnaryn's robe and tossed it to her.

"Come downstairs. We have time for a cup of tea before the

3

others wake."

### 

Trebeh entered the kitchen and, with the slightest wave of her hand, created small candle-like flames in the two wall lamps. The light bounced off the large windows, the room immediately as bright as midday.

Trebeh motioned Regnaryn to sit. She poured two cups of tea from the always-full pitcher, then sat across from the massive wooden table and watched Regnaryn sip the cool sweet tea.

"Tell me more about your dream, child."

"It was so real, and that voice." She shuddered. "He was taunting me... accusing me... blaming me. He said he would help me if I gave him my power." She looked at Trebeh. "What was he talking about? I have no power."

Regnaryn's words immediately evoked a distant memory in Trebeh. The yekcal fought hard to hide the shock she felt. "I know it felt horrible, dear, but it was just a dream."

"You are right, Mama." Regnaryn set aside the empty cup. "But he was so real, so vicious, that I..." She stared into the darkness beyond the window for a few seconds, then shook her head. "I am too old to act so."

"Child, even grown men, great warriors, can be dropped to their knees by such things."

"Why would I have such a dream, Mama?"

Trebeh smiled. "Ah, if we only knew what causes us to dream the things we do."

### 

:*Ayirak, love, are you awake?*: Trebeh whispered to his mind.

It did not matter how quietly she called her mate, he always awakened to her voice. This time proved to be no exception. He reached for her only to find himself alone in the large featherbed.

:*Trebeh, where are you? Is something wrong?*:

:*I am in the kitchen with Regnaryn. She had a bad dream.*:

4

*:Is she alright? She has not done that in years, not since she recovered from the fever. Should I come down?:* He felt her considering his offer in her mind and quickly added, *:I certainly could use a cup of tea and a good morning kiss, since that is all I can expect in the kitchen with one of the children there.:*

*:Why you dirty old cat,:* she said, her voice reflecting the grin she dared not show Regnaryn.

He growled back a sound shared only between lovers. She fought to keep herself from laughing. *:I think it better if you do not bring the dream up unless she does.:*

*:I understand,:* Ayirak replied.

### 

"Your father is awake and coming down, child."

"Do not tell him about the dream, Mama," Regnaryn pleaded. "I do not want him to think I am acting like one of the littles."

"If that is your wish," Trebeh said.

Regnaryn nodded. She no sooner placed a cup of tea at her father's place at the table when Ayirak appeared, his massive frame nearly filling the doorway. He paused for a moment and then entered.

"So, what has you two up before the sun has even risen?" Neither answered. "Whatever it is, it must be important to pull you out of bed so early, my little sleepyhead."

He crossed the room and wrapped his arms around Trebeh's waist. She turned and kissed him on the cheek.

"You could have at least run a comb through that mop." Trebeh laughed and ran her long finely manicured fingers through his brown spotted mane, trying to tame the sleep-induced rumple.

"Ah, I would have, my dearest, but the thought of being away from you another moment far outweighed my desire for grooming."

Regnaryn and Trebeh laughed. Ayirak feigned a look of hurt.

They sat in idle conversation until the first glimmer of sunlight shone through the window. Trebeh sighed and pushed back her chair.

"It is time for this lovely quiet to come to an end. The others will be up and about shortly. Regnaryn, help me prepare breakfast."

"I believe that is my cue to leave," Ayirak said and stroked his fur-covered chin. "So, I will go upstairs to make myself more presentable as my lady previously requested."

He rose and strode from the room.

Trebeh smiled. "I think this may be the first time in your seventeen years you have been awake to help with the morning meal."

Regnaryn sheepishly nodded. "Um, I guess so, but I always help with the other meals."

"So you do, child, so you do."

Trebeh told her what needed to be done. Breakfast was ready just as the quiet was shattered by the sounds of voices and footsteps bounding down the stairs to the kitchen.

*So it begins,* Trebeh thought with just a hint of disappointment at the loss of the rare calm.

# CHAPTER TWO

AS THE LAST of the sun's rays dwindled over Hammarsh Keep, servants bustled around the dining hall, laying platters piled high with meats, vegetables, breads and other delicacies on the long tables in preparation for the annual banquet held to welcome spring. The gathering, begun generations ago when the stewardship of the land was awarded to the family, represented a tradition open to all regardless of social or political station. It was by far the most anticipated event in this part of the kingdom of Alexandrash.

Outside the castle, several servants appeared to light the torches. The awaiting crowd, many of whom had travelled great distances, quieted in anticipation. A few moments later, the massive doors opened. The Lord and Lady of the Keep, Emmaus and Prescia, appeared. The couple, clad simply, acknowledged their guests with a deep bow and a curtsy. A loud cheer sounded from the gathered guests.

Emmaus raised his hand. "Welcome, friends, we are honored by your presence. Please grace us further with your entry into our home."

With that, the Lord and Lady stepped to the side and the

crowd entered in a single file procession, each personally greeted by their hosts.

Once everyone was gathered in the Great Hall, Emmaus and Prescia entered and stood in front of the massive stained glass window at the far end of the room. The crowd fell silent as Emmaus signaled for the lamps on both sides of the window to be lighted.

The guests stood in awe of the window's beauty and splendor in the dancing lamplight. The unique window, renowned for its size, intricacy of detail and color, filled most of the Great Hall's back wall in width and height, and, though many had tried, it had never been duplicated.

The window depicted a scene of a tall black-haired man resplendently clad in silver, purple and green armor flanked by two creatures. On his left, a golden drageal, the rarest of the fabled feathered dragons; to his right, an unknown horse-like being with piercing blue eyes, antlers and silver hair that fell like knotted ropes to the ground. The scene inspired awe, even among those who saw it daily. It was said, when light – from sun or torch – hit upon it, the eyes of the window's inhabitants looked into your very soul and their gaze followed you about the hall.

### 

As the night's festivities turned from food to dance and other activities, Graeden, the nineteen-year-old son of the Keep's sovereigns, sought out his friends. He found them and several of his brothers eyeing a group of young ladies across the room. The girls, fully aware of the attention they commanded, pretended not to notice as they giggled and whispered among themselves.

"So, runt, which one will you bed this evening?" Gantell asked, leering at the girls. He emptied his flagon of brew and took the one from Graeden's hand.

Graeden hated when Gantell called him that, but, as always, ignored it. He looked again at the young women, not the only such group in the hall, twittering and posturing like a flock of chattering magpies.

8

He sighed. "I am not sure I want to bed any of them."

A look of amazement fell upon his friends' and siblings' faces. "What?" they all cried.

"You must be joking," Graeden's friend Kendeth said. "Every girl in the province is here. Surely at least one can meet even your high standards."

"They are all addle-brained ninnies whose only concern is how good they think they look."

"We are not looking to bed their brains, little brother," Danforth said as the rest of the boys laughed in agreement.

"In fact, the more addle-brained they are, the better I like them," Gantell added, almost belching out the last word.

"You would," Graeden said only half under his breath.

"But you must agree," Danforth said, "Gant has a point, though I am sure that was not his intent."

"I just think it would be nice to carry on an intelligent conversation with them," Graeden said.

More laughter erupted.

"Once we are caught in the marriage trap, with only one woman to bed, *then* we will talk to them," Gantell said. "Until that time, it is all about the pleasure of the lovemaking. Leave the chatter to the old people."

"I, for one, am far too young to be tied to one female's bed," Danforth said. With a twinkle in his eye, he added, "For more than one night, at least."

The group again broke into laughter.

"What has come over you, Grae?" Danforth asked, only partially curbing his laughter. "I have never known you to be so serious or unwilling to bed a fair or even not-so-fair maiden."

Graeden mulled over his brother's words as the banter among them continued. The more he thought about it, the odder it seemed. Danf was right. He rarely gave a second thought to bedding any one of a dozen girls. But lately, it was different. He could not explain it, it was just... something. A sensation. No. A voice, whispering and gnawing at the back of his mind, telling him there was something more, something different out there for him. Once again, as he had done in recent weeks, he dismissed it, though he still felt its niggle.

"You had best be careful, if the girls hear of this new attitude of yours," Danforth said, snapping Graeden back to the conversation at hand, "the good ones will run from you like the plague, and the others will be plotting to wed rather than bed you."

Gantell, downing yet another flagon, slurred, "It is not like you have a lot to offer, you know. After all, you are not very bright or good looking or..."

"Good at sports or hunting or..." another of the boys teased.

"Going to inherit Father's lands or title," Danforth chimed in.

"Or, according to my sister's friends, very good in bed," Kendeth added and burst into laughter.

"Are you sure that was not you they were describing, Kendeth? I have never had a complaint or a refusal, polite or otherwise, from any of my bedmates. You, on the other hand, cannot make the same claim," Graeden answered with a wry smile, trying to join in the spirit of the moment.

The group again broke into peals of laughter as the good-natured insults continued.

"You know, Graeden," Gantell said, "I do not see why any of the girls want to have anything at all to do with you. So, tell me what is it that makes you so damn popular?"

Before Graeden could answer, Matteus, the eldest of the brothers, spoke up. "Be serious, Gant, you know exactly what it is."

Gantell shook his head.

Matteus laughed. "Just look at him – dark gray eyes, charming smile and that long black hair. All he has to do is smile at a girl, and she is half-smitten. Once she sees that mane of his, well, she will follow him around like a puppy."

Matteus turned to Graeden, winked and, with a glint in his eye, added, "Just make sure you net yourself a good one before you lose those looks, little brother. Otherwise, you will be spending all the nights of your old age alone."

Graeden flashed his brother a look of gratitude. Matteus nodded slightly, steering the conversation to a different topic. After a bit, the young men dispersed to find fairer company to share the evening's merriment.

Soon enough, Graeden's physical desires overruled his earlier objections. He, like all of the other young men and women at the party, focused on finding a bedmate to bring the evening to a more intimate conclusion. Happily, he found himself with Jerrilyne, a girl whose beauty could take one's breath away; porcelain skin with just the slightest blush to her cheeks, the palest of yellow hair and dark purple eyes reminiscent of the finest sapphire.

On their way to one of the private rooms set aside for the couples, a very drunk Gantell confronted them. He seized Graeden by the shoulders and violently shook him. The night's drink had done nothing to weaken his vise-like grip. Graeden struggled to break free. The more he fought, the more Gantell's grasp tightened.

"Just how did this worthless creature get a beauty such as you to agree to share his bed?" Gantell leered at Jerrilyne. "He has nothing to offer, you know."

Jerrilyne, afraid any response would anger Gantell further, stood in silence. Graeden nodded for her to leave. She hesitated a moment and then motioned that she would meet him back at the Great Hall. Gantell, too absorbed in his diatribe, failed to notice her departure.

"I have come to a conclusion," Gantell said, his slurred voice becoming more vicious as he poked a finger into Graeden's chest. "You really do not have any worth. No worth whatsoever. I truly believe Father made a mistake by not drowning you at birth like the runt kitten you were. He wanted to. Not sure what stopped him. Oh, wait... I remember, it was Mother, she has such a soft spot for strays and runts. And even now, you still fit that bill. Yes, Father made a mistake by not getting rid of you," Gantell continued, laughing at his own humor.

That final straw prompted Graeden to wrench himself free. He punched Gantell square in the nose, quickly followed by a blow to the stomach, which succeeded in knocking the much larger man to the ground. Gantell sat, shocked to find himself on the floor.

"I *am* worth something, damn it. And I will prove it!" Graeden shouted.

Gantell howled with laughter as his younger brother stormed off.

Graeden, so angry at himself for allowing his brother to affect him, could barely see. The thought of the waiting Jerrilyne cooled his anger, if not his blood.

On his way to the Great Hall, Graeden heard Jerrilynne's voice in one of the side rooms. He immediately knew she was not alone. He stopped and listened just long enough to realize she was with Kendeth, and conversation was not the only thing they were engaged in. Rage welled inside of him.

*That is it, I will show them all that I have worth*, he angrily thought as he raced toward the stairs that led to his room. *And that I am more than just eyes and a smile!*

Graeden ran into his twin sister, Taaryn, halfway up the stairwell.

"Where are you going in such a rush?" she asked.

"What do you care? What does anyone here care?" he shouted.

"Whoa, just a minute, Grae. I asked you a simple question."

Graeden glared at her, but he did not answer.

"What is wrong with you?"

Graeden grumbled something under his breath. He tried to push past her, but she grabbed him by the shoulders and shook him.

He pulled free. "First Gantell and now you. Just leave me alone, all of you."

"Is that what this is about? Something Gant did?"

Graeden did not answer.

"Come on, Grae, you know what he is like. One too many brews, and he turns from a pussycat into an insensitive lout. What was it this time?"

Graeden related the conversation after dinner and the most recent event. She listened without comment until he finished.

"Is that all?" she asked.

"All? How much more do you want? Maybe he should have killed me?"

Taaryn shook her head. "Now you are being dramatic."

"I am not. You did not hear him."

"Oh, please! Stop acting like a child. You are not the only one who has been on the receiving end of one of his tirades. Tomorrow, he will not remember half of what he said, and what he does remember, he will be sorry for."

A part of Graeden wanted to agree with Taaryn, but, he felt too angry. Angry and hurt.

"I am tired of his abuse and so-called apologies. You... you just do not understand!" he shouted. "You are just like him, all of you are."

"What? Fine, think what you want." She stormed off.

Graeden watched her leave. *How could she say that to me? And take Gantell's side! She of all people should know him, know me.*

He raced to his room, crammed some things into a bag and headed down the back stairwell that led to the kitchen. He grabbed a few supplies from the pantry and ran out the door. In the stable, he quickly saddled his mare. He wanted to get away from this place without running into anyone else.

### 

For probably the thousandth time in the last three days, Graeden chided himself for his silly pride. As soon as he departed the Keep, the cool night air, followed by the first gleams of sunrise, made him realize the foolishness of his actions. He had behaved like a spoiled child running away from home, yet he could not bring himself to turn around.

He knew Gantell's hurtful words were the result of drink, not malice, but a part of Graeden believed them. He had always thought of himself as worthless in the deepest reaches of his soul.

"Merlona, do you have any idea where my head was when I dragged you from your warm, comfortable stable to travel to who knows where?" he asked the butter-colored mare.

She turned her head and, as expected, had no answer.

"No, I did not think so and even if you did, you are too much of a lady to tell me."

So here he sat after three days on the road — in the middle of nowhere.

# CHAPTER THREE

THE CHILDREN bounded into the kitchen, shattering the calm. The youngest, twins Norellan and Katalanar, their yellow and white kitten fuzz so alike no one outside the family could tell them apart, argued over whose doll was best. Their sister, Nelluc, reminded them, yet again, that the dolls were identical. The twins never believed Nelluc, no matter how often they were told. The goading of older brothers Ennales and Neshya only escalated the quarrel.

"Mama, tell them." Nelluc threw her hands in the air and shook her head in surrender, her short-cropped black and white fur bouncing.

"Ignore them. You and Regnaryn acted the same at their age," Trebeh replied with the patience and calm only a mother could exhibit.

"Yeah, and you never listened to what we told you," Neshya chimed in as he entered the kitchen. "Hold on. Is that Regg? In the kitchen? For breakfast?" He rubbed his eyes to make sure he was not still dreaming. He turned to his younger sister. "What are you doing up so early? Normally, we have to drag you kicking and screaming to get up before midday, never mind joining us for breakfast."

He playfully pulled at Regnaryn's hair. She grabbed for his fluffy grey ear. He laughed and leapt out of reach.

"And when you do, you are too grumpy to be around," Ennales said.

"And sulk the rest of the day," Neshya added.

"Enough," Trebeh said. "Breakfast is ready. Now, where is your father? Neshya, go see what is taking him so long."

The words had no sooner left her lips when Ayirak entered the room.

"Looking for me, love?" he asked.

Ayirak walked to the stove as Trebeh placed the last of the meat on the large platter. She turned and wrapped her arms around his neck. He leaned over to kiss her upturned face. "I knew you could not bear to be without me for more than a few minutes."

She laughed, and he kissed her again.

"I am hungry, Mama," Katalanar whined.

Ayirak shrugged and walked around the table, kissing the top of each child's head before settling himself in his chair. Trebeh turned to lift one of the heavily laden platters.

"Why are none of you helping your mother?" he asked. The children immediately jumped to their feet. He motioned to Trebeh. "Love, come and sit down. You have done enough. Let the children serve."

Trebeh sat beside him as the boys carried the platters of gooey honey cakes and meat to the table. The girls served the twins milk and porridge before they poured tea for the others. Then, all sat and the chatter began anew.

After the meal, Trebeh and Ayirak settled into the sunroom while the children proceeded to clean up after the morning meal.

:*What do you think of Regnaryn's dream?*: Ayirak asked.

Trebeh shook her head, :*It could be just a simple nightmare.*:

:*It is not like her to have bad dreams, not since....*: Ayirak winced. Even thinking the words proved painful.

:*After the sickness. That is true. Yet, this dream seems to be very*

16

*different. It brought up her power.:*

Ayirak's expression changed. *:You do not think it has something to do with Karaleena's prediction, do you?:* He looked at her. *:You do!:*

*:I am not sure,:* she replied surprised he recalled Regnaryn's mother's words from so long ago. *:But there is just something about this dream, something... Perhaps I should talk to Phrynia.:*

*:Yes, that sounds like a good idea.:*

The noise from the kitchen filtered into the sunroom as the children argued over nothing and everything. Neshya, true to form, played his younger sister against his older brother, and he enjoyed every moment of it.

"Can they do nothing but argue?"

Trebeh smiled and shook her head. The teasing voices trailed off as the children left the kitchen to tend to the rest of their chores.

"What are your plans for the day?" she asked.

"There have been reports the latest storms caused damage around the Grove, especially to those whose homes are not as sturdy as ours or as sheltered as the drageals'. Now that most of the snow has melted, we need to see the extent and determine what can be done to fix it."

"If we suffered damage, I pity those outside Reissem Grove's protection," she said.

Ayirak nodded his agreement.

"Do Vilera and the other weather mages think the worst of the winter is over?" Trebeh asked. "That would be such a relief."

He shrugged.

"They gave no prediction at all?"

"The best they would say was that spring would arrive in a few weeks. What kind of prediction is that? Even I know spring will arrive within a few weeks. As for the weather until then, you know how vague they are. Never a direct answer, almost as cryptic as you seers."

Trebeh saw the playful glint in his eyes. She smiled.

"You know, my dear, it is not always that the predictions are vague, but rather those hearing them...Oh, how should I say this to be polite? Some are of a mind so enshrouded by the mundane they fail to grasp the deeper meaning of the words."

"Ha! See, that is exactly what I mean. You never come out and say anything to the point. Lots of words with little substance when you actually analyze them!" He grinned.

Trebeh smiled coyly and let the discussion, ongoing for more years than she wished to admit, drop.

Ayirak walked to the floor-to-ceiling windows and looked off into the garden. Save the occasional patch of snow still on the ground, the bright sunlight and the warmth of the sunroom almost made him forget the chill he knew still filled the morning air.

"It looks to be a beautiful day," Trebeh said. "I hope it will be a bit warmer. The children really need to go outside."

He returned to the couch and sat beside her. "The children will not mind a bit of a chill in the air."

"True. It certainly would be nice to have some time to myself after having them cooped up inside almost every day this winter."

"Well, that is a first," Ayirak said. "You putting yourself ahead of the children! Will wonders ever cease?"

She hit him over the head with a pillow. He grabbed her and tickled her sides until she could barely breathe. He pulled her close and kissed her. She purred, wrapping her arms around him.

"As always, you two seem unable to keep your hands off each other," a deep voice said from the garden doorway. "One would think, after all these years and at your age, well..."

"The better to keep you in nieces and nephews, brother," Ayirak answered. He kissed Trebeh once more and released her from his embrace.

"You are out and about early, old man," Trebeh said with loving sarcasm. "To what do we owe the honor of your company? "

Jombah ran his large hand through his sleek black and gray mane then wagged his finger at her. "I am not sure how long you two have been, well, doing whatever it was you were doing..." He waved his hand in the air. "...but it is not all that early."

Trebeh wrapped her fingers around the now cold cup and realized it had been quite some time since they had finished their morning meal. In the distance, she heard the children's muffled voices.

"And now, my fair lady, I must take him away from you for it is nearly time for us to meet the others."

Before Ayirak or Trebeh could answer, Jombah was overrun by children. The twins wrapped themselves around his massive legs. Neshya and Ennales jumped on his back, and Nelluc hugged him around the middle.

He laughed. "Hold on, kitlings, you will kill this old man if you are not careful."

"Well, he got the old right, eh, Enn?" Neshya said.

Jombah reached around and swatted his head, the gray kitling tumbled to the floor as if mortally wounded.

"Enough, children," Trebeh broke in, "leave your uncle alone."

The older children immediately obeyed, but the twins still clung to him. He reached down and picked them up in one arm, and they snuggled into his chest.

"Where is Regnaryn?" Trebeh asked.

"She left, Mama," Ennales answered, "nearly knocked me down she was in such a rush."

Before Trebeh could ask more, Neshya chimed in, "Up before breakfast; out before midday; she sure is acting strangely. Wonder what has gotten into her."

Jombah saw the look on Trebeh's face before she masked it.

:*You look concerned, sister. It is not unusual for Regnaryn to go off on her own, is it?*:

Trebeh was momentarily taken aback by Jombah's question.

:*What do you mean?*:

:*I have known you a very long time, Trebeh, since you were a mere kitling yourself, and have watched you through good and bad times. You cannot hide your feelings from me,*: he said with a chuckle.

*:It is nothing, I am just worried that she did not dress warmly enough. You know how children are at the first hint of warm weather. Regnaryn is so susceptible to a chill.:*

Jombah nodded. He sensed something else was on her mind, but could see she did not intend to discuss it. He thought of asking Ayirak, but noted his brother showed no similar concern. Whatever troubled Trebeh was likely unknown to Ayirak.

"Well, we need to be off," Ayirak said as he tousled the twin's hair.

"Papa, you messed my hair," Norellan pouted.

"Oh, I am so sorry, child," he said.

He kissed Trebeh on the cheek, and the two men left the house.

# CHAPTER FOUR

REGNARYN RAN into Ennales, literally, as she tried to slip unnoticed from the house. No matter, he would not follow. She hurried down the path.

She paused to look at the barren ground and the last remnants of winter – bare trees intermingled with ones that never lost their color and the few patches of scrawny winter grass along both sides of the foot worn path. An explosion of color and life would soon engulf the Grove, but today her thoughts were far from the approaching spring.

She walked slowly, unsure where to go. She knew to avoid the path that led to the ferret-like chetoga's dwellings. She was in no mood for their overly cheerful chatter.

No, this morning she needed to be alone, in silence. She needed to think. To reflect. No matter what Mama said, Regnaryn knew what she had experienced was more than a nightmare. Mama did, too.

"What could put you so deep in thought that you do not even see me standing here, little sister?" Immic asked as Regnaryn ran into the wall of pale purple feathers that was the young drageal. He caught her shoulder in his massive foreclaws to keep her from falling backward. "Or have I become so commonplace that I am now invisible to your eyes?" he teased, despite her uncommonly somber look.

She smiled weakly, steadying herself in the feathered dragon's gentle grasp. "You invisible? As if that were possible."

She hoped her flippant response would end his prying. She should have known better.

"Hmm, that may be true, but you still have not told me what had you so enthralled."

She stepped back. "Oh, you know me, Imm, my mind is rarely in the same place I am."

"But what if I had been a beast hunting its dinner?"

She snickered. "And when was the last time you saw such a thing within the Grove?"

Both knew no creature intent on doing harm had ever been within the confines of Reissem Grove.

"Why are you here? Are you following me?"

Surprised by her questions and tone, he did not respond.

"I guess all the females have finally found you out and will have no more to do with you and your vanity." She tried to sound playful.

"I am offended." He lowered his head into the massive wing that now wrapped around the front of his body. The glint in his eye made Regnaryn smile.

"Silly drageal," she replied.

He raised his head and opened his wings, beckoning her closer. She took a step forward. In an instant, she surrendered to the soothing cocoon of feathers. She purred softly as his comforting embrace momentarily drained the troubles from her mind. Her reaction did not escape the young drageal, and he silently held her for a few moments.

"Tell me what weighs so heavily on your mind that you pay no heed to your steps," he urged.

"So, you have been spying on me," she snapped. "Is there

nowhere in this place that I can be alone without someone watching me?"

Immic was taken aback by her sharp response. They had been the best of friends for as long as he could remember, and he had never seen her act so. Even as a young child when she struggled to keep up with the others – bigger, stronger and faster than she – and could not, she never reacted with ire or exasperation.

"Hold on," he said, trying a different tactic. "You ran into me as if I was not even there. And, if I were going to spy on anyone, especially a female, it certainly would not be you, little sister. Gads, you cannot even fly!"

The playful tone of his voice broke her mood. She smiled faintly, but said nothing.

"Regg, is there something you want to talk about?"

She shook her head, studied her feet for several moments, then softly said, "No."

"If you change your mind, I am always here for you." He waited a moment. "Now, you had better get yourself home, it is far too cold for you to be out with no cloak since you have neither feather nor fur to warm you. Look, you are shivering."

At that moment Regnaryn felt the cold and shivered. She nodded. Immic took a few steps back and gently lifted off the ground, only the slightest air disturbance in his wake. He ascended, noting she had not moved.

"Get going, Regg. What are you waiting for? If you catch your death, both my mother and yours will blame me."

She turned, briefly thought of staying, but knew Immic would not leave until she did. She took off at a fast pace, arriving at home within a few moments.

### 

Trebeh thought about Regnaryn's dream as she tidied the house. She tried to convince herself it was merely a simple nightmare, yet the reference to power still concerned her. Regnaryn had never been told of Karaleena's vision, and Trebeh had nearly forgotten it herself.

She mindcalled to Phrynia.

*:Good day.:* Phrynia said and quickly added, *:You sound distressed. Is something wrong with one of the children?:*

Trebeh smiled. *:Ah, I can keep nothing from you, can I?:*

*:We have known each other far too long to not feel tension in the other's voice, even in a mindcall.:*

*:How true.:* Trebeh chuckled, then took a steadying breath. *:Regnaryn had a bad dream last night.:*

*:Hmm, she has not done that for many years.:*

*:This was different.:*

*:Is that what concerns you?:*

Trebeh relayed the details of the dream.

At the mention of power, Phrynia interrupted. *:Karaleena's prediction!:*

*:I hoped you would not say that or, at least, tell me I was being silly. I had almost forgotten about it.:*

*:That is the mother in you. Regnaryn may not be your natural child, but you have raised her as if she were since Karaleena and Grenwald's tragic deaths.:*

The mention of Regnaryn's long deceased parents still generated a sense of loss in both women even these thirteen years later.

Trebeh replied. *:It was not difficult. She has always been such a sweet child.:*

*:A sweet child that may possess more power than any of us can imagine.:*

*:You really do not think...:*

Phrynia shook her head. *:She is well on her way to womanhood, and that could be the impetus for the powers of Karaleena's prophecy to awaken.:*

*:But the prophecy is not certain. I do not recall all the details, but there was more to Karaleena's vision and...:*

Trebeh could almost feel Phrynia shaking her head.

*:Yes, if memory serves, there will be another of her kind who will stand by her side,:* the drageal said.

*:Yes, and that has not come to pass. She is the only human here.:*

*:True.:*

*:And she has demonstrated no special abilities,:* Trebeh added.

*:Except animal speech.:*

*:But that does not indicate power. It is just a talent,:* Trebeh replied defensively.

*:Perhaps.:*

Trebeh did not answer.

*:When will you tell her of the prophecy?:* Phrynia asked.

That question had been circling Trebeh's mind all morning, but she was doing her best to ignore it. *:Not just yet. I see no reason to concern her with something that may not come to pass, especially if this was nothing more than a child's nightmare.:*

Phrynia did not press. There was, after all, a hint of truth in Trebeh's words. Until more of the pieces of the puzzle fell into place, there was no reason to mention any of it to Regnaryn.

### 

Trebeh had just poured herself a cup of hot tea when she heard the front door open. She walked to the kitchen doorway as a shivering Regnaryn quietly entered the house.

"Where have you been?"

Regnaryn stopped and looked at her mother. She had hoped to slip in without being noticed.

"And without a cloak, you will catch your death," Trebeh said. "You are shivering and your lips are nearly blue."

Regnaryn rolled her eyes, certain Trebeh exaggerated.

"Sit by the fire, and I will bring something to warm you."

Trebeh turned back into the kitchen. Regnaryn knew better than to argue. She settled on a large pillow by the fire. Trebeh came in and handed Regnaryn the cup of hot tea. She grabbed a heavy throw from the chair and wrapped it around the girl's shoulders.

"You spoke to Phrynia about the dream."

Trebeh let out a single nervous cough. "Why do you say that?"

"I can see it in your eyes. You have questions about it, so naturally you would ask Phrynia's opinion."

Trebeh did not respond.

Regnaryn turned back to the fire. "I know I am right. What are you keeping from me?"

Trebeh thought for a moment. She was still not convinced the dream had anything to do with Karaleena's vision, so no good would come of telling Regnaryn of it.

"Yes, I am a bit concerned," Trebeh began. "You probably do not remember, you were so very young, but there was a time when you had nightmares almost every night."

Regnaryn gave her a blank look. "I did?"

"Yes, just after you recovered from the illness that took the other humans from us. Every night, you would wake up screaming from a nightmare you could not put into words. I guess I was concerned that..."

Regnaryn turned to Trebeh as the yekcal wiped a tear from her eye. Regnaryn pulled the blanket tighter around her. She did not remember those dreams, and this was the first time she recalled anyone speaking of them. Her curiosity roused, she could tell by the look on Trebeh's face, this was not the time to ask about them.

"I tried looking into your future. I hoped to see more of this dream's meaning," Trebeh continued, "but I saw only mist and shadow. I thought Phrynia might be able to see something I could not."

"Did she?"

Trebeh shook her head.

# CHAPTER FIVE

NOW, FIVE DAYS after running away from home like a petulant child, Graeden finally admitted it was not his brother's drunken rantings that kept him from returning, rather it was his own self doubt. His fear that Gantell's words were indeed true. So, here he stubbornly sat, uncomfortable and aching, looking for a way to prove something that no one else cared about.

He ate and tried not to think of his mother, likely the only one who might notice his absence. Graeden had sent a message on the first day, but knew that would not stop her worrying. He needed to find a village to replenish his supplies, so he resolved to send another note from there.

As he brushed the crumbs from his shirt, Graeden suddenly experienced a strange sensation. Now, along with the familiar muffled voice constantly mumbling in the back of his brain, he felt a strange tickling, no more of a tingling feeling, as if icy fingers were running down his spine.

He tried to ignore it as he cleaned up and packed his belongings onto the horse. The voice returned, more persistent than before. He continued to ignore it. This time, it refused to be ignored. It became so loud, Graeden felt sure someone, some woman, stood nearby yelling at him.

He spun around looking for the one making the horrid sounds, but all he could see were trees and his mare — no one else was there. The voice cried out again. Louder. More shrill. Graeden instinctively put his hands over his ears, but that did not muffle the shrieks. They lived inside his mind. His head felt like it would explode. He lowered his hands. Once again, the voice fell silent. He stood terrified. Had he gone mad?

Graeden tilted his head, tapping it against the palm of his hand – as if the voice was water in his ears after too much time spent swimming in the pond. He waited. The voice did not return.

He sighed with relief and mounted the mare. He pulled the reins to the west, but the normally obedient horse refused to move. He dug his heels into her sides several times. No response. Graeden dismounted and pulled the reins again. She stared at him, but did not move.

He turned to walk away. Suddenly dropping to his knees, he struggled for breath as if punched in the stomach by someone even stronger than Gantell. The voice returned. Loud. Demanding. It refused to be ignored. He surrendered. Listened.

The voice, calm, soothing, and clear, told him to travel northeast. He nodded. The air returned to his lungs.

He rolled onto his back, motionless save for the heaving of his chest with each welcome inhalation. "What in all that is holy was that?" he cried.

He slowly sat up and shook his head in disbelief. Surely he had merely imagined it. He recalled the gnawing feelings he experienced before leaving home, but they had never been anything more than a niggle. He could make no sense of it.

Graeden found no acceptable reasons for what had just happened. Others might blame magic or spirits, but he gave no credence to such things. He shook his head again, slowly rose, turned and saw the mare facing northeast. "So, you heard it, too?"

The mare turned and stared. For just a second, he thought she might speak, perhaps to express her readiness to depart, but only to the northeast. Instead, Merlona walked over and nudged him. Graeden closed his eyes, trying to bring himself back to reality. "Voices in my head... My horse dictating the route... What next? Will the beasts of fantasy rise up from the wood? Perhaps one of the legendary feathered drageals of myth will suddenly swoop down and carry me off to who knows where. Yes. Oh yes. That is just what I need to complete this insanity."

He sighed. "I have been alone on the road a bit too long for my own good. Yes, that must be it." He nodded, hoping to convince himself as he mounted the mare. "Alright, this way is as good as any."

The mare leisurely headed off to the northeast. Graeden put the morning's strangeness out of his mind.

### 

Just before sunset, rider and mount arrived in a village somewhat smaller than the one they had passed a few nights before.

"I am sure you will be as glad to be in a stable tonight as I will be to sleep on something softer than the ground," he said as the village's inn came into view. "Right now, even a lumpy mattress would feel wonderful."

The voice had remained silent during the day's travel on the appointed course. Graeden hoped it would allow him the luxury of sleeping in a bed for a night or two before it returned. He shook his head. Did he now believe this nonsense?

Before he could answer his own question, a fair-haired lad of no more than ten jumped off his perch on a barrel by the side of the inn and bounded up to greet Graeden.

"Good evenin', sir," he said cheerfully. "Will you be staying with us for the night, or are you just looking for a good meal?"

"Both," Graeden answered. He dismounted, flung his saddle bag over his shoulder and handed the reins to the boy.

"That is wonderful, sir. Ma is a great cook, and she has outdone herself with tonight's stew," the boy said, smacking his lips as he led the horse in the direction of the stable. "I am thinking you will be wanting this beauty to get equally good fare, as well."

Graeden nodded and flipped a copper in the boy's direction. "Make sure she is well tended, and there may be another one in it for you."

The boy caught the coin and bowed without missing a step. "I will see to it, sir. You should be getting inside before all the stew is gone and you wind up sharing her meal." He grinned. "If she will let you."

Graeden followed the boy's advice. He approached the doorway. He thought he felt a slight tug at his sleeve. He glanced around, but saw no one as he entered.

Immediately overcome by the aroma of home cooking, he knew he had not smelled anything so inviting since the last time he had stolen down into Cook's kitchen. Before he finished savoring the delicious scent, a young girl, obviously the stable boy's older sister, greeted him.

"Will you be wanting a room and dinner, sir?" she asked, noticeably sizing him up for his ability to pay. "Would that be a private room, or will you be staying in the common area?" she added at the end of her inspection.

"A private room." He realized that, even through the layers of dirt and grime, he had managed to pass her assessment.

"Very good, sir, and how long do you think you might be staying with us?"

"That depends. I was thinking of only one night." He took her hand and gently kissed it. "I am not in any particular hurry, so I might stay longer if given good enough reason."

She lowered her eyes and coyly smiled at his not so subtle suggestion. Graeden, somewhat surprised at his own boldness, noted she neither accepted nor declined.

"The storm that is coming may give you good enough reason," a gruff voice said from behind Graeden. "Selera, your mother says the second batch of stew is ready. Go help her."

When she did not immediately move, the bearded, grey-haired man lightly swatted the back of her head. "Now! Folks are waiting!"

"Yes, Papa." She appeared more embarrassed by his reprimand than by being caught flirting, and quickly ran off.

"So, it is a private room you are wanting," the innkeeper said roughly.

Graeden nodded.

"That will be two coppers a night." Still warily eyeing the road worn traveler, he added, "Up front."

"Of course." Graeden retrieved the money from the small purse on his belt. The sight of the coppers softened the older man's expression.

"I was serious about the impending storm, boy. Neither you nor your mount will want to be caught on the road when it strikes."

"I saw no sign of a storm," Graeden replied.

"Ah, that may be, but the Old One sent word of it," the innkeeper answered. "Said it would come in tonight and last at least a few days, maybe a week."

"Aye, and I for one have never known her to be wrong," said a neatly dressed shopkeeper, who paused beside Graeden. "She said we had all best not be caught out in it. I have every intention of heeding her words," he continued. "You would be best served to do the same, young man. See you soon, Areth. Tell the Missus the stew was the best yet. Be safe."

"G'night," the innkeeper answered as he waved to the departing man.

"Now, boy, I am willing to bet that you have not had a good meal in..." Areth rubbed his bearded chin and looked Graeden over, "oh, I would say five, maybe six days. Am I right?"

Graeden nodded in amazement. The innkeeper laughed.

"Having raised three boys of my own, and seeing as many travelers as I do, I am usually spot on when figuring the time 'tween good vittles. So, enough chattering, you need to get yourself into the dining hall. Selera will bring you a double serving of stew. I will have someone take your bag to your room. Is there anything else on that horse of yours that you need?"

Graeden shook his head, turned and entered the dining area. Almost before he sat on the wooden bench, Selera set a large bowl of stew and a loaf of warm black bread before him.

"Papa must like you. He does not usually give double portions." She smiled and returned to her duties.

Within a blink of an eye, a younger blonde-haired girl placed a tankard of ale in front of him. Her quick departure prevented him from thanking her.

He took a mouthful of stew. It surpassed both the stable boy's praise and his own initial response to its aroma. He ate slowly, savoring every delicious bite. Between spoonfuls, he surveyed his surroundings.

The inn was not as large as some, but it felt comfortable and homey. The room adjacent to the dining area was filled with all manner of chairs and tables, arranged as if to invite guests to linger and enjoy the fire or a game or two of cards.

Graeden, engrossed in savoring his dinner, failed to notice the approach of the cloaked figure who sat down beside him. It seemed odd with the room nearly deserted that this person would choose that seat. Graeden's first thought — the fellow was up to no good, a thief or worse. But there was something else, something different, something strange about this man. Something Graeden could not quite put his finger on.

*Lack of sleep is causing me to imagine danger and intrigue around every corner.* Graeden pushed up from his chair, surprised when the figure grasped his arm.

"Do not leave just yet, Master Graeden," the cloaked figure whispered. "Stay and have a drink with me."

The raspy voiced man's knowledge of his name caught Graeden off guard. He found himself rooted where he stood. Almost against his will, Graeden sat. The figure filled two tankards from a pitcher

Graeden had not seen.

The stranger emptied his tankard in two gulps. Without looking at Graeden, he said, "I am here to warn you. Leave this place quickly, lad. Tonight! Now! Nothing but danger dwells here, and your true destiny awaits elsewhere. Go where your heart is directing you."

Graeden stared as the stranger refilled his tankard and motioned for him to drink. Graeden did so. When he lowered the tankard, both the stranger and the pitcher were gone.

Graeden called to Selera, busy cleaning the table in the corner, and asked her about the figure. She told him no one had been seated beside him all night. The look she gave him made Graeden abandon the topic.

"I must have nodded off. Sorry. Too long on the road," he added in an attempt to cover his uneasiness. "I had best be heading to my room."

He climbed the stairs, trying to push down the fear welling within and convince himself that this latest occurrence was no more than a fatigue-related dream.

In his room, he stripped off his clothes and settled into a bed that was far more comfortable than he could have imagined.

A bright flash of lightning illuminated the room, followed immediately by a loud clap of thunder that shattered the quiet.

*I guess the old woman was right. There will be a storm tonight. Hope it does not last too long.*

He listened for the rain to start, but soon fell asleep, his slumber far from restful. The words of the voice inside his head and those of the mysterious stranger ran through Graeden's dreams.

# CHAPTER SIX

THUNDER ROUSED Graeden. He wanted to lie there and listen to the falling rain. His growling stomach told him, regardless of the darkness, it was time to rise.

He reluctantly got up and splashed cool water from the washstand's basin on his face to erase the last remnants of sleep from his eyes. He dressed and headed downstairs, hoping the morning meal was ready.

"Well, the young master is finally awake. You must live a very soft life if you are in the habit of sleeping past midday meal," Areth said with what felt like a forced cheerfulness.

"I did not realize it was so late," Graeden apologized.

The rumble from his stomach made Areth laugh.

"Do not fret. We saved food for you." Areth motioned Selera to bring the meal.

"Thank you, sir, and please thank your Missus. I am sorry if I caused anyone extra work," Graeden replied. "I did not realize how exhausted I was, or how good a real bed would feel."

Areth nodded and pointed Graeden to a table by the window. Graeden noticed the large room was empty save those few – two priests, three traders and himself – staying at the inn.

He ate his meal, listening to the others discuss their inability to depart due to the inclement weather.

The traders seemed delighted by the delay, which Graeden thought peculiar. Every trader he had ever met in Hammarsh Keep would trudge through hellfire to reach his destination.

*Perhaps this is the end of their route and the delay will cost them nothing more than time,* Graeden thought, thankful for a rational explanation.

He finished the last of his meal, took the last sip of the honeyed brew and rose from the table. Just as before, the strange figure appeared and motioned Graeden to sit. Again, Graeden could do nothing but obey.

The stranger spoke so softly, Graeden leaned in to hear him. "You must leave here at once. It is becoming more dangerous with each passing moment. I know you sense something is not right."

Graeden appeared unaffected as the stranger continued, "I beseech you, listen to your own feelings. There is little time to waste."

A noise made Graeden shift his glance. When he turned back, the stranger had vanished.

Fear of impending madness again took form in Graeden's mind. Could this man be real or an apparition? No, that was impossible. Such things only happened in stories. He contemplated his sanity. After several minutes, he gave up and went to the stable to check on Merlona.

### 

Graeden returned to the inn and saw the others huddled together, whispering. When they saw him, they immediately dispersed. Something seemed off-kilter. Their movements appeared unnaturally stiff, their voices strained, their words forced. Everything felt wrong.

Throughout the day Graeden noticed the others continued to

watch him, then quickly averted their eyes when he glanced their way. Each wore a large black amulet. Had they always been there? Graeden could not recall. He decided the amulets must be talismans to ward off the storm.

He climbed the stairs and entered his room. He reached out to hang his cloak and felt the startling sensation of someone's hand covering his own. Graeden leapt aside, readying himself for a fight. The stranger removed his hood and locked eyes with Graeden.

Graeden stared in surprise at the stranger. With short brown hair and a weather-worn face, he appeared only a few years older than Graeden, but his dark, sorrow-filled eyes seemed to carry the burden of many lifetimes.

"Graeden, I implore you one last time. Leave! Surely you feel the change in this place, in the people, how they watch you yet avoid your glance," he said, his tone quiet and controlled.

"And why should I believe what you say?" Graeden sounded calm, but inside he trembled. "Are you not one of the stranger things here? Explain yourself, and perhaps I might give credence to your warnings."

The stranger shifted his stance. He closed his eyes and sighed. "I can tell you nothing of myself. I can only advise you to leave."

"And if I refuse?" Graeden asked, steeling himself for an attack.

The stranger did not move. "Then all is lost. I beg of you, reconsider. Leave. If not with me, then on your own. Quickly, before this day ends."

The stranger left the room. The sound of his footsteps disappeared long before he reached the stairs.

### 

The following morning brought the same stormy darkness. Graeden paused halfway down the stairs when he heard the others talking.

"Can we not just kill the boy and be done with it?" one of the priests asked.

Graeden froze.

36

"The Master does not want him dead," snapped one of the traders.

"Then what does he want with him?" the innkeeper's wife asked, her voice raspy and cold.

"We are not privy to such things, nor do we dare speculate. The one that will speak for the Master will be told, when the time is right," the other trader said, touching the black amulet. "I suggest you do as instructed without question, else you too will face the Master's wrath."

"For now, we have merely been instructed to take the boy," the third trader replied.

"Where?" Areth asked.

The traders laughed.

"It is not his body we are to take. The Master has other plans for that. Plans that I am sure..."

Graeden reached for the rail. The stair beneath him creaked. The trader stopped talking. Graeden quickly recovered and proceeded down the stairs as if he had heard nothing. Out of the corner of his eye, he saw the group quickly disband.

Selera came around the staircase to meet Graeden. She led him to the table by the garden window. She went through the normal motions, but there was something about her tone, her movements, that felt wrong. Graeden did his best to maintain his composure in light of what he had just heard. He wanted to bolt, but saw both doors guarded.

He waited for his meal, praying he had misunderstood. Graeden now realized the stranger had, indeed, been his ally when he warned of impending danger. Danger he would now face alone.

Graeden forced himself to eat slowly, barely tasting the food, half sick with worry that it might be was poisoned. But not eating would confirm he had overheard them.

He finished the meal and returned to his room, hoping the stranger would again be there. Graeden found himself alone. He stuffed his belongings into his pack and decided the window would be his best means of escape. As he opened the shutter and reached for the latch, the door behind him flew open and the innkeeper's wife entered with the others standing behind her.

"Going somewhere, boy?" The innkeeper's wife's voice sounded different, deep and guttural, her eyes demented, her stance unnatural. With each word the black amulet around her neck pulsated as she held it in one hand and stroked it with the other.

The others rushed in. The priests pulled Graeden away from the window and shoved him toward the woman.

"I asked you a question, boy," she hissed as she stroked the now glowing amulet.

Her tone sent a wave of pure fear through Graeden. He bolted past her, only to be knocked to the floor by the traders waiting in the hall. They grabbed him, dragged him back into the room, and dropped him at the woman's feet.

"Go now," she told the others, "I want to be alone with him."

Graeden tried to get up, but she put her foot on his shoulder, pinning him to the floor. She was not an overly large woman, at least two heads shorter than him and neither thin nor stout, yet her strength seemed far more substantial than even the strongest of men.

"You still have not answered me. Were you going somewhere?"

The words slithered from her lips and the cold, dead look in her eyes frightened Graeden to his very core. She fed off his fear, sniffing the air and drinking it in like a heady wine. She lifted her foot from his shoulder. With a great deal of force, she stomped down on him. He cried out at the impact.

"It is your misfortune to have heard those idiots. Had you not, they would have just drugged you with this evening's meal and you would not need to endure this pain," she said. "Although, before I am done with you, this will feel like mere child's play."

"Who are you?" Graeden asked.

She ignored his question and lifted her foot again, this time bringing it down upon his other shoulder. She smiled viciously at his screams.

Completely helpless at her hands, Graeden resigned himself to his fate. He would die. With that realization, all fear drained from him. He stifled a laugh.

"How dare you smirk?" she screeched in anger.

"How dare I, indeed?" Graeden felt almost giddy as a strange sense of calm settled over him.

She removed her foot from his shoulder. Graeden breathed a premature sigh of relief. In the next moment, he felt her icy cold fingers wrap around his throat as she lifted him up until his feet dangled above the floor.

She tightened her grip. Graeden grinned widely.

He barely felt her throw him across the room. The impact with the wall knocked all breath from him. He lay there motionless. She strode across the room, kicking him until he lost consciousness.

### 

Graeden came to. No light, no sound, and no sensation of floor nor wall. The only thing he felt – pain. He had no idea where he was.

*Perhaps this is death*, he thought, remembering the rage of the creature that had been the innkeeper's wife. *It would not have been difficult for that thing to have killed me. Yet...*

He tried to move and screamed in agony. The pain unbearable. He heard snickering somewhere far in the distance, then a voice boomed in his head.

"Why are you going there? How do you know of that place?"

Graeden's pain subsided, and he answered, "Going where? I have no destination."

"You say that, yet you travel on a direct course to that place. To her," the voice accused as it unleashed another wave of agonizing pain. "Is she already your lover?"

Graeden cried out, "I speak the truth! I know nothing of any such place or person."

His answer displeased his captor. The voice repeated the same questions. Graeden gave the same answers with the same consequences. He pleaded with the voice, telling it that if he knew what it wanted he would tell it.

"Do not lie to me!" The voice continued to inflict the pain until the boy fell into unconsciousness.

Graeden woke again to the pain. He took a shallow breath, and he sensed something hovering nearby. He feared it was there to resume the horrific game. He waited, but the pain did not come. He realized whatever was nearby was different – kind and loving and oddly familiar. A trick conjured by his tormentor? Or had his mind, at last, snapped?

He needed to warn it of the danger, to send it away before the others could capture it. Before he had a chance to do anything, Graeden's tormentor unleashed another wave of pain upon him.

As Graeden screamed, the new presence moved closer. He felt a warm glow spread over him. For that brief moment, his pain was relieved, his hope restored. Then the comforting glow receded. Graeden thanked the presence for the momentary respite. And then it was gone. He found himself praying for its return.

# CHAPTER SEVEN

THE WEATHER finally warmed, and the Grove folk gathered together. In the new grass of the fields around the square, the littles raced around with energy only ones so young could muster. Their excitement heightened as they met face to face after the long isolated winter.

The older children, glad to get away from their own confinement as well as their babysitting duties, quickly drifted from their parents' sight. They talked and played games in the warmth of the day. As evening approached, the eldest of them paired off and headed to more secluded areas.

Regnaryn remained with the younger children until just after sunset, then returned to her parents. They were surprised to see her so early; all the others her age were elsewhere and would more than likely need to be mindcalled when it was time to return home.

"Child, what are you doing here?" Trebeh asked.

"I am heading home. I thought I would take the twins so you can stay and enjoy yourself."

"That is very sweet of you, Regnaryn, but why are you leaving so early? You really should be with your friends."

"They are being silly."

"Silly how?" Ayirak asked.

"Oh, you know, the usual," she answered, aware that her father would not be happy to hear everyone, including Nelluc, had paired off. Ayirak was well aware of what went on. Like most parents, he chose to ignore it.

"If you are sure that is what you want to do, then yes, we will accept your offer. Thank you," Trebeh said.

Regnaryn approached the littles. Some still played, though with far less energy than a few hours earlier, while others slept amidst the sweet smelling flowers. She found the twins, who put up far less resistance than she had expected.

They had not gotten very far when the twins stopped, refusing to go any further. They plopped down beside a large tree and started to whine. Within the blink of an eye, both fell fast asleep, a frustrated Regnaryn standing over them. The twins, though mere toddlers, were too big for her to carry them both. She considered leaving one while she took the other home, and then returning for the second little. No real danger existed, yet if the one left behind woke to find herself alone, the youngster might be frightened. Also, the ground remained very cold, and Regnaryn would feel horrible if one of them became ill.

"You look like you could use a bit of help, little sister."

She jumped, almost tripping over the sleeping kitlings, at the unexpected sound of her eldest brother's voice. Javis caught her around the waist, breaking her fall.

"You startled me."

He chuckled. "Yes, I see that. I probably should have called out, but I thought you would hear me."

"Guess I was too busy trying to figure out how I was going to get them home," she replied, pointing at the sleeping kitlings.

"Simple, I will carry them."

He reached down and scooped them both up in one arm.

"I can take one of them, Javis."

"Do not be silly, Regg. They are quite a handful. Why should you struggle with one when I can carry both? For once, let your big brother do something for you."

"Well, if you insist," she replied with a smile. "I knew there was a reason I liked you best."

As they chatted on the walk home, Regnaryn noticed, for the first time, how much Javis, now raising a family of his own, reminded her of Ayirak.

They reached the house. Javis took the twins upstairs to their room and set them in their beds. Regnaryn wanted to change them, but he scooted her out.

"Leave them be. Sleeping one night with a little dirt on their faces will not kill them," he said as they descended the stairs.

She knew better than to protest. It was the same as arguing with their parents – useless. He offered to stay so Regnaryn could return to the gathering, but she told him she was tired. Both knew she did not speak the truth, but Javis did not press her. He stayed long enough for a cup of tea.

Regnaryn washed the cups and went up to her room. She changed into her nightclothes, climbed into the large feather bed, and reached for one of the few books in the library she had not yet tackled. She opened it. After reading just a few pages of the mundane history of a country and a people she neither knew nor cared anything about, she fell asleep.

### ###

Regnaryn opened her eyes to an unnatural blackness, but it was not just the darkness that felt strange. As her eyes adjusted, she saw the shadowy outlines of her surroundings and immediately knew this was not her room. No, this was no place she had ever been.

But there was more. Her body, her nightclothes, everything about her felt different. She was engulfed in an aura that reflected a light source she could not see. With each movement, the glow caressed her. She was fascinated to find she was floating above the ground.

Suddenly, the sound of a muffled scream shook Regnaryn from her musings. She spun around, desperate to determine the source. She saw nothing.

She waited. The cries began anew. As she moved towards them, Regnaryn saw something on the ground. She could not reach it, her path was blocked by an invisible barrier. She focused on the spot, which at first appeared to be a pile of rags. Then it moved, revealing a figure enveloped in a slimy blackness. The thing writhed and screamed. The sound, no longer muffled by distance, made Regnaryn cover her ears. Dampening the cries did nothing to stop the sound or the being's terror from assailing her mind.

She swallowed hard, closing herself off from the creature whose emotions had so quickly washed over her. She concentrated and slowed her choppy breathing. Once she regained her composure, Regnaryn tentatively reached her mind out to the being. She immediately recoiled. Even a light touch revealed a depth of pain that nearly overwhelmed her. But she also sensed something besides the pain, something foreign yet familiar; something that compelled her to help.

Regnaryn thought for a few moments as the poor creature cried out again. She took a deep breath and gathered her strength. She opened her mind and sent the strongest wave of comfort she could muster toward the figure, then quickly shut her mind behind the most formidable shield she had ever created.

She breathed heavily, as if nearing the conclusion of a foot race. The next moment she sensed something touch her mind. She readied herself for an attack. Perhaps the being's tormentor sensed her actions and intended to retaliate.

She checked her shielding and found it untouched. The energy winnowed its way in. She could not stop it. She prepared to defend herself. Suddenly, she realized it was not an attack, rather a surge of gratitude mixed with hope.

Before she could determine what this creature was and how it had breached her defenses, something grasped her shoulder. She turned, poised to strike.

"I will not be taken without a fight!" she screamed.

### ###

"Regg," Neshya said as he gently shook her. "Hey, stop hitting me!" She flailed violently. He pulled her up, wrapped his arms around her, and called her name as he nuzzled his face into her hair.

"Wake up, little sister. You are dreaming."

She recognized his voice and ended her struggle. Regnaryn opened her eyes to see the soft gray fur of her brother's face. He smiled down at her. She reached for him and held fast.

"I am here. Nothing will hurt you, I promise. Are you alright?" he asked with none of his usual sarcasm. "You were muttering in your sleep."

She nodded, but the look in her eyes betrayed her lie.

"Do you wish to talk?"

Regnaryn found no words to describe her experience. She shook her head in frustration after several incoherent utterances escaped her lips.

"It is alright," Neshya said, wiping a tear from her cheek. "We can speak later."

"Thank you. Thank you for not making fun of me. I mean, it was just a dream, another stupid dream, and I... I... please do not tell anyone about this."

Her pained expression made the ever-teasing jokester choke back his own emotions.

He nodded. With a wink and a broad grin, he said, "But if you tell anyone I was nice, not only will I deny it, but I will be sure to make your life miserable from that day forward."

She smiled. "Is everyone else sleeping?"

"No, they are not even back yet."

Before they could continue, the front door opened. They heard Trebeh shushing Nelluc and Ennales so as not to wake the twins.

# CHAPTER EIGHT

*:DO NOT PANIC, young master, I have come to help.:*
The stranger's voice was so loud and unexpected in the darkness that, had Graeden been able to move, he would have jumped.

"Where are you?"

*:I am with you and yet not,:* he answered. *:I cannot physically break through their barrier.:*

"What barrier? What is going on here? And if you are not here, how are you speaking with me?"

*:Calm down,:* the stranger answered. *:There is no time for details.:*

"But..."

*:You must trust me, Graeden, fully and completely. Your life depends on it. Do you understand?:*

Although surprised, he did.

*:Good. You need not speak, merely think and I will hear.:*

*:What should I do?:* Graeden wondered, while telling himself he had truly gone mad.

*:You are not mad, dear boy. Madness would be easier to escape.:*

*:What is going on here?:* Graeden asked.

*:When you are safe, I will explain.:*

The stranger sounded so sincere, Graeden put aside his doubts.

*:You must do exactly as I instruct, any hesitation could lead to your demise. I am going to join with your mind now, it will be faster than my explaining what needs to be done.:*

Before Graeden could respond, he felt the stranger's strength merging with his own.

*:How are you doing this?:*

*For now, think of it as a kind of magic that has joined our minds.* Graeden heard and thought simultaneously, and he felt his broken bones snap back into place. *Try to move.*

Graeden watched as first his right and then his left hand moved, drawing strange signs in the air. Their voices, merged as one, both recited words Graeden did not understand. The movements and words were recounted for each direction – north, east, south and west.

At the completion of the fourth repetition, the smallest sliver of light broke through the utter blackness. Graeden's hope soared.

He performed a flourish of different hand movements accompanied by more unknown words, repeated for dark then light.

The room rumbled and the blackness that had enshrouded him exploded into hundreds of glasslike shards, which quickly dissipated in the light.

Graeden's eyes soon adjusted to the brightness. He saw he still occupied his room at the inn. He saw blood – his blood – splattered everywhere.

*They are coming,* both minds knew. *We must be prepared to kill them, if necessary.*

The stranger felt Graeden's hesitation.

*They are no longer the people you met on your first night. If it comes to you or them, they must be the ones sacrificed.*

Graeden reluctantly agreed.

*The window!* they thought together. Graeden grabbed his bag, flung open the shutters, and climbed onto the ledge. Behind him, the door crashed open. Voices sounded the alarm of his escape. Graeden crawled along the ledge and leapt toward a sturdy tree branch, relieved when his feet landed solidly on the perch.

He shimmied across the limb to the center of the tree, took a breath and listened to ensure no one waited in the shadows below. When both minds seemed satisfied, Graeden jumped down, crossed the courtyard and darted into the stable.

He ran to Merlona as the others burst into the courtyard.

*Hurry! There is no time to saddle her.*

Graeden threw himself on the mare's back and grabbed hold of her mane. As soon as Merlona felt Graeden's fingers, she bolted for the open door and burst into the courtyard. His captors raced toward them. Graeden pulled out the short sword, now prepared to use it.

The inn folk rushed at horse and rider in a blind rage. Though unarmed, their crazed looks and incoherent screams terrified Graeden.

Merlona charged. Graeden swung the sword with one hand and held fast to Merlona with the other. The flat side of the blade landed square on one traders' skull. Graeden heard the crack and saw the man crumple to his knees and then onto his face. Merlona reared, hit one of the others on the shoulder with her front hoof, and then galloped toward the village's main street.

Graeden heard screams in their wake as they headed northeast. He dared not look back for fear of slowing Merlona and, more importantly, for what he might see.

Graeden wrapped his arms tightly around Merlona's neck. They raced past townsfolk, who seemed unaware of the shouting from the inn or the fleeing horse and rider. Graeden took no time to wonder why. Merlona continued at a full gallop until they reached an area well beyond the village.

*We are on our way.* Graeden felt the stranger say to someone.

Without warning, he felt all but the slightest bit of the stranger leave his mind.

*:Follow this trail until you come to a clearing by a small stream,:* the stranger thought to Graeden. *:I will be waiting.:*

# CHAPTER NINE

THE PATH WOUND its way into a forest. Graeden rode on but soon enough the low, thick branches forced him to dismount and continue on foot. As he approached the clearing, he heard the stranger speaking in a language unfamiliar to his ears. Somehow, he understood.

"I had no choice. They were going to kill him. Or worse. Is that what you wanted?" the stranger asked angrily.

*Or worse? What could be worse?* Graeden's mind raced.

"Do not be ridiculous. Of course, I did not want anything bad to befall the boy," the high pitched voice replied with more than a hint of annoyance.

The second voice, emanating from thin air, startled Graeden. He stumbled, snapping a twig underfoot. The voice stopped and the stranger turned, his hand gripping the hilt of his sword. Seeing Graeden, the man removed his hand from the weapon and smiled. Graeden looked past the stranger. He saw no one, save an extremely large ferret, which stood on its hind legs on a rock. The creature looked at Graeden and curled up on the rock, his snow white fur in sharp contrast to the dark gray stone.

Graeden turned his attention to the stranger. "Who were you talking to?" he demanded.

"Talking to?" the stranger answered. "I spoke only to myself"

"No! There was someone else here. I heard him. I heard both of you."

"Now, now, Graeden. As you can plainly see, there is no one else here. You have been through a great ordeal, perhaps..."

"Do not patronize me," Graeden shouted. "And do not dare say I imagined it. I know what I heard. What did you, both of you, mean? Who is he, and why was he going to kill me or worse? You said you would explain when we were away from that place."

The stranger toyed with the idea of telling the boy the full truth.

*:He already knows more than he should, Ellyss,:* the second voice snarled into the stranger's mind.

*:His mind is teetering on the edge of madness...:*

*:And you do not think revealing who I am, what all of this is, will not push him over the edge right now?:*

*:No, Aloysius. I do not,:* the stranger snapped. *:Not knowing the truth is what distresses him. And...:*

The ball of white fur sighed.

"As you wish," the high pitched voice said in Graeden's tongue.

Graeden swung around to see the voice's source but saw no one other than the white ferret. The look on the boy's face revealed he feared himself mad.

*:I told you,:* Aloysius said with a sense of smug satisfaction.

Ellyss glared at him.

Aloysius laughed aloud, uncoiled himself, and stood upon the rock on all four legs. He sat, curling his black tipped tail around him.

"If you are going to tell him, Ellyss, you had better do it before he faints dead away."

The stranger grabbed Graeden's arm before he crumpled to the ground.

"That was uncalled for," Ellyss said angrily. "You truly are a

51

surly old chetoga. I do not know how Varlama has put up with you all these years." His tone lightened, but a hint of anger remained beneath the surface.

"Who are you? What are you? What is going on here?" Graeden demanded.

"All in good time, Graeden." Ellyss released the boy's arm then retrieved his pack from the side of the rock where his companion sat. He returned to the boy's side and held out a small bottle filled with a green liquid, motioning him to drink. Graeden took the bottle without once taking his eyes from the strange, talking creature.

"Did that ferret really talk?" Graeden asked.

Ellyss winced in anticipation of the tirade he knew calling Aloysius a ferret would cause. The wait was short.

Aloysius snapped his head around and glared at Graeden. The boy drew back as the fluffy white creature's expression changed from harmless pet to dangerous beast with bared teeth and raised hackles.

"How dare you call me a ferret, you little whelp," Aloysius growled. "A ferret of all things. Does he actually think I look like one of those... those dumb animals?" he asked no one in particular.

He leapt from the rock, delighting in the fear in Graeden's eyes as the boy wondered if the ferret intended to attack him. Graeden tried to scramble away. Aloysius' move landed him nose to nose with the frightened lad.

"I will have you know, *boy*." The pitch of his voice now sounded higher than before. "...that ferrets are scrawny, stupid, ugly little creatures. Chetoga, on the other hand, are larger, more intelligent and," he continued smugly, "far more attractive beings. It is so obvious, one would think anyone with eyes or an iota of intelligence could clearly see the difference."

Graeden said nothing. Frozen in place, mouth agape, he stared in awe at what he now knew was definitely *not* a ferret.

The chetoga shook his head and indignantly stalked away from the frightened boy, muttering, "Ferret, the nerve of that damn human!"

Ellyss grinned and helped Graeden to his feet. "You will have to forgive Aloysius. He tends to overreact to being mistaken for a ferret. Though, how he would expect anyone who has never *seen or even heard* of a chetoga to be able to distinguish between the two, is beyond me." He directed his comment at the annoyed chetoga.

"Uh... um..." Graeden stuttered, unable to form real words.

Ellyss laughed, put his arm around Graeden and led him to the campfire. "You have had quite the time of it these past few days, young sir."

Graeden said nothing as he sat beside the campfire, trying to make sense of recent events.

"Stop acting so," Graeden heard Ellyss say to the chetoga. "We do not have time for such histrionics."

Aloysius stopped pacing, looked at Ellyss, and saw the eyes of a friend who knew and accepted all past transgressions and triumphs. Aloysius grinned and shook his head in mock hurt. He walked back to the rock by the campfire and sat down, still muttering, "A ferret..."

"Allow me to *properly* introduce you two." Human and chetoga nodded. Ellyss continued, "Come to think of it, we have not yet been introduced, either. My name is Ellyss, and that surly creature is Aloysius. He is, in fact, a chetoga, a race of highly intelligent – at least by his account – beings that some, present company excluded I am sure, say evolved from the common ferret."

"Hrmph," Aloysius snorted.

"I... I do not understand," Graeden said.

"And just *what* do you not understand, boy?" Aloysius asked with slightly less contempt than before.

"Er, well, all of it, sir," Graeden answered.

Aloysius chuckled. "I am not surprised."

Ellyss interrupted. "I need to tend to your wounds. The enchantment I left with you will not hold much longer."

Graeden had almost forgotten his ordeal at the inn. Now, as Ellyss spoke, the pain began to resurface.

"Drink this. All of it." Ellyss handed him the small green bottle Graeden had dropped when Aloysius pounced. "It tastes horrific, but it will dull your pain and help your wounds heal quickly."

Graeden did as instructed, nearly gagging on the thick acrid liquid. He wiped his mouth on his sleeve and handed the empty bottle back to Ellyss.

"Now you need to rest." Aloysius pointed to the bedroll by the campfire.

Graeden nodded, crawled into the bedroll and fell fast asleep.

### 

Graeden awoke to the bright light of day. He thought over all that he had dreamt: torture, magic, strange creatures. He sat up and saw Ellyss and Aloysius. Not a dream, he realized.

"Morning, boy," Ellyss said cheerily. "How are you feeling?"

"Fine, I think," he answered.

"Good, but you must take it easy, your wounds are not yet fully healed."

Ellyss handed Graeden another bottle of the green liquid. Graeden drank it without hesitation, noticing there was a bit less of the awful liquid than the night before.

"Well now, you must be hungry," Ellyss said.

Without waiting for an answer, he handed Graeden several pieces of jerky. The hungry boy greedily snatched them and gobbled them down.

"You, my friend," Ellyss said to Aloysius, "will have to fend for yourself. I am not in the habit of carrying freshly killed game in my pack. Since you will not eat jerky, you are on your own."

"It is just as well," Aloysius replied, "you probably would not know how to care for it. It would most certainly spoil and be no good to anyone. So, then, I am off."

Ellyss handed Graeden more jerky and a hunk of hard tack. He poured a cup of tea. Graeden gulped everything down so fast, he barely tasted it.

Swallowing the last of the jerky, his hunger still not satisfied,

Graeden asked, "Ellyss, just how long has it been since..."

"Rest a bit more now. There will be time for your questions later." Ellyss handed the still hungry young man the last of the jerky and hard tack. "I see I will need to catch something for our dinner."

Having no sooner said that, Aloysius bounded back into the campsite with two large rabbits dangling from his mouth. He leapt onto the rock and placed the carcasses before him. The two men looked enviously at his kill, but said nothing.

The crafty chetoga picked up a rabbit, bent it in half so that the snap of its spine and the tearing of its flesh was audibly uncomfortable to the men. Aloysius bit into the exposed muscle and wrenched a piece free. The two men silently looked on with a sense of awe at the precision with which the chetoga devoured his meal. Aloysius paused, turned his now blood-stained face to them, grinned and tossed the second rabbit to Ellyss.

"I was going to eat both," he lied, "but the sight of two grown men drooling is just too pathetic to bear. Of course, since you two refuse to consume it as it was meant to be," he said, taking another bite from the partially eaten rabbit, "your meal will be delayed."

"Thank you very much," Graeden said softly.

Aloysius nodded and tore another chunk of raw meat from the bone.

"I am sorry I offended you earlier, sir," he continued, remembering their initial encounter. "It was not my intent. It is just that I have never met anyone like you before, and..." he hesitated, not knowing what else to add.

"Apology accepted, boy. Just do not make the same mistake with the next chetoga you run into. They may not be as forgiving."

Ellyss stifled a laugh, earning a glare of icy contempt which Graeden already knew was a facade.

"As I was saying, before being rudely interrupted," Aloysius continued with a hint of disdain, "if you ever again meet another chetoga, do not make the same mistake. We are a fiercely proud race and do not take kindly to having our honor besmirched."

Graeden nodded.

Ellyss roared with laughter. "Being a tad dramatic, eh, you old dog?"

"Oh, so now I am a dog," Aloysius replied. "First a ferret, now a dog. Will the insults never end?"

Graeden sat silently as the two friends traded insults. Ellyss prepared the rabbit while Aloysius cleaned the last of the meat from the bones of his.

At last the meat was cooked and the two men ate. Aloysius walked to the stream to clean up, mumbling about how humans just did not understand the proper way to enjoy meat. He returned a few moments later, still grumbling.

Graeden found the constant banter between the friends amusing. He remembered that he and his siblings, especially Taaryn, acted much the same. He now longed for the Keep and the lifestyle he had so foolishly discarded.

"You look like you have something on your mind, boy," Aloysius said.

Graeden nodded tentatively. "I have so many questions about what went on back there. But, I am not sure I really want to know. The inn. You. All of it... so strange. No offense."

The chetoga nodded.

"It is up to you how much you want to hear. And you need not take it all in at once. We are in no rush to part company, so take your time," Ellyss said.

*:What are you saying? We have already spent far too long here.:* Aloysius mindspoke to Ellyss. He received no response.

"Thank you," Graeden answered then quickly changed the subject. "Here, let me clean up, it is the least I can do."

As the boy stood, he experienced a pain that took his breath away.

"Ah, it is as I said before, you are not yet fully healed," Ellyss said, grabbing Graeden's arm. "I feared this morning's small amount of potion might not be enough. Aloysius, if you could get me another vial…"

The chetoga handed Ellyss another small bottle. Ellyss nodded and led Graeden back to his bedroll.

"Drink this. You need sleep more than you need answers right now."

:*That will help his wounds, but what of the Master? Will he not find the boy once we are gone?*: Aloysius asked.

:*As soon as he is asleep, I will cast a cloaking shielding around him. It will keep him hidden until he reaches his destination.*:

Graeden took the bottle and drank the liquid, welcoming the restful sleep he knew it would afford him.

"I want to thank you again for rescuing me, and for helping to bolster my resolve and strength before that, as well," he said and drifted off to sleep.

"Before?" Ellyss and Aloysius asked each other.

# CHAPTER TEN

WRENCHED FROM their slumber by a scream that shattered the night's calm, Ayirak and Trebeh flew from their bed and into the hall. They stood frozen in place, trying to determine who or what had made the horrific wail. They heard the twins cry out, watched Nelluc rush from her room to comfort the littles, and then saw Neshya and Ennales, faces filled with fear, running toward them. The next instant, another scream tore through the night. All realized Regnaryn was missing. They ran to her room, unsure what they would find.

Trebeh reached the door first, but entry was blocked by an unseen barrier. The others ran into her, not expecting the doorway to be obstructed. Despite the force of the three male yekcals behind her, the barrier held. None could enter. The boys cried out, prompting Ayirak to raise his hand to silence them.

Trebeh peered into the room and saw that Regnaryn sat upon her bed; body stiff, eyes staring blankly, and mouth agape.

*:What is it, Trebeh?:* Ayirak mindspoke to her, trying not to increase his sons' panic.

*:I am not sure.:* She displayed a fear he had not seen in her since

they had first escaped their homeland so many years before. *:But, whatever it is, it is not good.:*

"Boys," Ayirak said, "Take everyone downstairs to the far end of the house. It will be quieter there so the twins can calm down."

Ennales nodded and grabbed the reluctant Neshya, pulling him toward the twins' room.

Trebeh mindcalled to Regnaryn. She was immediately thrown backwards into Ayirak as if her thoughts physically rebounded off the barrier. The yekcals stared at each other.

"This is worse than I thought," she said. "I do not think I can do this alone."

"I am of no use to you in these matters, you know that."

Trebeh smiled weakly and nodded. "I will contact Phrynia. She can help."

Ayirak agreed.

"Take the children away from the house. To one of the stables. They will be safer there."

Her words faded. Ayirak did not need to hear more, her meaning was clear.

### 

Ayirak settled the children at the stable and returned to find Trebeh leaning against the wall, her breathing labored and her face drained.

She shook her head. "Phrynia is on her way. She is of no help from a distance."

"But she cannot come up here, the stairwell is too small." Ayirak gently stroked her face.

She held her fingers to his lips. "I know, but if she is downstairs in the sunroom or by the fireplace, perhaps that will be close enough." She paused a moment, then whispered, "It must be."

*:I am here,:* Phrynia said, shocked to feel Trebeh's exhaustion.

*:Ayirak, do not allow her to touch the barrier,:* the drageal said. *:It is tainted with an evil that is draining her strength and that of*

59

*anything it contacts.:*

*:What are you saying? Regnaryn is in there.:* Trebeh reached for the barrier, only to be restrained by Ayirak. *:We must get in to save her!:*

*:We will.:* Phrynia continued calmly, *:Sacrificing ourselves before we do will not help the child. We must find a way to get through it without physically touching it.:*

*:I found a small crack. But what if we alert its caster to our presence?:*

Phrynia shook her head. *:We will deal with that if it happens. Show me the weakness.:*

Ayirak broke in, unable to remain silent any longer, *:How could something like this enter Reissem Grove? It is absolutely unheard of, not once since this settlement was founded has such a thing happened.:*

*:Only Regnaryn will be able to tell us that,:* Phrynia answered.

At that moment Regnaryn's pained screams began again. It took all of Ayirak's strength to keep Trebeh from throwing herself at the barrier. The crazed mother only stopped struggling when Regnaryn's screams subsided.

*:We must hurry!:* Trebeh cried.

The two women joined minds and created a slender thread of thought they hoped would slip unnoticed through the tiny crack. As the first thought crossed the barrier into Regnaryn's room, the women paused, waiting to see if their encroachment had been detected. With no reaction, they wove thread upon thread, directing them towards Regnaryn.

They cautiously touched Regnaryn's mind with their tapestry of thought, but they were not prepared for what they found, what Regnaryn was experiencing. It took every bit of resolve not to reveal themselves.

The room appeared completely engulfed in flames. Flames wrapped themselves around Regnaryn's neck and body, strangling her like the tendrils of a choking vine. As the fingers of flames tightened around Regnaryn, she screamed in terror and pain. They discerned something else, a distant presence that laughed at her agony. When the flames subsided, the women heard mumbling, but they could not understand the words.

They realized Regnaryn's mind was fully entwined with her captor, making it impossible for them to directly communicate with her. Instead, the women insinuated thoughts to her – thoughts of comfort, love and, most importantly, strength. They sent these thoughts one after another along the already established threads, hoping some part of Regnaryn's mind would recognize them.

At last, they sensed Regnaryn's acknowledgement. They watched in awe as she took their thoughts and added them to her own, creating a tapestry of strength. Regnaryn's resolve multiplied with each new thread she combined with her own thoughts.

She attempted to free herself, but her captor held fast. She did not relent. She tried again and again until she finally succeeded. Once free, the barrier dissipated and her tormentor's presence vanished. As it did, Phrynia heard the distant sound of cursing in a vaguely familiar tongue.

Regnaryn collapsed back onto the bed, face pale, breathing shallow. Trebeh rushed into the room, Ayirak close on her heels.

Trebeh gathered Regnaryn into her arms, rocking her gently and purring softly. Regnaryn's eyes fluttered open as the color returned to her cheeks.

:*Should I get the children now?*: Ayirak asked.

:*Not yet. Go stay with them while Phrynia and I talk with her first.*:

Ayirak nodded, kissed the still sobbing young girl on the head and left.

Regnaryn looked up into her mother's large, almond-shaped eyes. "Oh, Mama, it was horrible. Did you and Phrynia see it? Feel it? That horrible taunting voice laughing as my skin burned. Oh, it was so real, I can still feel the heat."

"It is over now and you are safe," Trebeh replied. "How did you know we were there?"

"Before I broke free from his grasp and brought down my barrier, I felt a glimmer of you within my mind."

"Wait, that was *your* barrier?" Trebeh asked in total shock. "But it had such an evil imbued into it. How could it be yours?"

"As soon as I realized that thing was attempting to overpower me, I tried to build a barrier to protect the rest of you. But he took control of it. Then, he told me if I did not surrender my power, he would wrench each of you through the barrier, torture what was left of your bodies, and murder you in front of my eyes."

Regnaryn trembled as she spoke. Trebeh gently stroked her head.

"Come and have something cool to drink. It will make you feel better," Trebeh said.

Regnaryn nodded, and she followed Trebeh from the room.

### 

"Sit here by me, child," Phrynia said as Regnaryn joined her by the fireplace in one of the few rooms the drageal could comfortably enter. "There is much to discuss."

Regnaryn sat on the chair beside the cascade of pillows the large drageal had settled on.

"You heard what I told Mama?"

The drageal nodded. Trebeh entered the room and handed glasses of tea to them.

"You do not seem surprised. You knew it was my barrier."

Phrynia smiled. "Yes. It contained all of your characteristic signatures. But I also saw it was tainted by something not of your making."

Regnaryn shot up from her chair. "Where are the others?" she asked fearing the worst. "I... it... we did not harm them, did we?"

"Calm yourself, child. They are all fine," Trebeh said soothingly. "Ennales took them to the stables. Your father is with them now."

"Please bring them back," Regnaryn pleaded.

"There are things we need to discuss without the others

around."

"I promise to answer all your questions, but I need to see that everyone is alright."

### 

It took only a few moments before the front door opened. Neshya was the first one to enter. He smiled with relief when he saw Regnaryn sitting there, exhausted but looking nothing like she had in her room. Ayirak followed, carrying the sleeping twins. Regnaryn could see the others behind her father, trying not to push, but eager to enter.

Ayirak nodded to Regnaryn as the others clamored around her. He climbed the stairs to put the sleeping littles back in their beds. When he returned, he found the elder children bombarding Regnaryn with questions.

"That is enough," he said with sufficient authority to silence them. "It is time for you three to return to your beds. Regnaryn will be here when you wake to answer your questions."

Ennales and Nelluc immediately left the room, whispering as they climbed the stairs. Neshya lingered.

"Was it the same dream as the night of the party?" Neshya whispered.

Before Regnaryn could answer, Trebeh asked, "What dream? I know of no dream on the night of the party."

"Uh," Neshya mumbled under his mother's glare.

"It is my fault, Mama," Regnaryn said. "I made him promise not to tell."

"Hmm," she said with a look that told both children this was not the end of the discussion. "Very well, young man, it is off to bed with you. We will talk in the morning. And you, young lady, have seen the rest of the family, so..."

Neshya hugged Regnaryn and left the room.

"Before we go any further," Trebeh said, "tell me about this dream that you and Neshya have kept secret."

She lowered her gaze and gently kicked her feet against the chair. After a few moments, she related the details of the dream.

When Regnaryn finished, Phrynia asked, "Have you any idea what it was?"

Regnaryn shook her head. "No, but there was something about it. Something familiar but yet not, I cannot really explain it. And now..."

"Child, what is it?" Trebeh asked softly.

Regnaryn looked away. "This is my fault. I do not know why, but I searched for the being tonight. I was worried and wanted to see if it was alright, but it was not there. I searched and searched, but I found no trace of it. I lowered my shieldings, fearing it had become too weak for me to sense through them, but it was nowhere to be found. I guess I forgot to re-establish them when I left. The next thing I knew, I felt overcome and could not break free. That was when I tried to build the barrier around my room. I am not sure why, but I felt I needed to protect all of you. It knew what I was doing, though."

Regnaryn turned to her mother. "I am so sorry to have put everyone in danger. I probably should have told you about the dream, especially after the first one, but... it was different... there was no evil in whatever being it was I found in that place."

Trebeh embraced her.

*:Well, now we know how that thing got into the Grove,:* Ayirak mindspoke to the women.

*:Yes, but knowing brings up even more questions,:* Phrynia answered.

Ayirak agreed.

Regnaryn abruptly pulled away from Trebeh. She looked into the distance as her body stiffened. Tears flowed down her cheek. Her focus returned to those around her.

"Mama, it was the same voice!" She shook her head. "These are not just nightmares. They are real! He is real!"

Trebeh reached for the terrified girl and gathered her into her

64

arms. She rocked Regnaryn, gently purring as she tried to comfort her.

Regnaryn pulled away. "Is it true? Did I murder my parents and all the other humans? Am I to blame?"

"Child, no one murdered the humans of Reissem Grove," Trebeh said firmly.

"You know what happened. We have told you the story many times," Ayirak added.

"The humans of the Grove all died of an illness, a fever," Phrynia added. "Even you were afflicted, and we feared you would be lost, as well."

"But why? Why was I the only one to survive? The voice said I was the cause. The evil inside of me made it happen," Regnaryn sobbed.

"Child, there was no evil in you then, nor now, that would allow you to cause such a thing," Ayirak replied.

It took several more minutes before Regnaryn believed them.

"You have been through enough tonight," Phrynia said. "You should go to your room and rest."

Regnaryn turned to the drageal with a look of fear in her eyes. "No, I do not want to go in there ever again." She tearfully buried her face in her mother's mane.

"It is alright, child." Ayirak stroked her head. "You do not have to go into your room if that is your wish. Come upstairs with me. You can lie in our bed." He saw her tense at his suggestion. "You do not have to sleep. We can talk or read or..."

Regnaryn clung tightly to the large yekcal's hand as they silently climbed the stairs.

"Trebeh, she must be told of the prophecy," Phrynia said when she felt certain no one could overhear their conversation.

"Now? But there are so many elements that have yet to come true."

Phrynia stared at the yekcal.

"Yes, you are right," Trebeh conceded.

"Give her a little time. You do need to tell her. Soon," Phrynia said.

Trebeh nodded her agreement.

"What needs to be done immediately is to strengthen her shieldings," Phrynia continued. "She must keep that thing from entering her dreams ever again."

Trebeh agreed. "I will work with her on that tomorrow."

# CHAPTER ELEVEN

GRAEDEN WOKE to Merlona's nudge and anxious whinny. Was she trying to alert him to danger? He grasped the hilt of the sword beside him and listened. He heard nothing save the normal sounds of the woods and the nearby stream.

"Alright, alright, I am awake. The sun is barely risen, dear lady. Is there somewhere you need to be?"

For just a moment, he thought he saw a glint of agreement in her eyes.

"I have been alone too long if I expect conversation from my horse." He laughed but part of him did not find the notion absurd.

He stretched and felt a twinge of pain, shook it off and got up to begin another day of his journey. As he restarted the fire, he noticed the fish wrapped in leaves and ready to roast though he did not remember preparing it. He washed up at the stream and brought water back for tea. Something sweet sounded good, like what Cook always made especially for him. He shook off the memory and tended to Merlona.

After breakfast at the water's edge, Graeden caught a flash of white fur scurrying away. For just a moment, he felt he had forgotten something. Something important. He stared into the distance, but nothing came to him.

He finished clearing the campsite and grabbed Merlona's saddle. Again, something did not feel right. Was this the same saddle he had always had? But, how could it not be? He shook his head and saddled the horse.

Graeden mounted Merlona and tried to get her to go due west. She refused. She looked at him. He remembered the odd tugging sensation and the voice that had provided him direction, so he let the reins go slack.

"Fine, go where you want."

Merlona turned and headed northeast at a brisk pace. For the first hour or so, she kept to that speed, ignoring Graeden's attempts to slow her. Graeden finally surrendered to the horse's will.

After some time, Merlona slowed to a walk and then stopped as if she had reached her destination. Graeden knew it would do no good to disagree.

She leisurely nibbled at the grass as Graeden ate bread and cheese from his pack. He noticed several trees lush with apples, picked one and took a bite. Delicious. He shared half with the horse, then picked more apples and stashed them in his bag. He packed up. They returned to the trail, again heading northeast.

"We are almost out of supplies, I hope we come across a village soon," he said, more to break the silence than to actually talk to the horse. He immediately grimaced. Even stranger, Merlona tensed beneath him. Graeden continued on at Merlona's chosen pace. Just before nightfall, the mare found a suitable clearing for their evening's camp.

### 

The morning was chilly and sunless, the sky gray with clouds. Rain seemed more of a certainty than a possibility. Graeden considered staying put until the rain passed, but the sensation that drew him ever northward tugged just hard enough, and the voice again whispered to ensure he did not linger. He broke camp and set out.

After a short distance, light rain fell. It was merely a thin veil, enough to annoy you by slowly soaking you to the bone, but not enough to send you dashing for cover. So, they trod on. The sky turned ugly and dark, but the rain neither strengthened nor diminished. Graeden considered stopping, but Merlona persisted.

Mid-afternoon, Merlona turned down a path off the main road. Graeden, half asleep in the saddle, barely noticed until she came to a halt jerking him awake.

"So I guess you have had enough of this muck, eh, girl?" He slid off her back.

He looked around and saw a cave further up the path. From the opening, it looked large enough to accommodate them both.

"How did you find this place?" He shook his head. "Well, however you did it, I thank you most heartily." He smiled and bowed to the mare. "Let us see if that cave is as good on the inside as it looks from here."

The mare did not wait for him. She approached the cave's entrance, and confidently strode into the darkness. Graeden followed, knowing she would not walk into danger. A thin shaft of light fell upon a pool of water at the rear of the cave.

"So, you just followed your nose, or was it your ears this time?" he asked the horse as she drank from the pool. "A double turn of good luck. First shelter, now water. If I can find some firewood, we could be quite cozy here."

Graeden stepped outside into the still drizzling rain. He found a few bits of wood dry enough for the fire and returned to the cave just as the rain intensified.

He walked toward the pool, carrying the firewood. "Dinner tonight will be the apples I found yesterday. Good thing I picked so many."

He dropped the wood in what appeared to be a fire pit to the side of the pool. Obviously, they were not the first to discover this place. Graeden started the fire, hoping the airshaft that admitted light would act as a flue. It did.

With the fire started, Graeden surveyed the illuminated cave. He whistled in amazement at the sight of barrels and boxes piled waist high along the wall. He worried he had intruded on someone's home, but quickly recognized it as an emergency shelter probably stocked by the locals. He found all they required and more.

"I was wrong, girl. Tonight we will not only enjoy the comforts of a cozy, dry shelter, we will eat almost like royalty, as well."

### 

Graeden arranged his pallet and stretched out to rest. Before he closed his eyes, the darkness was splintered by distant lightning followed by a loud clap of thunder. A shiver of fear raced down his spine, and he felt overcome with an unexplained dread.

He lay there several moments then fell into a sleep filled with dreams of strange storms and even stranger people; of darkness, pain and torment. He woke several times during the night to brilliant flashes of lightning and deafening claps of thunder. Each time he woke, it was with an unexplained feeling of terror, more intense than either the storm or his dreams should have caused.

### 

By daybreak, the storm passed. Graeden rose and went to the cave's entrance. The sky was bright and cloudless, a sharp contrast to the previous day. The morning sunlight danced off the raindrops that clung to tree and bush. He breathed in the wonderful fragrance that only happens after rainfall.

The landscape looked muddy, but not impassable. Merlona joined him, seemed to agree with his assessment, and ambled outside.

Graeden considered staying at the cave another day. He could use a better night's sleep, but he quickly dismissed the idea as that tugging sensation again returned.

Merlona nibbled on a patch of grass as Graeden gathered wood to replace what he had used. He packed extra supplies in his bag and left enough coin to cover four or five times the cost of what he had taken.

They departed mid-morning, once again with Merlona dictating speed and destination.

"You know, Merlona, even with what I took from the cave, we will still need to stop at a village soon." Both stiffened with tension at the suggestion.

### 

Just before sunset, they came upon an ordinary looking village. Their arrival was met with the usual mix of reactions from the villagers – a few smiled, others sneered, and some took no notice whatsoever. Still, Graeden felt uneasy. He sensed a similar response from Merlona.

They rode directly to the dry goods store. He tethered Merlona and entered. He was greeted by a rotund, red-faced, balding man, who quickly swallowed the bite of cake he chewed.

"What can I do you for?" he asked, eyeing Graeden's shabby appearance. "Been on the road a while, by the looks of you." Graeden nodded and the man continued, "I accept only coin for my wares, no trades, and I need no help around the shop."

Graeden nodded and reached for the coin purse in his pocket. The storekeeper smiled. "So, what is it that you will be needing today, sir?"

Graeden rattled off his list, glad to discover the shopkeeper had everything on hand.

"Will you be staying at The Spotted Hen tonight?" the tradesman asked as Graeden handed him the money. "The inn you passed on your way here. It is quite respectable and has quite a good reputation among travelers – tasty food and clean sheets and, if you are inclined..."

"No," Graeden said curtly.

Graeden quickly packed the supplies on the nervous horse and rode off.

Once on the open road beyond the village, both relaxed. Merlona stopped at a clearing on the side of the road about an hour later. There they made camp.

# CHAPTER TWELVE

TREBEH KEPT a watchful eye on Regnaryn. Not surprisingly, she seemed as jittery as a chicken in a skulk of foxes. The sight of the normally fierce girl so cowered broke Trebeh's heart.

Everyone was kept away from her. Everyone but Neshya. After their little secret, the siblings had formed an even closer bond. When alone, Neshya showed both an uncharacteristic tenderness and a healthy amount of teasing; the combination seemed to help.

Days passed and life returned to its usual routine, Regnaryn again ate meals with the family and resumed some of her regular chores. Still, she fought sleep to the point that it took a physical toll upon her, her exhaustion apparent to everyone in the household, especially Neshya.

"Regg, you really need to get some sleep," Neshya said. "You are going to make yourself sick."

"I am fine."

Neshya grabbed her arm. "No. You are not!"

She glared at him.

"Regg, it is the middle of the night, and we are sitting staring into the darkness."

She walked to the window. "If you want to go to bed, go."

"But..." he said, taking her arm again.

She pulled away. "I said I am fine, so leave me alone."

She walked into the other room leaving him unsure about what to do.

When Regnaryn was like this, it was best to leave her be. But how could he? Why had Mama not done something, said something, to make Regg come around? Was he seeing something that was not there?

### ###

After just a few hours of sleep, Neshya came downstairs to find Trebeh cleaning up the kitchen.

"I am sorry."

"Sorry for what, son?"

"For oversleeping and missing breakfast. For not getting to my morning chores..."

Trebeh turned and smiled. "You have been doing something far more important than your regular chores. You are helping your sister. Now sit, I saved you some food."

Trebeh put a plate in front of him.

"What is wrong?"

Neshya nearly choked on the mouthful of food. "What makes you think something is wrong?"

Trebeh laughed. "Child, I carried you in my belly then suckled you at my breast, I have watched you go from infant to gangly kitling to near manhood. Do you think you can truly hide your feelings from me?"

"It is Regg."

Trebeh waited.

"She is making herself sick," he continued. "She refuses to sleep save the few moments when her eyes defy her determination to keep them open. Surely you see that."

Trebeh said nothing.

"Why have you not done something?"

Trebeh ignored the frustration and anger in his voice. She

understood. "What would you have me do?"

Neshya shook his head. "I do not know. Surely, there must be something."

Trebeh smiled. It was nice to think that, even on the threshold of manhood, he still thought she could fix everything.

"So I gather that you do not think she will come around on her own?"

"No."

Neshya's sadness almost brought Trebeh to tears. She reached across the table and took his hand in hers. "I will not let it go on much longer, child. I promise."

### 

It did not surprise Neshya to find Regnaryn fast asleep in the chair in the sun room that night. He carried her upstairs to her bed. Her eyes briefly fluttered open, then closed. Neshya pulled up the covers and watched her.

"You need not stay. She will not wake until morning."

"I know, Mama, but..."

Trebeh nodded. "Do not stay too long, son. You have not been doing much sleeping lately, either."

"I promise, Mama, not too long."

Trebeh walked away, knowing she would find him asleep at Regnaryn's bedside come morning.

### 

"What have you been doing to me?" Regnaryn snarled.

"Have I been doing something?" Trebeh replied without looking up from her book.

"Yes. Something to make me sleep."

Trebeh looked up.

"You can stop now. I will sleep on my own."

"How has your sleep been? No more intrusions since we strengthened your shieldings?"

"None."

Trebeh nodded, "Good."

The yeckal knew it was time to tell Regnaryn about her mother's prophecy. She avoided this moment. First, by trying to convince herself it was not related and then, after the incident, by saying Regnaryn needed time to recover.

"Come sit by me."

Regnaryn did as instructed.

"How much do you remember of your mother, Karaleena?"

Regnaryn thought the question odd. "Only what you and Papa have told me."

"I thought as much. After all, you were very young when we lost her... and the others."

"No one really talks much of them anymore and when you do, you all look so sad."

"I suppose we do." Trebeh sighed. "Not only were your parents instrumental in the founding of Reissem Grove, they were our dearest friends." She paused and took a deep breath, "Did I ever tell you that your mother was a card caster of some repute?"

Regnaryn shook her head.

"Your mother spoke of many things that would come to pass, including a prophecy just before you were born."

"About me?"

"Yes."

"Why do you bring this up now?"

"Karaleena foretold that you would grow to be a powerful magicker, perhaps the most powerful to ever live. And with the mention of your power in the dreams..."

"What? You knew this and never told me?" Regnaryn railed.

Trebeh looked away.

"Why did you not tell me of this after the first dream?"

Trebeh did not respond.

Regnaryn stormed out.

The sound of the front door slamming echoed through the quiet house.

# CHAPTER THIRTEEN

SPRING TURNED to summer, though this far north the warmth Graeden was accustomed to never materialized. The weather was pleasant and the further into summer it got, much to Graeden's relief, fewer storms occurred.

After traveling the same road in the same northeasterly direction for days on end, Merlona suddenly changed course and chose the path that headed due north.

Graeden tugged on the reins to stop her. "What are you doing?" he demanded, fearful that terrible sensation would again strike him down.

She ignored him.

He jerked the reins.

Merlona whipped her head around, snorted and proceeded.

Graeden held his breath, waiting for the voice in his head to once again scream. For the breath to be torn from his chest. But nothing happened.

They rode into another nondescript village, heading directly toward the shop.

"Where are you headed, lad?" the shopkeeper asked as he

gathered the requested supplies.

"Nowhere in particular." Graeden regretted his answer as soon as he saw the suspicious look that crossed the man's face. "North."

"This is the last village in Alexandrash. I suggest you take the path leading west when you leave here."

Graeden did not respond.

"The road north will end in about a day's ride and turn into nothing more than a footpath leading into the Darklands," the shopkeeper said.

"Darklands?"

"Yes, a very odd, evil place." The shopkeeper shuddered at the mere thought. "It is said that strange, horrible creatures live there. Any who enter are never seen again. Take the road west. There is no reason for any sane man to enter that place."

Graeden nodded, paid the man and departed, knowing full well it was not up to him to decide the path he would travel.

### ###

Graeden and Merlona traveled due north another day when, just as the shopkeeper said, the terrain changed. The road became nothing more than a footpath. Thick trees blocked the sun. But Merlona kept to her course without hesitation. For several days, they traveled through the thick foliage.

Then, as suddenly as the trees had thickened, they thinned. Graeden found himself facing the most treacherous rocky tract he had ever seen. It looked impassible, but Merlona confidently pushed on, navigating the terrain as if she had a map.

On the third day, the landscape changed again. An endless grassy field lay before them. Nearly overcome with exhilaration, Graeden urged Merlona to quicken her pace. She refused.

Graeden considered dismounting and leading her, but he hesitated. He looked down and spotted a large hole, an invitation for injury or death had he tumbled into it. After that, he neither urged Merlona to move faster nor dismounted without her approval.

At sunset, she stopped. Graeden realized they had not traveled very far, as he could still see the rocky tract from that morning. He knew Merlona was exhausted.

He slept more soundly than he had for quite some time. His dreams, filled with glimpses of things that seemed both new and unknown, yet also felt familiar and beckoning.

An overwhelming sense of childlike excitement roused Graeden from his slumber long before sunrise. He needed to get to the place in his dream. The place the voice within his head had been directing him towards. He rose, noting Merlona's readiness to move on.

"Since we are both anxious to be on our way, we might as well be off."

They set out before dawn. Even in the diminished light, Merlona traveled at a quick pace, again confident about the path she should travel. Exhilaration gripped Graeden.

After midday, he realized Merlona moved even faster than before, as if she knew her destination was at hand. Graeden saw nothing more than the grassy plain that seemed to go on forever. Suddenly, directly ahead, a large forest loomed maybe an hour's ride away.

Graeden rubbed his eyes, certain he was imagining it. No matter how many times he blinked, the trees did not disappear. Merlona began to gallop, a pace the mare rarely initiated.

# CHAPTER FOURTEEN

DURING AN afternoon flight, Phrynia saw Regnaryn sitting alone. Days had turned to weeks. Still, the young woman had not been told the details of Karaleena's prophecy. The drageal decided to take matters into her own hands, regardless of Trebeh's wishes.

Regnaryn sat with a book in her lap, staring blankly into the distance. She jumped when Phrynia touched her shoulder.

"I am sorry, child," the drageal said. "I did not mean to startle you. I thought you heard me."

Regnaryn leaned over and picked up the book. "I guess my mind was elsewhere."

Phrynia chuckled, "It must have been quite the daydream, child, you have been fidgeting for the last..."

Before the drageal could finish, Regnaryn snapped, "First Mama, and now you!"

Regnaryn jumped to her feet. Before she could bolt, Phrynia grabbed her shoulder. Regnaryn turned, the furious expression on her face surprising the drageal and loosening her grip. Regnaryn took the chance to escape.

"Leave me alone, all of you!" she shouted.

Phrynia now understood Trebeh's problem. Still, Regnaryn needed to be told.

Something was coming. Phrynia sensed it. She could not see it clearly, but every fiber of her being told her it involved the prophecy.

Phrynia mindcalled Trebeh, telling her of Regnaryn's reaction.

*:Yes, that is her response to everything and everyone, except Neshya.:*

Phrynia laughed. *:Perhaps he should tell her.:*

*:That thought has crossed my mind.:*

*:Still, the way she is acting – so out of character.:*

*:What are you thinking, Phrynia?:*

*:I wonder if it is just the dreams that have her in this state, or if there is more to this than we are seeing?:*

*:More?:* Trebeh asked, not sure she really wanted to know.

*:Could this be part of the prophecy?:*

*:Or is it just a phase human children go through at this age?:*

*:Either way, she must be told. We cannot put this off any longer.:*

Trebeh nodded. *:You have seen her reaction to merely being approached. Any mention of the prophecy or Karaleena elicits far worse.:*

*:If we have to, we will hold her down until she listens,:* Phrynia replied only half-jokingly.

Suddenly they were interrupted by the news of an approaching stranger. A human!

*:That settles it. Surely, you can no longer deny Karaleena's prediction. Regnaryn must be told. Immediately!:*

It was true. Even if the approaching human was not the one of the prophecy, his arrival, coupled with recent events, erased any doubt Trebeh previously held.

*:Yes, the time has come.:*

### ###

The two women found Regnaryn, once again gazing off into the distance. Trebeh approached. The girl rose, ready to run.

81

"So now you have come together," Regnaryn said as Phrynia silently landed behind her to block any escape.

Trebeh nodded. "You refuse to listen to either of us. What other choice is there?"

"I do not wish to hear any of this," Regnaryn said flatly.

"You have made that clear," Phrynia replied.

"Apparently not clear enough."

Trebeh was no longer shocked by Regnaryn's bitter tone. "Does that not tell you the importance of the matter?"

Regnaryn shrugged and sat down. "If you must." She sighed. "Apparently, the only way to stop this constant harassment is to hear this prophecy you suddenly think so significant."

"Regnaryn," Trebeh began, "it is true we were told of the prediction before your birth. You know seers well enough to realize not all that we foretell comes to pass."

"Still, you have not thought it necessary to tell me until now," Regnaryn said, the cold edge again present in her voice.

"In all honesty, child," Phrynia replied, "we had forgotten about it."

Regnaryn turned toward Phrynia, a look of shock on her face. Before she could speak, the drageal continued.

"Regnaryn, you must remember, your mother only told us of her vision in passing. She did not go into great detail. Then, with all that went on after that, well..."

"And," Trebeh added, "you have never shown any extraordinary abilities, nor have there been any signs leading us to believe the prophecy would come to pass."

"Until now," Regnaryn answered.

Trebeh nodded. "The mention of your power in the dream awakened our memories of Karaleena's words. I hoped it was nothing, but after the latest incident..."

"And just what was this prediction?" Regnaryn asked, her voice just a bit less cold.

"Your mother said you would be a great magicker, perhaps the most powerful the world has ever seen."

Regnaryn stared at the two women. "That is what you told me before. But you said yourself, I have never shown any unusual or extraordinary abilities."

"They may still lie dormant."

"Perhaps, both the prophecy and your interpretation are wrong," Regnaryn snapped.

"Maybe, but there was more to Karaleena's vision," Phrynia replied. "She spoke of a struggle, a power struggle between you and another. A struggle that could decide the fate of many."

Regnaryn laughed. "Me? Powerful? Deciding the fate of many? Does that not sound just a little absurd? I do not believe any of it."

Phrynia nodded. "True, we could be looking at the predictions from the wrong view, and they may not come to pass. However, with your dreams and some of the odd feelings Trebeh and I have been experiencing, we thought it best to inform you of the prophecy's existence."

Regnaryn looked a bit puzzled. "Odd feelings?"

"Little things. Like a sense that we have forgotten or not seen something that was right in front of us."

"Nothing we can put our fingers on," Trebeh said.

*:Should we tell her of the approaching human?:* Trebeh asked.

*:No. Let us wait to see if he actually comes here.:*

Trebeh breathed a sigh of relief at Phrynia's words.

### 

On the sixth day after the traveler was first seen, Ayirak stood at the edge of the forest and watched his approach. From both path and speed, Ayirak knew the rider would enter Reissem Grove this day. He sighed and mindcalled Regnaryn to meet him.

"You sent for me, Papa," Regnaryn said. "We missed you at breakfast."

Ayirak smiled, glad she seemed in better spirits than in recent days.

"You did not have to run, child," he said, brushing the hair from her eyes. "I need you to come with me. A stranger is approaching, and you need to greet him."

Regnaryn looked at him blankly. "A stranger? Here?"

Ayirak nodded.

"But how? I did not think outsiders could find this place."

"Most cannot. But, if one is meant to be here, then the path is clearly visible." She stared at him as he continued, "That is part of the mystery of Reissem Grove."

"But why would you need me?" she asked. "Surely he should be met by one of his own kind, not me."

"You *are* his kind. He is a human, like you," he answered calmly.

Stunned, her expression hardened.

"How can that be?" she shouted. "I am the last human. You told me that yourself. I... I do not understand."

"No child, you are merely the last human *here*. There are many others of your kind outside Reissem Grove."

"First the prophecy, and now this. What else have you all kept from me?" she demanded.

Ayirak gently pulled her close to him. She looked into his large yellow-green eyes, eyes that could offer comfort or cut you to the quick. The betrayal she felt did not allow her to accept his support.

She pulled away. "How could you let me go on thinking I was alone? Why?" Her words trailed off. She turned and saw Trebeh.

"We never told you of the other humans or the prophecy, child," Trebeh said, "because we did not think there was a need. In all the years we have been here, no humans, save the group that founded this place, have ever come."

"You still should have told me," Regnaryn fumed. "Instead, you allowed me to be treated as an outcast. An oddity. Never fitting in, never being accepted. Always being alone."

Regnaryn regretted her words as soon as they left her lips. They were lies. She had always been accepted. No, more than that, she had been loved like kin by everyone.

"I am sorry, Mama," she sobbed. "I did not mean that."

"You have a right to be angry, child. We should have told you. We were selfish, fearful if you knew there were other humans, you would leave to find them. After losing your parents and the others, we could not bear to lose you, too."

Trebeh turned to Ayirak, tears wetting the white fur of her face. He held her gently. Regnaryn ran to them. Ayirak wrapped his massive arms around both.

"We were wrong, Regnaryn," Ayirak said sadly, "and we are deeply sorry for that."

*:Ayirak, he is getting closer. It is time Regg goes to meet him,:* Immic, who had been watching the traveler's progress, mindcalled to him.

*:We will be there shortly.:*

Ayirak released mother and child. He wiped the tears from Regnaryn's cheek. "It is time for you to greet our guest."

# CHAPTER FIFTEEN

SUDDENLY, THE FIGURE of a young woman appeared at the edge of the trees. Graeden could not see her face, but instinctively knew she was beautiful.

He was so focused on her, he did not realize Merlona had stopped until he heard the girl's muffled laughter.

He dismounted and tried to regain his composure. Even clad in breeches, she was more beautiful than he had imagined. He stood mesmerized by her porcelain white skin, huge green eyes and tawny red hair. Merlona's nudge brought him back to the moment.

Regnaryn eyed him with curiosity. He did not look much older than she. And there was something about him that seemed familiar. She felt she knew him. But that was impossible, she had not seen another human these past thirteen years; had not even known there were any other humans. Still...

"My lady," Graeden began.

"I am not your lady," Regnaryn snapped.

"I am sorry, my..." he hesitated. "I am sorry, I do not know your name, and My Lady *is* the correct form of address in these situations. At least, that is the case where I come from." His hint of superiority was not lost on Regnaryn.

"And is it the custom where you come from," she replied with haughty emphasis, "to not offer your name first?"

Graeden could not help but notice the glint in her eyes as she chided him. *Those eyes*, he thought, and realized it was more than that. There was something else, something he could not put his finger on... something familiar.

"You are right," he answered, choosing not to use any form of address at all. "I most humbly apologize." He bowed deeply at the waist. "I am Graeden, sixth son of Lord Emmaus and Lady Prescia, Stewards of the province of Hammarsh in the southernmost region of the Kingdom of Alexandrash." As the words left his lips, he realized they sounded pompous and empty. "I am sure that means nothing to you, but you did ask."

She nodded.

"And may I have the honor of knowing your name?" He waited a moment, but she did not respond. "Lady? Your name?"

"Oh, I am sorry, my mind was elsewhere. I am Regnaryn."

"Lady Regnaryn, a lovely name and so fitting for such a beautiful lady," he said, smiling broadly.

She was about to snap at him, but his smile looked so sincere, she merely said, "It is Regnaryn, just Regnaryn."

He nodded. "What is this place?"

"What do you mean?"

"What is this place called?"

"Reissem Grove."

"Ah, that is a lovely name also. It is so beautiful, though quite the perilous trek to get here."

She did not respond.

"Do you live nearby? And where are the other people?"

"Yes, my home is close by. I am the only human," she replied.

"You say that as if there were something other than humans," he said, half joking.

Surely he could not be so stupid to not know of the others, she thought.

"Of course, there are. Yekcal and shanassi, queetok and yawalla." She saw no recognition in his face. "And chetoga all live here."

He showed a faint glimmer of recognition at that name.

"And, of course, drageal."

"My dear Regnaryn, you are mocking me," he said. "Everyone knows drageals are mere myth, the stuff of children's bedtime stories."

She chuckled. "I think you will have a hard time convincing Immic and the others of that."

He looked bewildered.

"Now, if you and your lovely companion will follow me."

She smiled, and he nearly fell over his own feet. She walked away. Graeden watched how her clothes hugged her body, how the fabric moved as she did with near-liquid fluidity. She turned, grabbed the end of her braid which now lay between her firm breasts, and flipped it over her shoulder. She motioned him to follow. He did so, mesmerized by how, with each step, her braid swayed in opposition to her hips. He felt a desire rising deep within him, reminding him just how long he had been alone.

She stopped, waiting for him to catch up. "Was he always this slow on the road, pretty lady?" she asked the mare as he reached her side.

Merlona shook her head.

"Come on," Regnaryn grabbed his arm and pulled him towards her so they could walk side by side.

The mere touch of her hand sent shivers through his body. He wanted to seize her and make love to her on this very spot but, as he looked into her face, she seemed much younger and more innocent than he had originally thought. He chastised himself for his lustful thoughts.

"Let me tell you what I know of this place."

She spoke about Reissem Grove, pointing out foliage and paths and whatever else she saw. He questioned her on politics and economics, topics important in other places but not here. Things Regnaryn neither knew nor cared about.

"Regnaryn, you say you know nothing of these things I ask, yet you speak perfect Alexandrashi. How can that be?"

"It was the language of my parents and the other humans."

He waited for further explanation but none came. When she did speak, it was of the beauty of the place and its people. Graeden met her ardor with skepticism.

*:Speak to his mind, child, not his ears,:* Ayirak thought gently to her.

She did as instructed and reached out to Graeden's mind. What she found surprised them both.

"By all that is holy," Graeden blurted out. "It is *you*!"

She shook her head in disbelief. "You are real. And you are here."

He excitedly nodded. "As are you. I remember now. The inn... those things... the pain... and you."

He grabbed her and kissed her with gratitude. She stood frozen in place, too shocked to move.

"You saved me! It was you who kept me from going mad. You gave me hope."

He wrapped his arms around her and kissed her again. This time with more than gratitude. The intensity of the second kiss did not escape Ayirak and the others. Ayirak broke from the cover of the trees, grabbed Graeden's shoulder, and swung him around. The yeckal gripped his shirt front and lifted him off the ground until the two were face to face.

"What do you think you are doing?" he shouted in Alexandrashi, his deep booming voice thundering in Graeden's ears as he was dangled above the ground.

Graeden, stunned by the fierceness of this strange, massive cat-like beast, who held his life in its huge hand, feared the beast's deep and rumbling voice would make his heart explode. How was it, he wondered, that the beast also spoke Alexandrashi?

Graeden could not speak. He just hung limply in the beast's grasp.

"Papa, leave him be," Regnaryn cried.

Graeden heard her voice, but he failed to grasp the meaning of her words. All he could think about as he faded from consciousness was his fear of this talking beast.

Ayirak sneered, dropped him to the ground, and slowly walked away.

"Neshya, take care of him," he growled.

Neshya picked up the limp body and swung it over his shoulder. He grabbed Regnaryn by the hand and dragged her along, "I suggest we stay away from Papa for a bit."

"What is going on?" she sobbed. "Did Papa kill him?"

Neshya shook his head. "Nah, the poor thing merely fainted. Just as well."

Regnaryn refused to walk, forcing Neshya to drag her.

"I want to know what is going on," she demanded when he finally stopped. "What made Papa so mad?"

"Oh, no." Neshya laughed. "Not me, little one."

"Do not call me that, I am not a little. I am almost as old as you are," she said angrily. "You never call Nelluc little one, and we are the same age. I am so tired of being treated like a child."

Neshya was surprised by her reaction, he had always called her little one.

"Be that as it may, Regg, I am not the one to give you that talk. Ask Papa. No, that would not do." The thought of Papa discussing that with her made Neshya start laughing again. "You had best ask Mama that question."

He readjusted the bundle on his shoulder and took his bewildered sister's hand, tugging at her until she again followed.

*Poor thing*, Neshya thought. *She really has no idea why Papa reacted so.*

###

:*Ah, at last, the young ones have met,*: the female voice stated.

:*All will be well now. They will defeat the Master,*: Ellyss said.

:*Perhaps.*:

:*Have you seen something? Something to say there is more trouble to come?*: Aloysius asked.

:*We must wait and see. But for now, farewell, my friends.*:

Ellyss turned to Aloysius. "I hate when she is so evasive."

Aloysius laughed. "And when have you known Jucara to be anything but cryptic?"

# CHAPTER SIXTEEN

TREBEH WAITED in the hallway. She directed Neshya to bring the stranger to his room and stay with him. Regnaryn silently followed.

Neshya dropped Graeden's limp body on the spare bed.

"Be careful, you will hurt him," Regnaryn said as Graeden nearly bounced off the bed.

"He will be fine, do not worry. You can stay with him and hold his little hand until he wakes up," he teased. "Just hope Mama can calm Papa."

Regnaryn still did not understand Papa's anger. She sat in a chair by the side of the bed. "Oh, Nesh, look at him," she wailed as Neshya lighted the lamps. "Papa must have hurt him. Look at his face."

Neshya wiped Graeden's face. "It is only dirt. He is not hurt." He sat in the chair just beyond Graeden's line of sight. Neshya did not think the newcomer would repeat his previous action, but he stayed to make sure he did not, for everyone's sake.

Regnaryn held Graeden's hand and recalled what she had seen earlier when she touched his mind. Papa's actions had almost made her forget.

"Nesh, do you know who this is?"

"Not a clue," Neshya replied. "But you seem to."

"He is the one from the dream; the one being tortured and tormented."

Graeden stirred. The young yekcal sat back in his chair, allowing the shadows to engulf him.

Regnaryn moved closer to Graeden. He looked puzzled. Then, he remembered.

"Regnaryn." He sat up. "What happened? Where am I?" She stroked his hand.

"Wait, I remember now. You, you somehow got inside my head. Like in my dreams. How did you do that?" he asked but did not wait for an answer. "I kissed you. And then, there was a beast, a huge beast that yelled at me in... in Alexandrashi! I was terrified it was going to kill me."

He looked at her tear-streaked face. "And you talked to it." He searched her face, looking for anything to bring sanity to the situation. "What is going on?"

"I do not know what happened. I do not know why. I..." Her sobs devoured her words.

Graeden instinctively put his arms around her.

"I would not do that," Neshya said quietly.

Both Regnaryn and Graeden jumped at the sound of the yekcal's voice and pulled away.

Neshya leaned forward. Graeden's eyes widened at the sight of the same kind of beast he had met earlier. This one was much smaller and, at the moment, less violent It, too, spoke Graeden's tongue.

As Neshya sat on the edge of the bed, Graeden drew back in fear.

"Stop it, Neshya. You are scaring him," Regnaryn said, glaring at her brother.

"I am here to protect him... and you. What do you think Papa would do if he came in here and found you two holding each other like that?" Neshya asked with just a hint of sarcasm. Neshya turned to Graeden. "You understand."

Graeden nodded. Somehow, as odd as the idea of talking to a beast seemed, Graeden sensed a familiarity to it he did not understand.

"Rather than yelling at me, little sister, perhaps you should tell your friend here what is going on. I think he will take it better coming from your lips than from those of a beast." Neshya laughed at his sister's expression.

"I will stay to make sure the story gets told correctly. And you," Neshya continued, turning his attention back to Graeden. "You should think about closing your mouth before some other beast comes along, mistakes you for a fish, and hooks you for dinner."

Graeden snapped his mouth shut. Neshya laughed. Regnaryn's angry glare made her brother laugh even more.

"Where should I begin?" she mused.

She described the history of the first meeting of human, yekcal and drageal in Reissem Grove; of mindspeech and how it miraculously came to all that inhabited this place in a way that transcended language barriers. Graeden listened, but he did not comprehend.

"What of the talking beasts?" he asked.

Both she and Neshya threw their hands up in exasperation.

"Have you not heard a word I said, you... you stupid human? There are no beasts here. There are only people, different from you and me, but people just the same. Intelligent people. And far more intelligent than you will ever hope to be if your narrow-minded reaction is any indication of how your tiny brain works," she shouted at the stunned young man.

Graeden opened his mouth to speak. She would not let him.

"I do not know why Papa wanted to throttle you, but your stupidity has me ready to call him to finish what he started."

She left the room in a huff, leaving the stunned Graeden alone with the beast. Neshya shook his head and tried his best not to laugh.

"Whew, I have not seen anyone get her that angry since... No, I take that back, I have never seen anyone make her *that* angry, ever!" Neshya could no longer contain his laughter. "Oh, the others are going to be so upset they missed seeing this."

Graeden quickly turned away not sure how safe he was alone with the cat-like beast. Neshya leaned over, took Graeden's chin in his hand and turned the newcomer's face towards him. Graeden stiffened in fear as he saw the previously laughing face turn deeply somber.

"You are an idiot," Neshya began, eyes locked onto Graeden's. "If we truly were the beasts you think us, would you still be alive? Do you think Regnaryn is our pet? Did you hear anything my sister said to you?"

Neshya saw the look of disbelief on Graeden's face at his relationship to Regnaryn and shook his head in disgust. He released Graeden's chin.

"Yes, we are siblings. She has lived with this family as one of our own since her parents and the other humans died of some disease that affected only them." Neshya's voice hardened.

Graeden's thoughts swirled. "But surely you are joking when you say drageal live here? How can that be?" For the moment, the irony that he was asking one fantastical being about the existence of another was lost on him. "Drageals are myths, beasts..." Graeden caught himself as the word left his lips, "I mean, beings of fairy stories."

Neshya shook his head. "Are all humans, save Regnaryn, so incredibly dense? I am not sure saying it a fourth time will help, but if you wish, I will."

"That will not be necessary. I just do not understand how this can be? This is the stuff of fable. Or perhaps I am dreaming?"

"You hear the words, but you do not listen. Can you really be that stupid?" Neshya asked again.

"I am trying to listen, to understand, to believe. But this is all so... so different than what I have known. From all I have been taught." Graeden looked as baffled as he sounded.

Neshya nodded. "I suppose that is true. But I assure you, we are real."

Neshya stood. He turned back to Graeden as he reached the doorway. He said softly but sternly, "By the way, if you do *anything*, and I do mean anything, to hurt my sister, you will see the true ferocity of a yekcal when we protect our own." The young yekcal turned and departed, closing the door behind him.

Graeden stared at the door. The more he tried to make sense of all that had gone on, the more it made no sense – intelligent non-humans, humans living with non-humans, communicating with each other through their minds. But, somehow, all of this bore a strange sense of familiarity.

Graeden's head pounded. He closed his eyes and fell back on the pillows, half hoping sleep would make it all go away.

# CHAPTER SEVENTEEN

"I BROUGHT YOU dinner, young man," the female voice purred as she entered.

Graeden slowly sat up and stared wide-eyed at the beautiful cat-like creature who stood before him. She looked gentler than the others, and her smile made him feel she knew his thoughts. She set down the tray and motioned him to eat. He nodded silently and reached for the cup of steaming liquid.

"Be careful, dear, the tea is very hot."

Her tone reminded him of his mother. He withdrew his hand.

"Perhaps you should let that cool," Trebeh said from the chair beside the bed.

He nodded and picked up one of the meat-filled pieces of bread. He took a small bite, realized how hungry he was, and took another bite before he swallowed the first.

She laughed. "Slow down, boy, no one is going to steal your food."

He stopped and stared at her, remembering how often his mother had said the same thing when he and his brothers gobbled their food.

"Sorry," he mumbled, his mouth still full. He swallowed. "I did not mean to be rude."

"I just do not want you to choke on your first day here."

He smiled and took a sip of the tea.

"It is Graeden, correct?" she asked, and he nodded. "I am Trebeh. I understand you had a less than pleasant introduction to my mate, Ayirak. You will have to forgive him. He is usually not so aggressive."

Graeden winced at the memory of his meeting with the large yekcal.

"But dear boy, you must admit your actions toward Regnaryn were not exactly what *any* father wishes to see."

Graeden tried to think of something to say in his defense.

"I realize you think you did nothing wrong," she continued. "You merely kissed a girl."

Graeden nearly spit out the tea. That was exactly what he was thinking.

She continued, ignoring his reaction. "Where you come from, that behavior may be commonplace, but as Neshya told you, Regnaryn has been the only human in our community for quite some time, so she is not..."

Graeden looked at Trebeh and suddenly her meaning struck him.

"Oh, no," he said, shaking his head. "I meant no harm. I mean, I am sorry. It was just, well, when she spoke into my mind, I realized she was the one who had helped me through terrors I did not understand. Terrors I had forgotten until that moment. And there she was, standing right in front of me! Real! Flesh and blood! I was so excited to meet her, to see that she was not something my imagination had conjured, I..." He stopped, looked at Trebeh, and was relieved to see she understood. "I am truly sorry," he continued, his head bowed in apology, "I meant no disrespect."

"I hoped there was more to your actions than mere lust," she said as she brushed a strand of hair from his face. He did not pull away from her touch. "I was unaware of this bond you two share."

"How did you know what I was thinking?" He did not try to hide his suspicion.

She smiled. "I have several sons, and they all think the same. And, in a way, you told me. The more excited you get, the louder you shout your every thought."

He did not understand.

"Graeden, Regnaryn spoke into your mind, right?"

He nodded.

"Anyone who belongs here can communicate with their minds. It is called mindspeech."

He listened, actually hearing her words. "But if you can hear my thoughts, why can I not hear yours?"

"They are shielded," she said. *:Only when I wish to mindspeak to someone will they hear my thoughts,:* she mindspoke to him.

He jumped with surprise. "This is so unbelievable. I have so many questions."

"Yes, I am sure you do. There will be time for those later. Right now, I would like to help you shield your thoughts. You will need your privacy to sort things out for yourself."

Graeden nodded.

She took his hand and joined empathically with him. He watched as she built a wall around his mind, layering stone upon stone. When complete, he felt her leave his thoughts. Somehow, her departure felt oddly familiar.

"There," she said with a sigh of relief. "Your thoughts are now your own. It is not the strongest of shieldings, but it will be fine to keep your thoughts in and others out."

"Are you saying someone might try to enter my mind?" he asked.

Trebeh smiled. "Well... I can not guarantee the young ones would not try to find out who and what you are."

He stared at her.

"It would not be done with malice, just curiosity. You are the first human, besides Regnaryn, that many of them have ever seen."

"Of course."

"Good, and I see you are now more comfortable around this beast."

Graeden flushed and bowed his head. "Oh, you heard about that. I am sorry, I did not really mean it, I just..."

She smiled at him. "I know. I understand, even if Regnaryn and Neshya do not. Are you ready to meet the rest of the family?"

"Um, what about..." Graeden fumbled for the name of the first yekcal he had met.

"Ayirak?" she finished his question. "Yes, he is downstairs, too. But do not worry, I have explained what happened. I promise he will not hurt you."

She winked, and Graeden knew he was safe. He got up from the bed and looked at himself.

"Lady..." he began.

"Just call me Trebeh," she said.

"Trebeh, is there some place I can clean up? I look quite the mess." And then it dawned on him. "And what about my horse?"

"She has been taken care of. In fact, I believe Regnaryn and your mare have had quite the discussion about you."

Graeden was not sure what she meant, but he chose not to pursue it.

"As for cleaning up, yes... Now that I take a closer look at you, a good wash and a change of clothes are definitely in order."

"I do not think my other clothes are in any better condition than these," Graeden answered.

"I think I can find something that might work." She eyed him up and down and continued, "Not a perfect fit, but they will do for the time being. I will have Neshya bring them to you. In the meantime, the bathing chamber is through that doorway. Just a quick wash-up for now. You can have a full soak later on."

She left and Graeden headed for the bathing chamber. He stopped and marveled at the room with its walls that looked like polished marble. It was magnificent.

He grabbed a washcloth and towel from the open chest and stripped off his clothes. He stepped to the basin and uncorked the pipes affixed to the wall, which allowed water to flow. As he washed off the topmost layer of road dirt, he heard the soothing sound of water and saw a waterfall gurgling into a small pool. Beyond that, was a privy behind a half-wall.

He was almost finished when he heard Neshya return.

"I put the change of clothes on the bed," Neshya said. "Mama said not to dawdle."

"I am almost ready," Graeden answered from the adjoining chamber.

"I will wait in the hall."

Graeden returned to the bedroom and dressed. The clothes were luxurious to the touch and a decent fit. He pulled the pants drawstring tight around his waist and rolled up the legs and the shirt sleeves, the former owner was obviously taller and heavier than Graeden. He tied his freshly brushed hair back off his face and joined the waiting Neshya in the hallway.

### 

"I want to apologize for the way I acted earlier," Graeden said as Neshya led the way down the hall.

Neshya laughed. "Not to worry. It was worth it to see how angry you made Regg."

"We have not been properly introduced yet." Graeden extended his hand to the yekcal. "I am Graeden. And you are Neshya, correct?"

"Yes." The young yekcal shook Graeden's hand.

# CHAPTER EIGHTEEN

AT THE BOTTOM of the stairs, two bouncing balls of shrieking yellow and white fur assaulted Graeden. They wrapped themselves around his legs, forcing him to grab the banister to keep from falling on top of them. The kitlings squealed his name over and over as they jumped up and down. He looked to Neshya for help but the yekcal was too busy laughing to be of any assistance.

"Children, enough. Leave him be."

Graeden recognized the voice, not nearly as booming or angry as when he first heard it, but Ayirak's just the same.

The children immediately stopped their squealing and reluctantly let loose of Graeden's legs. They stomped away, pouting and muttering.

Ayirak stood in the doorway, glaring and clearly not amused at the goings on. Neshya tried to stop laughing with only limited success. Graeden stood frozen, unsure of what to do.

"Stop scaring the boy," Trebeh called out. "Come in here, all of you."

Neshya, still trying to stifle his laughter, led Graeden into the large room. He was barely seated on the couch facing the fireplace before the two yellow balls of fur snuggled beside him. Graeden instinctively put his arms around them and both beamed and chattered so fast, he could not understand one thing before they were on to another.

"Girls." Trebeh's voice sounded firm but loving. "Let him be." She turned to Graeden, "These little balls of energy are my babies."

Both pouted.

"I am sorry," she said, grinning. "These are my youngest kitlings; the twins, Norellan and Katalanar."

"I am very pleased to meet such beautiful young ladies," Graeden said and squeezed them tighter. "Twins, eh? I, too, am a twin."

"Really?" one of them asked.

"Does he look like you?" asked the other.

Graeden smiled and shook his head. "No. My twin is a sister, Taaryn. And I have been told she is much prettier than I am."

The twins squealed with joy, and Graeden noticed the look of satisfaction on Trebeh's face.

He realized the girls spoke Alexandrashi mixed with something that was a beautiful blend of purrs and trills along with other more word-like sounds, which Neshya or Trebeh would translate.

A few moments later, the front door opened. Two more yekcal, from the size of them also Trebeh's children, entered the room and kissed both Trebeh and Ayirak on their cheeks. They walked over to Graeden, introducing themselves as Nelluc and Ennales. Ayirak made a slight snort of disapproval, and Graeden saw Trebeh gently slap his hand.

"It seems you have angered Regnaryn to the point she does not even want to be in your company, Graeden," Ennales said.

Graeden reddened.

"Can you tell me how to do that so she will not want to be in my company once in a while."

Neshya and Ennales broke into laughter. Nelluc tried to stifle her own amusement. Even Ayirak's icy glare did not completely curb the children's amusement.

The next moment, Regnaryn entered the room. She smiled, mesmerizing Graeden once again. Her facial expression changed to a glare when she saw the twins wriggling all over him.

"They are not pets, you know," she snapped.

"Regnaryn," Trebeh said sternly. "You have no cause to speak so."

Regnaryn shifted her eyes downward, her face flushed. She did not apologize. "It is time for their bath," she said flatly.

She approached, but the twins did not intend to leave Graeden. She leaned over and grabbed their arms. They held fast to Graeden.

With her so close, he saw she was even more beautiful than he had originally thought. Again, his desire for her stirred deep within.

Trebeh had had enough of the twins' resistance. She spoke, and though he could not understand the words, Graeden recognized the tone, one that left no room for discussion. The kitlings reluctantly left his side and followed Regnaryn.

Graeden smiled as he watched them. "My little sisters are just like that. I guess little ones are the same no matter who they are."

Trebeh nodded. Ayirak scowled. Graeden summoned all of his courage, rose from his seat and walked across the room until he stood directly in front of the massive yekcal. He swallowed hard and bowed deeply from the waist.

"Sir, I humbly apologize for my actions earlier today. It was never my intent to hurt or take advantage of Regnaryn, or to dishonor you or your kin in any way."

Ayirak's expression remained glacial.

"There is no excuse for my behavior," Graeden continued. "I was so overcome by relief and gratitude at the realization Regnaryn was real, that she was flesh and blood, I could not help myself."

"That was no kiss of mere gratitude, boy," Ayirak answered, clearly holding back his rage. "She is a mere child, boy and you... you..."

Ayirak could not finish. He did not want to say aloud what

resided in his thoughts.

*:Ayirak, the boy has apologized,:* Trebeh said. *:Let it go. He did not realize what he was doing. You should not have been so hard on him.:*

*:But you did not see. He knew exactly what he was doing. You do not understand,:* he snapped.

*:I do. He kissed your little kitling. Her first kiss not as daughter, sister or friend. The kind of kiss you thought you would never see. Am I right, my love?:* she asked, although she did not wait for a reply. *:I understand, she is the child who holds a special place in your heart, and mine as well. But, in reality, she is not really a child, not any longer.:*

Ayirak did not answer, did not have to. Both knew she was right. He turned to her and caught the wink she gave him. Ayirak rose from his chair and looked down as Graeden waited nervously before him.

For an instant Graeden thought of bolting. He realized, even if he managed to escape, he had nowhere to go. Ayirak reached for him. Graeden flinched in anticipation of a blow. Instead, Ayirak gently put his hand on the boy's shoulder.

"I accept your apology, young man."

Graeden let out a sigh of relief, and flushed as he realized the others heard. Neshya, of course, thought it was hysterically funny and again burst into laughter.

Ennales left the room and returned with a tray laden with honey cakes and tea. He placed it on the side table and poured the cool drink. He brought a plate of cakes and a glass to his parents, then did the same for Graeden, Nelluc and finally himself.

"Hey, where is mine?" Neshya asked.

"You, little brother, can get your own if you are finally done being annoying."

Neshya shook his head, playfully mumbling about the cruel mistreatment he had to tolerate.

"They are in bed, Mama," Regnaryn said as she reentered the room.

Trebeh nodded. Regnaryn accepted the plate and glass Neshya offered.

"See, brother," he said to Ennales, "*that* is how you treat sibs."

Ennales nearly spit out his tea, making Neshya laugh again. This time, though, all, including Graeden, joined in.

"I see you now socialize with talking beasts," Regnaryn snapped as she sat on the floor cushion beside Trebeh's chair.

Graeden reddened with embarrassment. The look Regnaryn received from her mother instantly rebuked her.

"Well, Graeden," Trebeh said, "now that you have had time to adjust to some of what is going on around you, do you have any questions?"

Graeden nodded. "Oh, yes, many. But, I guess my biggest question is probably unanswerable." He swallowed hard and continued, "How is it possible that you, well… that you *are*? That you exist."

Regnaryn threw up her hands in disbelief. Trebeh just nodded.

"You are right, that is unanswerable but not at all out of line. Honestly speaking, when we first arrived here, we asked the same thing about each other."

Regnaryn looked at her mother in amazement. She had never heard such things.

"To all born here, living in harmony with beings of other races is perfectly natural. But, when we first came here, our initial reactions were very close to Graeden's. We had never heard of such things as drageal or human."

The children listened intently. They had heard the story of the Grove's founding before, but this was new.

"Before I try to answer you, Graeden, let me ask you" Trebeh said, "how is it that you, a human, exist?"

Trebeh waited and watched as Graeden thought for a moment and shook his head.

"That is my point. The only answer any of us can give to that question is, we exist because we do."

The room was quiet as everyone digested Trebeh's words. It was several moments before the silence was broken by Graeden's next question.

"How do you know Alexandrashi? You all speak it so well, even the little ones. "

"Oh, good," Neshya laughed, "a question even I can answer. It is called Alexandrashi, eh? We speak it because it was the tongue of the humans who helped to establish this place. Not everyone in Reissem can or does speak it, but Papa always said Regnaryn needed to keep some part of her heritage."

Graeden nodded. "But the twins also spoke words I did not understand. What language was that?"

"We also speak yekcal and Reissem. The twins blend all three, more often than not within the same sentence," Nelluc replied.

Graeden listened, but found himself constantly looking towards Regnaryn. She totally fascinated him. Her deep green eyes held a richness he had never before seen. When she smiled, even if it was not at him, he felt himself go weak inside.

"Reissem?" Graeden asked after Neshya nudged him back to the conversation at hand.

"Reissem, named after this place. Remember? Reissem Grove. It is our common language," Ennales answered. "It consists of words and sounds all groups that live here can make."

"Yes," Neshya chimed in. "Each group still has its own language. But not all groups are capable of creating the correct vocalizations for each language."

"Take, for instance, drageal. Only a drageal can make those sounds," Ennales added.

"Ah, drageals," Graeden said.

# CHAPTER NINETEEN

"NOW, DEAR BOY, it is time for you to tell us about yourself," Trebeh said.

Graeden looked down at his hands. "I do not think there is anything about me that you would find interesting."

"Oh, I am sure we will," Trebeh replied. "It has been quite some time since we have had the privilege of greeting anyone like you."

He nodded, took a deep breath and began, "I am the sixth son of Emmaus and Prescia, the Lord and Lady of Hammarsh. My father's holding is not large enough to allow his eight sons – five older and two younger than me – to inherit land and title. That will go to the two eldest, Matteus and Gantell.

"There is nothing of distinction about me. As long as I can remember, I have competed with my siblings, searching for something that I could be known for. Something to be best at. Everyone, even my younger brothers and sisters, have found at least one thing they have mastered. Everyone but me." His words were filled with anguish at his own shortcomings.

He had not planned on revealing why he had so abruptly left Hammarsh Keep, but before he realized it, he had told them everything about his last night at the Keep and of Gantell's drunken comments. He admitted that, almost immediately, he knew his brother's words were not the reason he stayed away.

"For days I wandered, enjoying both the solitude and the warmth of spring. One morning, and I fear you might think me insane, the voice I had been hearing in my head as a whisper suddenly insisted I pay attention to it. After that I was overcome by a feeling. No, much more than that, a compulsion, to travel to the northeast. My mare apparently felt it, too, for she refused to travel in any other direction." Graeden looked at the others. "I know that sounds a bit odd, but..."

"Actually," Trebeh replied with a faint smile, "I understand completely. But that is a tale for another time. Do go on."

"Yes, Graeden, go on, we are all ears," Neshya said.

"...and tails..."

" and claws..."

" and teeth..."

"and fur," the others added.

"Sorry, yekcal humor," Nelluc said.

Graeden noticed Regnaryn laughing along with her siblings. *That smile,* he thought yet again.

"Truth be told, my horse was the one who decided when and where we traveled. So I guess she brought me here, in more ways than one."

"That is not much of an adventure," Neshya said. "Surely something exciting must have happened on such a long journey."

Trebeh watched Graeden's face, which showed his internal struggle with the memories Regnaryn had reawakened. But there was more, as if he was searching, peering into a darkness he could not fully penetrate. After a moment, Graeden shook his head. "Nothing."

"But you met Regnaryn in that place," Trebeh said.

He nodded. "Though, I did not recall any of that until she spoke into my mind in the wood. Only then did I remember her.

And still, I only recall bits and pieces of what went on there." He looked at the others, not sure if anyone believed him. He only half believed it himself. "I know that sounds bizarre, but..."

Ayirak grumbled something under his breath. *:That is absurd. Does he really expect us to believe such drivel?:*

Trebeh squeezed his hand. *:He speaks the truth as he knows it. There is more to this than meets the eye, my love.:*

Ayirak said no more.

"There are many things that happen in this life we cannot understand, at least not at first glance," Trebeh said.

Everyone but Regnaryn chatted. Her silence did not escape Trebeh. After some time, Nelluc stifled a yawn and all realized the hour. Nelluc and Ennales excused themselves and went upstairs.

"You will sleep in the extra bed in Neshya's room, where you were earlier," Trebeh said.

Graeden nodded.

"Come on then. I guess I am stuck with you," Neshya said.

Graeden started to apologize but saw the grin on the yekcal's face.

Graeden bowed and thanked Trebeh for her hospitality. He turned to follow Neshya.

### 

"What is the matter?" Trebeh asked Regnaryn as they picked up the glasses and plates from around the room. "You barely said two words all night."

Regnaryn remained silent.

Ayirak was ready to scold the young girl for not answering but Trebeh motioned him to let it be. He reluctantly complied. He stopped Regnaryn as she walked to the kitchen and kissed the top of her head. She did not respond.

*:Why is she acting so?:* he asked Trebeh as he climbed the stairs.

*:She is still trying to sort out his presence. She is coming to grips with a lot, you know. Give her time.:*

*:Hrmph. I will never understand why children have to make such*

*a fuss over everything. Do not be too long, my love.:*

Trebeh smiled at the unspoken invitation. She walked into the kitchen, put the dishes down beside the sink, and looked at her daughter.

"Let them sit until morning," she said, taking Regnaryn's hand. "Tell me what is on your mind. You were awfully quiet this evening."

Regnaryn followed her mother back into the other room. They settled onto the couch. The yekcal could see the girl was weighing her words before she spoke.

"I... I do not trust him."

"And why do you say that? After all, he was able to find this place, which means..."

"I know what it means!" Regnaryn said sharply. "But there is just something about him. About his attitude. Do you know what he called you?"

"I do," Trebeh answered, choosing to ignore her insolent tone. "As a matter of fact, he not only told me, he apologized."

Trebeh continued, "Think how shaken you were when you realized you were not the only one of your kind. That boy came here, never realizing our kind existed. He reacted as he should have. Shocked. Confused. I would be more worried if he had not had that reaction!"

"But he called you beasts. As if you were less than he."

Trebeh nodded. "Again, expected."

Regnaryn shook her head in disbelief at Trebeh's words.

"You have read the tales and myths of your parents' land. Do not all of them describe anything that is not a human as beast? As something to be feared? Or tamed and dominated?"

"Yes, but, he is not a little. He should have known they were just stories, not truth."

Trebeh laughed. "And just how could he have known that? This is all perfectly natural to you. You were born into a world where humans were just one of many. He was not. Those stories are his only reference, so he recalled and reacted. He meant neither harm nor disrespect."

"Perhaps not," Regnaryn replied.

Trebeh sensed the girl still did not fully accept her explanation. "You trusted him before," Trebeh said.

Regnaryn stared blankly at her.

"When you met him in your dream, did you not trust him then?"

Regnaryn looked away.

"Surely there was something about him that made you want to help him?"

Regnaryn shrugged. "I did not know it was him. It was just some thing in pain."

"I see," Trebeh said.

# CHAPTER TWENTY

A LIGHT RAP on the door disturbed his slumber. It took Graeden a moment to remember where he was. Another rap, and a voice announced breakfast.

Graeden did not move.

Neshya grumbled under his breath. He got up, stretched and yawned, then headed toward the washroom. "If I were you, friend, I would not dally. If you are late to breakfast, you will not only go hungry, you will incur Mama's displeasure," Neshya said. "And you do not want to do that!"

Graeden nodded and followed the yekcal. The two young men quickly washed, dressed, and headed downstairs.

### 

They entered the dining room and encountered Ayirak's glare. Both apologized for their tardiness, took the two remaining empty chairs, and quickly filled their plates.

Graeden, amazed at the amount of food, took a bite of the flavorful fare.

"Where is Regnaryn?" he asked.

The children smirked at his question.

"Oh, she never comes to breakfast," Ennales replied.

"And when she does," Neshya said, "it is far from pleasant."

The children nodded and snickered.

"Enough," Trebeh said softly.

"I tried to wake her. I went in and shook her, but she told me to go away and pulled the covers over her head. Really, Mama, why do you even make me try?" Nelluc whined.

"If you want, I will get her up," Neshya offered with a sly grin.

"No, young man, let her be," Trebeh said. "We all remember the last time you got her up." Everyone laughed.

Graeden looked puzzled until they explained how Neshya had taken Regnaryn, bedding and all, and dumped her into the bath to wake her. Graeden tried not to laugh but he could well imagine the outraged expression on her beautiful face.

### ###

It was not until well after everyone had eaten and the room had been cleaned that Regnaryn came downstairs. She paused in the doorway at the sight of Trebeh and Graeden seated at the table talking. She said nothing.

"Come sit with us, Regnaryn," Trebeh invited.

Regnaryn took a honey cake and a glass of tea, then sat down beside her mother.

"I was just telling Graeden that you took care of his mare yesterday."

"Yes," Graeden said, "and I am very grateful."

"She is quite the beauty," Regnaryn said.

Graeden nodded. "That she is, though she can be stubborn," he said, trying not to stare at her. "Trebeh tells me you have a way with animals."

"I guess so," Regnaryn replied, not sure she appreciated Trebeh talking to him about her.

"Do you think, when you have a few moments, you could take me to her? Not that I do not trust that you took excellent care of her, but we have been together, just the two of us, for so long, I guess I miss not waking up beside her."

Trebeh smiled at the young man's embarrassment.

"We could arrange for you to sleep in the stable."

"Ayirak might prefer that," Graeden said, only half joking.

Regnaryn remained unclear about Ayirak's reaction to Graeden the previous day, and this joking by both Graeden and Trebeh confused her more. She wanted to ask Trebeh about it, but not in front of Graeden. Instead, she sat in silence.

"After you finish eating, Regnaryn, perhaps you can take him to the stable," Trebeh said.

Regnaryn nodded.

"Good, then I will tend to my chores."

Graeden watched Regnaryn eat. She made no effort to hurry, and he felt content to sit and look at her.

"Why are you staring at me?" she asked.

Graeden flushed. "I am sorry. I did not mean to."

She stood and carried her dishes to the sink. "Come then, if you want to go to the stable."

She strode to the front door. He followed, running to catch up with her as she headed down the path.

"Is the stable not close by?" he asked as they walked further away from the house.

"Yekcal do not keep horses. They have no need for them. The stable is down closer to where the humans lived."

"Are there really no others?" he asked.

"No." She walked on ahead.

Graeden was taken aback by her lack of emotion and wanted to ask her to explain. Yet he could tell the topic was closed.

He caught up to her and changed the subject to the beauty of their surroundings. Regnaryn nodded and mumbled some form of agreement.

"Regnaryn," he said after a few moments, "I must apologize for my attitude and behavior yesterday. It was..."

She stopped and turned toward him. "I understand. Mama explained why you called them beasts."

He caught his breath at her beauty, so innocent yet so inviting. "Yes, well, I really wanted to tell you how sorry I am for being so forward in kissing you the way I did."

"Oh, that," she replied as if it meant nothing.

Graeden was confused. She acted as if she was used to being kissed, yet he was led to believe, by Trebeh's words and Ayirak's actions, that she was an innocent. He was still pondering this when they reached their destination.

The modest-sized stable looked sturdy and well-kept. Odd if no one used it. Inside, it was bright and comfortably cool, even in the already warm morning. Stables back home were dark, stuffy, and either stiflingly hot or freezing cold. He realized this stable had been built more like a house than a stable. The community appeared more sensitive to the needs of their animals. At least, Regnaryn certainly seemed to be.

The mare whinnied a greeting and walked to Regnaryn's side.

"Good morning, Merlona," Regnaryn said, rubbing the horse's neck. "I hope you are enjoying your accommodations. Your master certainly enjoyed his."

Taken aback, Graeden asked, "How did you know her name?"

Regnaryn said, "She told me."

"She *told* you?"

Merlona looked at Graeden and shook her head. Regnaryn laughed.

"Mama told you I speak to animals. You do not listen very well, do you?"

Graeden flushed. "She said you had a way with animals. I presumed she just meant you were good at handling them."

She was amused by his befuddlement though he clearly believed her.

"So you can actually talk to them, like in a language?" he asked.

"Sometimes. Usually it is just images not words."

He shook his head in amazement. "Unbelievable." He caught the slight look of disapproval beginning to form on her face. "I mean... incredible."

Her expression softened, and he breathed a sigh of relief.

"Well, since you know her name, I will take it that she speaks."

"Yes, Merlona is extremely intelligent. Most other animals are limited to a mere phrase or two. She is the exception. You should count yourself fortunate to have such a companion."

Graeden's mind whirled. "Yes, I think I have always known she was special. I hope she has not been telling you any of my deep dark secrets," he teased.

Regnaryn smiled. "No, not any of the deep dark ones. Not yet, anyway."

Graeden nearly choked.

"So you see, she is being taken care of quite nicely," she continued. "I guarantee when the littles hear of her, she will have more affection than she can handle."

"She will enjoy that."

Regnaryn smiled. "Well, if you are satisfied, we should head back. Papa wants to take you to meet some of the others."

The look of dismay that came over his face made Regnaryn forget any mistrust she harbored. She took his arm and nuzzled her head into his shoulder.

"Do not worry, it will be fine. I am sure Mama will not let anyone eat you."

She hugged his arm tighter as they walked to the house. Graeden, surprised by her change of attitude, wondered if she had any idea what she was doing to him. Her closeness sent shivers of desire throughout his body. He was not sure how much longer he could control himself. He felt relieved when they reached the house and she ran inside.

# CHAPTER TWENTY-ONE

*:AYIRAK, SLOW DOWN. Stop making the boy run,:* Trebeh said.

Ayirak turned and chuckled into her mind. He slowed his pace, but only a little.

"Sir, may I ask a question?" Graeden asked. "Regnaryn said we are going to meet other..." He hesitated. "...beings. Who did she mean?"

Ayirak frowned.

Graeden's mind overflowed. He could not stop the jumbled words that poured out of his mouth. "Wait, that is not what... Damn, I am so confused."

Ayirak's grimace turned to amusement. He let the boy babble.

"Ayirak, stop it. Graeden, come walk with me," Trebeh said. She motioned Regnaryn to walk beside her father. "Maybe I can answer some of your questions."

Graeden's look of relief was not lost on either of the yekcals. He and Trebeh fell in a few steps behind Ayirak.

"What do you wish to know?" Trebeh asked. "We have a few moments before we meet Phrynia. She is a drageal."

Graeden drew in a breath. "The only drageal I ever saw is the one in the glass window in the Great Hall at home."

"You have a window with a drageal on it?"

Graeden nodded. "It is of some ancestor flanked by a drageal and some other being." He smiled and added, "I know this sounds silly, but I used to make up games about them and even recall having dreams where we went on adventures together. Silly, I know."

"Not at all, child. Not at all," Trebeh said, patting his hand.

He thought for a moment. "You do not think, no, that could not be, could it?"

"What, dear?"

"Trebeh, you do not think my ancestor actually fought alongside drageals, do you?"

"You will need to ask Phrynia. I know little of the history of drageals or humans."

Graeden nodded. "How will I talk to her? Will she mindspeak to me? Does she speak Alexandrashi? Will she accept me after what I said before?"

"Slow down, child," she chuckled. "Give me a chance to answer one question before you ask five more."

"Sorry."

"I understand your excitement." She took his hand. "If Phrynia chooses, she can speak to your mind. But you need not worry. Drageals speak Alexandrashi." She smiled. "... after a fashion."

His mind raced. Not only would he meet drageals of myth, they would also speak his language. "And the others? The ones that do not speak it?"

"Well, until you master Reissem or mindspeech, we will be here to translate."

A frightening thought suddenly entered his mind. "Will I ever be able to leave this place?"

Trebeh put her arm around his shoulder and hugged him. "Of course, dear. We can all come and go as we please, though most have nowhere else to go. Some leave to see the rest of the world, but often return once they realize life is not as pleasant beyond the Grove's borders."

"But what about that feeling? It would not let me go anywhere but here."

Trebeh smiled. "Ah, yes, that. It seems once you have been here, it disappears and you can travel wherever you choose. Maybe it is because you know this place will always be here for you."

He felt so relieved by her response, he did not realize they had entered a clearing. Suddenly, the wind picked up around him and a drageal stood before him.

"Always the dramatic entrance, eh?" Ayirak chuckled.

The large, golden feathered drageal nodded, stepped forward and extended a taloned hand. Graeden stared in awe at the being in front of him.

*She looks like the drageal from the window? No, she would be ancient. Perhaps all drageals look the same,* he thought as he took her hand. The drageal nodded and smiled.

"I am Phrynia," she began in a slightly whistled Alexandrashi. "It was my son, Immic, who first alerted us of your coming. I have been told you thought us myth."

Graeden paled and opened his mouth, but no words would form.

Phrynia laughed. "It is alright, boy. There was a time, long ago, when drageals thought the same of humans."

Graeden nodded, unable to take his eyes off her.

"What is it, child? Do I look that different from the pictures in your books?" she asked with a laugh.

He shook his head. "No, in fact you look exactly like the drageal in the window of the Great Hall in my home."

"Do I now?" she laughed.

"But that cannot be. That would make you hundreds of years old."

He looked into the drageal's eyes. For a moment, he thought she knew exactly what he was talking about.

"This must be quite a change from your homeland," Phrynia

said, changing the subject.

Her words pulled him away from the whirlwind in his mind. "It most certainly is."

The drageal's expression and the softness of her eyes relaxed Graeden.

"So, tell me how you came to join us here in Reissem Grove, Graeden," Phrynia encouraged.

A look of puzzlement crossed the boy's face.

Phrynia chuckled. "Yes, I am sure you have already told this story to the others."

"And you did not hear it, as well?" Graeden asked.

Phrynia thought a moment. "Oh, I see. You think because we speak into each other's minds, we hear all that goes on."

Graeden nodded.

"That is not how it works. Think about the amount of noise there would be if we heard everything everyone was saying and thinking and doing. It would be enough to drive one mad."

"Oh, yes, I had forgotten."

"So, Graeden, please tell me."

Graeden nodded and retold his tale.

"And you were not bombarded with everyone's thoughts when you first arrived?" Phrynia asked.

"I only heard Regnaryn and Trebeh's voices when they mindspoke directly to me. Trebeh did build a shielding in my mind."

"Yes, but not until you had been here several hours. You are right, Phrynia. With all that went on yesterday," Trebeh shot a glance at Ayirak. "I failed to notice that."

Graeden looked uncomfortable at being singled out.

"Well, I do not know why you are different but, let me tell you, not hearing all those thoughts at once is not a bad thing," Phrynia said.

"I can still recall the noise," Trebeh said. "That and meeting the others." She shook her head. "It caused nothing but fear and discomfort for everyone. Not until we finally calmed ourselves was everyone filled with a sense of... of..." She struggled to find the word.

"Rightness," Graeden supplied. "As if no matter what happened, how odd or different things seemed, this place is where you were meant to be."

"Yes, that is it precisely!" Phrynia said, pleased with his insight. "At first, we could not decipher each other's thoughts." She paused, remembering their beginnings here. "Then we heard ear-shattering thunder. When we spoke again, we all understood."

Graeden paled at the last revelation.

"What is it, Graeden?" Regnaryn asked, grasping his arm.

"I, I heard... or felt ... um... thunder."

"Of course," Phrynia said, "when you first arrived in the Grove. I am not surprised."

"No, it was before that. Before I knew where I was going," he explained.

"When?" Trebeh asked, astounded at his revelation.

He turned and looked at Regnaryn. "The first time I met you in that... that place."

"Ah, yes, we heard about that meeting," Phrynia said "Very unusual, very unusual, indeed. As was its aftermath."

Graeden had not heard of any aftermath. But from the tone of the drageal's voice, he knew it had not been pleasant.

Phrynia changed the subject. "I know you have many questions, but what do you most want to know about this place?"

"Who are the other beings that live here?"

With his permission, Trebeh entered Graeden's mind and showed him images of the others. He saw beings that resembled bears and deer and massive foxes, none of which meant anything to him. As the image of a chetoga appeared, a glimmer of recognition filled his eyes.

"Do not ever call them ferrets. They really do not like that," Graeden blurted out.

"Have you ever met a chetoga before?" Phrynia asked.

"I do not think so. I would think I would remember such a thing, but..." His words trailed off. The others could see his desperate attempt to find a reason for his comment.

*:There is only one chetoga I know who is offended when called a ferret,:* Trebeh said to Phrynia. *:How could Graeden know that?:*

### 

On the walk home, Regnaryn and Graeden stayed a few paces behind Trebeh and Ayirak.

"I am glad you are feeling more comfortable around everyone, Graeden." She smiled.

He was happy to see her attitude toward him changing. He could not believe her beauty – her smile, her eyes, everything about her. He pulled her closer to him and was about to kiss her when Trebeh's gentle cough brought him back to reality.

"Regnaryn, please walk with your father and keep him company," she said sweetly.

Graeden flushed as he remembered where he was and saw Ayirak's glare. Regnaryn nodded to her mother, unaware of her parent's motive. She left Graeden's side and bounded up to walk alongside Ayirak. His glare softened when she took his hand.

# CHAPTER TWENTY-TWO

"THAT IS ALL of them, Trebeh," Graeden said, handing her the last of the dinner plates. "I think I will go find Neshya and the others."

"Wait a moment, child, there is something I wish to talk to you about."

Graeden paled. Had Trebeh looked into his mind and seen his lustful thoughts about Regnaryn? No, she promised she would not do so.

"Come sit with me," she said and added, "you are not in any kind of trouble, that I am aware of."

Graeden sat across from her. "I am glad to hear that."

"Hmm, the fact you thought you might be makes me think perhaps I should keep a closer eye on you."

He flushed deeply, about to protest when he saw the grin on her face.

"Well, I do not cause any more trouble than Neshya."

"That, is not a comforting thought, Graeden. That child is always into one thing or another, but that is not why I wish to speak to you."

Graeden squirmed.

"You have been here how long now, Graeden?"

"Eight days."

He thought how much he had changed in that short time. How his disbelief in the Grove folk had been replaced by the knowledge that they were not always as they outwardly seemed. He marveled at the strength of the seemingly frail deer-like queetok, able to pull three times their body weight. While the shanassi, massive and bear-like, were the gentlest of beings and dismayed if they even harmed an insect.

"Everyone has been wonderful to me."

"Are you happy here?" she asked.

"Yes. Why do you ask? I have not offended anyone, have I?"

"No, no. It is nothing like that," she replied. "I was merely wondering about your plans."

"Plans?"

"Will you be staying?"

"I had not given it any thought. You did say I was free to come and go as I pleased."

"You are, indeed. You may stay or leave, as you wish. It is the weather that concerns me."

"Weather?"

"Winter comes early here and lasts a very long time. We would not want you caught in a winter storm, would we?"

"I guess not."

"You have a few weeks to make your decision before you run the risk of being weather-bound."

"I will give it some thought."

Trebeh desperately wanted him to stay. While she liked the boy well enough, her real worry was, if he left, Regnaryn would follow. That thought terrified her.

### 

"I have come to a decision," Graeden said after several days of avoiding Trebeh.

She looked at him, but his face did not reveal his thoughts. Her heart raced, and she held her breath.

"I want to stay in Reissem Grove and make it my home, if that is still an option."

"Of course, it is, dear."

"There is something about this place…"

Trebeh nodded, feeling very relieved.

"But I really need to find a way to get word to my family that I am alright. I fear they think I have been eaten by a wild animal or something worse." He smiled, but it only half concealed the pain he felt at not returning home.

"Write the message, and I will see that it is delivered."

"Really? I thought this place was cut off from the rest of the world."

Trebeh smiled. "No. There are some who reside beyond our borders and come and go from here."

"How? Who? I cannot see a drageal or any of the rest of you just showing up at the Keep with a message from me."

Trebeh laughed. "Nor can I. I do not believe your family would be quite ready for that just yet." She saw Graeden's puzzled look. "We have friends who maintain contact with humans."

Suddenly, the thought flashed across Graeden's mind that he already knew this. But as he tried to focus on the memory, it disappeared.

"Are you alright?" Trebeh asked. "You look like your mind is miles away."

"I was just thinking of home."

Trebeh ignored the obvious lie.

"Since you are going to stay, you will need to learn Reissem."

"Yes, then I will not be such a burden."

Trebeh shook her head. "No, that is not it. We do not mind helping you, but you should have your independence."

"Will you also teach me to mindspeak?"

"Of course."

"Good. I was afraid that might not be possible. It seems so instinctive to everyone else and well..."

"Everyone that has ever come to this place can mindspeak. Sometimes, they just need a little help to get them started."

He hoped she was right.

"Your Reissem lessons can begin tomorrow, if you like," Trebeh said.

"Oh, yes, that would be fine. But I must warn you, I have never been very good at studying."

Trebeh smiled. "Ah, but you are no longer a child. Now, you have a purpose to your studies, so you will excel. I am sure of it."

Graeden did not respond.

"Since you and Neshya get along so well, I think I will have him help you with the basics, those things a child would learn just growing up. Then, once you are ready to move on, you will be put in a group to learn the rest."

"Group?" he asked, wondering who else here needed to learn Reissem.

"The children."

"The littles?" he gasped, embarrassed by the prospect of being put with those less than a third his age.

She smiled. "You will be with whatever age group best fits your learning level. Remember, when it comes to Reissem you are one of the littles."

He nodded. "And mindspeech?"

"I was thinking you and I would work on that."

"When can we start?"

"Now, if you want."

"I would like that."

*:I thought so.:*

He jumped at her voice in his mind. "I thought you built a wall around my mind."

"It is called a shielding," she corrected him. "Yes I did, and it is intact. I just spoke to you. Think of it as a tap on the door to your mind. Mindspeech is like talking. If I want to speak to you, with mind or voice, I say something and then you decide whether to reply or not."

"I have not heard anyone else in my mind, so I assumed the shielding was blocking them."

"One can indeed build such a shielding, but most do not. Here in Reissem Grove, most shieldings are more like fences around our minds; gentle reminders of boundaries others will not cross uninvited."

"Oh, I see," he said. "Are there other kinds, as well?"

"Yes, but let us leave that discussion for another day.".

He nodded.

*:Alright then,:* she said glad he did not react with surprise at her voice in his mind. *:As I was saying, you will soon come to think and use mindspeech the same as you do your normal voice.:*

Graeden remained skeptical about that.

*:I can mindspeak in a whisper,:* she continued so softly Graeden strained to hear. *:Or IN A SHOUT!:* She laughed as the boy jumped. *:Or anywhere in between,:* she said in a more normal volume. *:Try to mindspeak to me.:*

Graeden stared hard at Trebeh, contorting his face as if trying to squeeze the thoughts from his mind to hers. After a few moments, he let out a deep sigh.

"Relax. Think of who you wish to speak to then gently toss the thought to them like you would a ball to a child," Trebeh said.

He nodded and closed his eyes.

"I cannot do it. It is impossible," he said. "I keep trying, but it is not working. Maybe I am just too stupid! Just look at me, I am sweating and out of breath. And from what? Thinking!"

He shook his head in disgust at his own failure, unable to find the words to continue.

"Do not be silly, Graeden. This is the first time you have tried."

"But I mindspoke to Regnaryn before. How could I do it then

and not now?" He shook his head. "Maybe I did not actually do it, maybe we just imagined it."

Trebeh put her hand on his shoulder. "What you and Regnaryn shared seems to be something on a more visceral level."

"But you said everyone else instinctively knew how to mindspeak on the day they arrived."

Trebeh nodded.

"Why can I not do the same?"

"Maybe you are fretting too much about it. I have no doubt that, with time and practice, it will come to you." She smiled. "Remember, you can try to mindspeak to me any time."

"Thank you."

"Well, you have had a busy day." She headed toward the kitchen.

Graeden followed her. "Can I help you fix dinner?"

"No, I will be fine. Find Neshya. You two can start on your Reissem lessons before supper."

# CHAPTER TWENTY-THREE

AFTER SEVERAL sessions, Graeden had yet to mindspeak a single thought to Trebeh. She tried to ease his frustration by having him recreate his shielding. Unfortunately, he fared no better at that. He understood to build it like a wall, with one block on top of another, but he could not get them to hold together for more than a moment.

"That is enough for today," Trebeh told him as he neared mental exhaustion. She effortlessly rebuilt the shielding in his mind.

"I am useless. I just cannot do this," he said. "Do I really *need* it to live here?"

"No."

Graeden grinned. "Good, at least I will not be tossed out into the winter's rage for my stupidity and lack of talent."

"No, we would never toss anyone out into the cold. We would wait for the spring thaw."

He smiled sheepishly. "I guess I am feeling a bit sorry for myself."

"I hear you are doing quite well with your studies of Reissem. Perhaps that is the problem." She took his hand and stroked it lovingly. "Dear boy, you said it your first day here. You have always wanted to be the best at everything you attempt, even though you know no one can do such a thing, no matter who they are."

"Well, I am obviously a good example of someone who cannot."

"Graeden, you are too old to pout," she chided. "Tell me something you do well. I have heard you are a pretty good archer."

He nodded. "I am adequate, not as good as..."

She interrupted, "Stop comparing yourself to others."

He nodded.

"So we agree. You are a decent archer. How long did it take you to achieve your current skill? An hour? A day? A week? As long as a month, perhaps?"

He laughed. "No, much longer than that. I doubt if anyone could master archery in just a month." He stopped, realizing her point. "But this is different. It is only thinking."

"Mindspeech is a skill, and it requires the same amount of work as any other skill. And you suffer the same amount of frustration when it does not go right. You need to be less harsh on yourself."

He knew she was right, but that was of little comfort.

### 

"Phrynia, what am I going to do with the boy? I have tried everything, and he still is unable to mindspeak."

"Well, he has already shown he is capable of it."

"Or was it Regnaryn's doing?" Trebeh asked.

"I do not think so. He is here, after all."

Trebeh nodded.

"Perhaps the problem is not the boy but the teacher," Phrynia said. "He obviously wants to learn. Otherwise, he would have given up by now."

"Yes," Trebeh said.

"Regnaryn should try to teach him. Perhaps their connection will allow him to break through whatever is holding him back."

Trebeh knew the drageal spoke the truth. The idea had crossed her mind, as well.

"Let me guess, Ayirak is what keeps you from letting her teach him," Phrynia said. "I know that old yekcal and would not expect him to react in any other way to this boy and his favorite kitling."

Both women laughed. Phrynia continued, "Let me talk to him. Maybe if the suggestion comes from someone other than you."

"Good luck," Trebeh said, certain Ayirak would not react well, regardless of who broached the subject.

### 

"So, what brings you here today, Phrynia?" Ayirak asked as he approached his waiting friend.

"I need to talk to you about Graeden."

"Hrmph," Ayirak said.

"Trebeh is having problems with his mindspeech training..." Phrynia began.

"Perhaps he is not as smart as you all seem to think he is," Ayirak interrupted.

"I have a suggestion that may help him," she continued without acknowledging his comment.

"And what might that be?"

Phrynia ignored the yekcal's glare. "Let Regnaryn try her hand at teaching him." She raised her hand to stop him from interrupting. "Hear me out, Ayirak. No matter your opinion of the boy, you have to admit they share a bond. And having one of his own instructing him might make it easier for him to relate and learn."

"He has no problem learning Reissem from someone else," Ayirak countered.

"That may be. But I think it is worth a try."

"I do not see that it will do any good, but no matter what I say, you and Trebeh have already made the decision."

Phrynia smiled. "Perhaps."

### 

"There you are, love," Trebeh said as Ayirak entered the kitchen. He crossed the room, wrapped her in his arms and kissed

132

her gently on the forehead to the disdain of the children at the table.
*:I can see by your expression Phrynia has spoken to you about Regnaryn and Graeden.:*
He did not reply.

"Where are Regnaryn and the boy?" he asked.

"Graeden and I are here," Neshya said as they entered the room.

"Yes, you always seem to come in when the work is done and the food is ready," Nelluc said as she laid the last plate on the table.

*:Relax, Ayirak, she will be here shortly. Since when do you keep such a close watch on her?:*
Ayirak said nothing.

The family sat and the usual banter made its way around the table. Ayirak no longer seemed concerned about Regnaryn's whereabouts. Midway through the meal, Regnaryn bolted into the room, apologizing for her tardiness.

"You are lucky you got here, Regg," Neshya laughed. "Graeden was about to gobble down your share of the food."

Graeden glared at Neshya, making the young yekcal burst into laughter.

### 

Trebeh sat on the couch across from Ayirak. She waited to see if her mate would bring up the matter of Graeden and Regnaryn. He remained silent.

"Is there something on your mind, dear?" she asked, breaking the silence.

Ayirak glared. "Does it matter what I have to say?"

"Of course, it does."

"You know damned well what I want to discuss," he growled. "I do not like the idea of Regnaryn and Graeden alone together."

"You cannot still be angry over that kiss." She looked at him. "You are! The boy apologized and there have been no further incidents."

"You have not seen how he looks at her."

She shook her head, but she said nothing.

"You may be the mother of sons, but you are female and do not understand the... well, the way a male thinks and... and..."

"You know as well as I do, Ayirak, newcomers are always taught by their own kind," she said, ignoring his previous remark. "It was only because of your feelings about the boy that I tried to instruct him myself."

He looked at her in surprise.

"Do not tell me you think I do not know how you feel. Everyone knows, even Graeden!"

"What do you mean?"

"Oh, please, you cannot believe the boy does not see that you have no use for him. Now who does not understand?"

"But..."

"But, nothing."

His expression changed to one of horror as another thought crossed his mind. "Does Regnaryn see that, too?"

"I doubt it, she rarely sees the negative side of any situation."

Ayirak let out a sigh of relief.

"I am done cleaning up, Mama," Regnaryn called from the kitchen. "I am going to go outside for a little while."

"That is fine, dear," Trebeh answered.

She waited for the door to close, then said, "I know you do not think having Regnaryn train Graeden is a good idea." She leaned forward and took her mate's hand. "If it was anyone other than Regnaryn, you would be the first to agree to this."

He opened his mouth, but Trebeh put her finger to his lips. "Do not try to deny it, love. I know you too well. I think what you are afraid of is..."

"I am not afraid of anything," he interrupted.

Trebeh smiled at his protest. "Yes, yes, I know, you are the big brave leader. But when it comes to your children, especially Regnaryn, you are quite the opposite."

Ayirak considered protesting, but realized, once again, how well his mate knew him.

"You are afraid if Regnaryn spends time with Graeden, whatever already exists between them will become stronger. Then you will have to deal with your most precious child growing up."

He reluctantly agreed.

"But if it is meant to happen, it will, whether you want it to or not." She gave him a moment to digest her words. "Now that we have settled that point. I think we should tell them," she said.

Ayirak shook his head. "I knew it! I really had no say in this whatsoever, did I?"

"Oh, dearest, you know I always value your opinion," she said playfully.

Ayirak started to argue, when the sound of the children bursting into the house stopped him. "We will continue this conversation later, my love."

"Children, is all this noise necessary?" Trebeh asked and they instantly quieted. "If I am not mistaken, all of you have things to do that do not require you to be downstairs."

The chatter began again as the children raced up the stairs.

"Regnaryn, Graeden, please come here," Trebeh said. "We want to talk to you."

Regnaryn plopped down on the arm of the chair beside Ayirak. Graeden sat beside Trebeh.

*:It is all right, son,:* she said to alleviate his trepidation.

"Let me get to the point," Trebeh started. "As you both know, Graeden has been having difficulties learning to mindspeak."

"I am trying," Graeden said in his own defense.

"I know. Your problems are not from lack of effort. But neither of us can deny that it is not progressing as well as it might."

Graeden grimaced.

"I want to try something different. Regnaryn will teach you now."

Graeden looked at Ayirak and met a glare that sent a shiver down his spine. He was certain Ayirak did not agree with this.

"Is that all right with you, Graeden?" Trebeh asked.

Her question broke the hold Ayirak's stare had on him. "Um, I am sorry," Graeden said, "what were you saying?"

"I thought tomorrow, after your Reissem lessons, would be a good time to start with Regnaryn," Trebeh repeated.

"Oh, yes, that will be fine," Graeden replied.

"Good. Ayirak and I have full confidence this will work."

Ayirak turned his glance to his mate, muttering an unintelligible answer.

The young couple nodded and left the room.

"I still do not like this, Trebeh," Ayirak said after the pair had gone.

"Oh, I think you made that perfectly clear to all of us," she answered in a tone that made Ayirak aware she was not at all happy with him.

# CHAPTER TWENTY-FOUR

"HOW IS HE doing, Regnaryn?" Trebeh knew that, over the last few days, the couple had spent almost every moment working together.

"I am not sure. He seems distracted. Things will be going fine, and then he will freeze up for no apparent reason."

"Maybe he just needs a little more time," Trebeh replied.

She knew what was concerning the boy. Ayirak. The yekcal always hovered nearby whenever Regnaryn and Graeden were together.

"Trebeh, where are you?" Ayirak called as he entered the house.

"In the garden, love," she answered.

He looked relieved to see only Trebeh and Regnaryn. "So, what are you two up to this fine afternoon?"

"Regnaryn is going to find Graeden so they can work a bit more before dinner." Trebeh motioned Regnaryn to leave.

Ayirak turned, ready to follow Regnaryn.

"Dear, I need to talk to you," Trebeh said

"What is it?" he asked.

Trebeh waited until the front door closed. "Oh, never mind, it was nothing."

Ayirak glared, knowing he had been outmaneuvered. "I do not think it is a good idea for them to be alone together."

"Yes, I know very well what you think," she answered. "But you see, they need to be alone, at least when she is trying to teach him. How can the boy concentrate on his lessons when he is wondering where you are lurking?"

Ayirak said nothing.

"Leave them alone for a day or so. Then we can see if you are the cause of his learning difficulties."

"Hrmph, the only reason he should be nervous around me is if he is planning something."

Trebeh laughed. "You are half again his height, and his first encounter with you left him bruised and terrified. Not to mention every time he is near, you glare at him. I would not be surprised to find you are growling into his mind, as well. Oh, do not try that look on me," she said. "I have known you far too long."

"I will give them a few days alone, but if anything happens..."

She took his arm and nodded. "I know."

### 

Days turned into weeks. Graeden continued to struggle. He worked hard, but he made little progress. His ability seemed erratic, and only on the rarest of occasions could he mindspeak a single word.

"I do not understand, Regnaryn," he said. "Why am I having so much trouble with this? Learning Reissem has been easy. It took me no time at all to get through those lessons."

She nodded. "Yes, your Reissem is very good, as if you had been speaking it your entire life. But you have come a very long way with your mindspeech, too."

The smile on her face gave him hope, though he was not sure either of them truly believed it.

"Thank you. I am trying."

No matter how little progress he made, she continued to

encourage him. Without Ayirak's presence, Graeden's attraction to Regnaryn resurfaced, but he realized her feelings for him were no different than those she had for anyone else. He tried, but he could not stop his feelings from growing. He constantly found himself distracted by her closeness, her smile, her mere presence.

### 

"Graeden, I think we should take a break from this," Regnaryn said, following a particularly intense session that yielded only minor results.

"No. Please do not give up on me," he cried. "I am trying. Really, I am."

"I know," she answered. "Maybe you are trying too hard. Perhaps you need a rest. Some time to allow you to gather your thoughts and try again refreshed. Or maybe if someone else helped you."

She reached for him, but he pulled away.

"So you think I am useless? Stupid? Does everyone else feel the same way? Are people laughing at me behind my back?" He stormed out.

She was confused. She did not consider him useless, just that he was working too hard.

### 

Startled by the sound of distant thunder, Regnaryn went downstairs and out onto the porch. The dark storm clouds in the distance threatened impending rain. The twins bounded toward her and wrapped themselves around her legs, swatting at each other.

Regnaryn laughed. "What are you fighting about now?"

The kitlings screeched simultaneously, making it impossible to understand a single word.

"Enough," Ayirak roared from inside the house.

The twins immediately quieted.

"Come on, you two, supper is ready." Regnaryn hustled the twins through the door.

"Where is Graeden?" Trebeh asked when everyone was seated around the table.

"I think I hurt his feelings. I am not sure where he went."

"Trebeh, do not put anything aside for him," Ayirak said. "If he does not have the consideration to show up for supper, he should go hungry."

"Whatever you say, dear."

Ayirak knew his words would go unheeded.

The family finished supper with no further mention of Graeden. While cleaning up, several claps of thunder boomed in the distance. Regnaryn looked concerned.

"What is the matter?" Neshya asked.

"I need to find Graeden," she said as she left.

Neshya shook his head as the front door closed.

# CHAPTER TWENTY-FIVE

REGNARYN ENTERED one of the unused stables and saw Graeden seated in the corner staring into the distance.

"Graeden, you missed dinner. Is something wrong?"

He did not respond.

"We should go back to the house before the storm hits."

He turned. "Everybody here thinks I am stupid, because I cannot learn to mindspeak. Damn, even the littles can mindspeak!"

"Graeden, no one thinks that. You are being silly," Regnaryn answered.

"First I am stupid, now silly. What next?" he muttered. "Why not just say I am worthless as well?" He was so upset, he trembled.

"I am sorry," she said and sat beside him. "I did not mean it that way. No one thinks you are stupid. Mindspeaking is not always easy to learn. And you are getting better."

He did not respond. She put her arm around his shoulder.

"Please, do not be upset."

She wrapped her other arm around him and hugged him tightly. Her show of affection and caring broke through his wall of self-pity and he smiled faintly.

"I am sorry. I have been acting like a spoiled child," he said quietly. "It is, just that, well, I guess I assumed mindspeaking would come easier."

Regnaryn reached to brush aside a strand of hair from his face. He took her hand and kissed it softly. She leaned in to him, put her arm around his neck and nuzzled her head against his chest, purring. He pulled her closer, raised her face to his and kissed her gently, tentatively. His passion quickly grew. He pushed her backwards and rolled on top of her. He continued to kiss her while his hands found their way under her clothes and explored her body. His desire reached new heights as he touched her bare skin. Overcome by his own passion, he failed to notice her fear.

At his touch, Regnaryn felt a flood of strange sensations coursing through her. He moved his hands and his mouth, and those sensations increased.

:*Papa! Mama!*:

Within moments, the door to the stable burst open. Ayirak flew across the room. He grabbed Graeden by the hair and lifted him. He held the boy, feet dangling in mid-air for just a second, then a single backhanded cuff from his massive hand sent the boy flying across the stable. Graeden bounced off the door and slid limply to the floor, a lifeless, bleeding lump.

Ayirak turned to Trebeh and angrily shouted, "Did I not tell you this would happen? I knew it was not safe for him to be alone with her. I knew this human," he spat the word out, "could not be trusted. Now do you believe me?" The large yekcal turned and started toward the boy.

Trebeh, already at Regnaryn's side, clasped her hand and was overcome by a flood of unexpected images. The shock of the vision made Trebeh release her hand. Regnaryn immediately ran and stood between her raging father and the motionless Graeden.

"Get out of the way, girl!" Ayirak roared, the look of fury in his eyes increasing.

"No, Papa," Regnaryn sobbed. "You are going to kill him."

Ayirak growled.

"Mama! Stop him!"

Graeden moaned. Regnaryn turned to see him struggling to move. His face appeared bruised from forehead to chin, his left eye already swollen shut. Blood flowed from his smashed nose and split lip. He pushed himself up on one arm, but it crumbled under his weight and he fell. Ayirak saw the boy move. His rage increased.

"I told you to step aside, girl!" he shouted.

"No, Papa, you have hurt him enough already."

"I said get out of my way. You do not know what he intended to do."

"No, she does not," Trebeh whispered in a voice almost too quiet to hear.

The emotion in her voice stopped Ayirak where he stood. Those few words, spoken in a near-whisper, shouted volumes to Graeden as well. He slowly lifted himself up on his other arm and staggered forward until he stood in front of Regnaryn and faced Ayirak.

"By all that is holy, I had no idea," Graeden cried. "I thought she knew... I mean, the way she acts. The cuddling, the nuzzling. And she is of marriageable age. Where I come from..."

"This is not where you come from," Ayirak growled. "You were told that."

"By the goddess, I did not... I would not..." Graeden stammered.

"But you did and you would have had we not arrived!"

Graeden turned and looked at Regnaryn's tear-stained, frightened face. "I am sorry. I am so sorry. What have I done to you?"

He took a few steps closer to Ayirak. "Do with me as you will, Ayirak. There is no punishment too severe for what almost happened here. I will make no excuses, there are none. I am supposed to be a man of honor. I should have known better. She is an innocent. I knew that. And yet I ignored it and..." He could not bring himself to speak the words, he just shook his head and looked at Regnaryn's scared expression, "I beg you, sir, punish me; for no matter what you do, it will never be enough to cleanse my conscience." Graeden fell to his knees, head bowed in utter and complete shame, softly repeating over and over, "I am sorry. I did not... I would not... I am sorry."

Ayirak took a step toward the boy.

Regnaryn shouted, "No! Stop! It is all my fault, it must be. Punish me, not him. He... I..." She bowed her head and whispered, "It is my fault. It must be."

Trebeh reached for Ayirak's arm.

"Stop," she said softly.

He turned and glared. The look in her eyes told him something else was going on here.

:I do not understand,: Ayirak said. :What have you seen?:

:I will tell you later. For now, just go back to the house, please.:

Ayirak growled under his breath and stormed out of the stable. Graeden and Regnaryn stared, confused by his sudden departure.

Trebeh sat on the bench at the back of the stable. "Come here, please."

They sat beside her, neither daring to look at the other.

"This is not your fault." She took their hands. Once again, she was bombarded by images; images that explained so much about these two, of their previous encounter and of what might come to pass. She took a deep breath to regain her composure.

Trebeh gently took Graeden's face in her hands. He winced slightly, and she looked at him as only a mother could.

"I am sorry he hit you. How badly does it hurt?"

"Not as bad as it should. Not as bad as I deserve."

Regnaryn rocked back and forth, sobbing.

"Stop, both of you," Trebeh said sternly. "The one at fault here is me."

Graeden said. "How can this be your fault? I..." He could not finish.

"I saw signs. I should have known."

Graeden and Regnaryn stared, confused by her words.

Before they could question her further, she continued, "We will talk of this later. Right now, I need to look at your injuries."

She looked more closely at him as her fingers deftly felt around his wounds. "The good news, none of the damage appears permanent. But you will not be very pretty for a while, and probably will be eating only broth," she said, choosing her words deliberately, trying to lighten the somber mood. "This is going to hurt a bit," Trebeh told him.

She gently grabbed then tweaked his nose to put it back into place. Graeden winced and bit back a yelp.

"Sorry, but that had to be done now or else it would never be as it was." She carefully felt the rest of his face for any other injuries. "Ah good, the rest are just superficial, painful but not serious. They will just need time to heal. When we get back to the house I will give you something to ease the swelling and the pain," she said, dabbing the blood from his face. "But this shoulder does not look good. Hmm, I will need to work on that."

"How can you treat me kindly after what I just did? Ayirak's reaction was understandable, but yours?" Graeden slowly shook his head, wincing with the movement. "Yours does not make sense."

Trebeh nodded. "I see where you might think that. At first sight, I felt the same as Ayirak. But now I realize there is more to this than either of you know."

She turned, leaving Graeden to stare in confusion. She brushed her hand over Regnaryn's face and purred softly. Trebeh once again took both of their hands in hers.

"Later, we will talk more about what happened. Right now, we need to get back to the house so I can tend to Graeden's injuries."

"But you do not know what I did," Graeden cried.

"I do."

"But how?"

"It was not difficult, with your emotions, both of you were

almost screaming your thoughts."

"Do you mean everyone knows?" she asked sheepishly.

"Not likely." Trebeh replied.

"But you did," Graeden said.

Regnaryn's face flushed scarlet. "I called them," she said, barely above a whisper. "I was scared. I did not know what else to do. I am sorry. It is all my fault." She burst into tears and tried to bolt, but Trebeh's hold kept her firmly in her seat.

"She did not know how to deal with what she was feeling or even what it was," Trebeh said. "When we saw what was happening, we came."

Graeden's face reddened, and he looked away.

Trebeh stood. "It is time to go back to the house."

Regnaryn pulled free of her mother and ran.

Trebeh shook her head, then turned to Graeden. "Come with me, please. The sooner I work on that shoulder, the better."

Trebeh held Graeden's arm to steady him as they walked. They stepped out into the night, only to be met by a blinding strike of lightning. Graeden froze. At that instant, Trebeh saw glimpses of what was in his mind. Flashes of faces, of sounds and unspeakable horrors inflicted upon him at some other time, in some other place. Things she knew he did not fully comprehend, memories purposely hidden.

*Who buried this part of his past and why? But more importantly, should I tell him of this?* she wondered.

Trebeh stood with him as the rain poured down. After several moments Graeden came back to himself. For the rest of the short walk to the house, he alternated between silence and begging forgiveness.

# CHAPTER TWENTY-SIX

GRAEDEN HALF-EXPECTED to find Ayirak and the others waiting to pummel him as he and Trebeh entered, but no one was there.

Trebeh led Graeden to his room. He tried to hide the pain as she removed his bloodied clothes. He sat on the bed and she went to get a cloth to clean his face.

"Come in, Neshya," Trebeh called to the knock on the open door.

No one entered. She shook her head, crossed the room, and took the tray. Graeden could not hear what was said, but sensed the anger in Neshya's voice. An anger Graeden knew was deserved.

Trebeh returned to Graeden.

"Now, where was I?" she asked.

She picked up the washcloth and wiped the blood from his face. She dipped her fingers into a bowl on the tray and proceeded to smear its earthy smelling ointment over his wounds.

"I know, it has a nasty odor," she said at the face he made. "You should have smelled it before we added the scent — horrible, absolutely horrible."

He did not respond. She finished and put the ointment on the table.

"Now about that shoulder."

"Leave it be. I do not deserve such compassion," he said flatly.

Trebeh shook her head. "Do not start that again. I am going to tend to your shoulder and any other wounds you may have whether you like it or not. And do not give me that look, it would not work under normal circumstances and with your face the way it looks right now, well, you just look silly."

He surrendered.

She ran her fingers lightly over his shoulder and arm, surprised to discover it was not the first time his shoulder has been severely injured. And the damage from the last time, though skillfully tended, was not fully healed.

"Your shoulder needs to be reset before I can tend to your arm. This is going to hurt."

"Good," he replied.

She ignored him and reached for the glass beside the ointment. She handed the dark orange liquid to him. "Drink this."

"No."

"I have already told you, I am in no mood for your petulance. It has been a long, trying night, and there is still much to do. You will either drink it, or I will pour it down your throat."

He took the glass and swallowed it down in one gulp. In mere moments, the potion took effect. She put her hands on either side of the break in the shoulder and with one quick movement adjusted the bones into their normal position. He barely reacted.

She went to the hall to retrieve the basket containing the additional items Neshya had left. Trebeh returned to see Graeden sitting there, half grinning, half sleeping. She took the sturdy strips of potion-infused bandages from the basket. She wrapped them tightly around his shoulder, knowing they would keep the bones in place and accelerate the healing.

She finished bandaging his shoulder, then realized Graeden was humming. *Ah, the wonders of a good potion.*

She took his arm in her hands. The bones had broken when he
hit the door and then shattered when he put his full weight on them.
She drew in a breath and asked assistance in this complicated
healing. She took several more deep breaths and began. Trebeh
wrapped her fingers around his arm and slowly moved her hands up
and down – from shoulder to wrist – gently drumming her fingers
to cajole the shattered bone fragments back into place. Had Graeden
not been so strongly medicated, the pain of this process would have
been unbearable. Though, after seeing even the few flashes of the
pain he had endured before, perhaps not.

After quite some time, she finally manipulated all of the tiny
pieces into place. She tightened her grip around his arm and
continued to skim her hands up and down the length of his arm,
sealing the bones together. She repeated this until she felt certain all
fragments were firmly in place, then wrapped his arm in the potion-
infused bandages.

Trebeh sat back in the chair, exhausted. Graeden grinned and
spoke, but his drug-induced words were incomprehensible. When
she nodded, he seemed content.

After a few moments, she picked up the second glass containing
a pale green liquid and handed it to Graeden. He drank it down. She
took the glass and helped him to recline.

"Sleep well, my child, there is much that awaits you." She
tucked the blanket around him. His eyes closed and he fell asleep.

She gathered his clothes and the basket of supplies and carried
them to the bathroom. She returned, took one last look at Graeden
and headed for the door.

"What is it, Neshya?" she asked as she locked the bedroom door
to keep the others out. Without looking, she knew he was still angry.

"How could you?"

"How could I what?" she replied knowing full well his meaning.

Neshya growled under his breath. She glared at him and he
stopped.

"How could you help him, heal him, after what he did to Regnaryn? Have you seen her? Seen the state she is in since he, he..." Neshya shook his head. "Yet you ignore her, your own daughter, and choose to tend to that, that... monster."

Trebeh did not react. She listened calmly, allowing him to rant.

"I cannot believe you," he said and turned to walk away.

"Neshya," she said softly. He stopped. "There is more to this than we knew."

He turned. "What? Tell me what could justify his actions."

She shook her head. "I cannot. Not yet. Soon enough all will become clear."

"That is not an answer," he growled and stomped toward the stairs.

Trebeh sighed, knowing this was just the beginning of the drama about to unfold. She turned toward Regnaryn's room. The closer she got, the louder the young girl's sobbing became. She shook her head and entered.

Nelluc stood by the bedside, trying to give the sobbing Regnaryn a cup of tea.

"You can go now, Nelluc. I will stay with her."

Nelluc hesitated.

:*Do not worry, dear, she will be fine,:* Trebeh told her.

Nelluc nodded and left. Trebeh sat beside Regnaryn. She watched the sobbing girl rock back and forth. It pained Trebeh to see her so consumed with guilt and anguish; there were so many things she wanted to say but knew this was not the time. Anything said now would not be heard. Not understood. Not remembered.

After several minutes, Regnaryn stopped rocking and looked at her mother. Trebeh held out her arms and the girl fell sobbing into them.

Trebeh held Regnaryn, gently stroking her hair.

"He is afraid of storms," Regnaryn said.

"I know. Is that why you went to find him?"

Regnaryn nodded. "But I never meant for anything to happen;

for him to get hurt." She looked up at Trebeh. "What have I done, Mama? Is this the evil the voice spoke of?"

Trebeh was surprised at Regnaryn's question. "Child, you are not evil."

"But it is my fault he got hurt. If I had not called you..."

Trebeh took a deep breath, "Shh. You did the right thing by calling us. You were afraid."

"But should I have been? I know Graeden, he would not have hurt me."

Trebeh shook her head. "Maybe not."

Regnaryn did not understand, and Trebeh did not explain.

Trebeh offered the now cold tea to Regnaryn. She drank it. Within a moment, the herbs in the tea took effect and Regnaryn fell asleep.

### 

Trebeh found Ayirak in the garden. "Where are the children?"

"I had Ennales take Neshya to stay the night with Javis," Ayirak replied.

"And the girls?"

"Nelluc is upstairs with the twins."

"Good, come inside. It is cold out here," she said, rubbing her arms. "Or are you still trying to cool that temper of yours?"

"This is no time for jokes," Ayirak replied, following her.

She settled herself onto the couch. He sat across from her.

"You said there was more to what went on tonight. Are you going to tell me what you saw, or must I guess?" When she remained quiet, Ayirak continued, "Maybe he should just leave. Yes, that would be ideal. I am sure we could find a way to get him safely away from here without having to wait for spring."

"What are you talking about?" she asked. "Did you not see how they acted?"

He stared blankly.

"I do not believe you! Did you not see the guilt they have for each other's pain? Pain they feel responsible for. Were you so blinded by your rage, you saw none of this?"

Ayirak did not reply.

"You may be sharp to the ways of the world, but you are dull to those of the heart." She sighed. "They are already deeply in love. And I think it may have started well before they met in the dream. That is what drew her to him in that place."

He just stared.

"Did you not hear what I said?"

"I heard, but I do not believe," Ayirak replied. "Not of this love or that place. It was just a dream they somehow shared."

"No, it was real. I saw the horrors inflicted upon him, most skillfully hidden from his recollection."

"Bah, drivel!" Ayirak snorted. "I do not care what happened to him before. I only care what he did this night. His actions were not born of love, he sought only to satisfy his own lust with no regard for her. And as for love, what does she know of such things? She is but a child."

Trebeh shook her head. "That is the problem. She knows nothing of love or sex or any of the human emotions one her age should, and she is most definitely not a child."

She paused and watched the effect her words had on him.

"And, there is something else."

"What could you possibly have to add to this?" he asked.

"Had I known the truth when he first arrived, I would have handled these two quite differently," Trebeh mumbled, momentarily ignoring his question. "I curse myself for not recognizing the signs." She looked into his eyes and in a near whisper said, "They are soulbound."

"What?" he sputtered nearly choking. "How can they be soulbound? It is not possible, they have just met... not him... not Regnaryn... they... she..." he stammered.

She let him ramble.

"How can you be certain?" he asked.

"I saw the thread that binds them. And it is one of the strongest I have ever seen."

"No, this just cannot be. You must have misinterpreted what you saw." He shook his head.

"Possible," she answered, trying to appease him, "but unlikely."

He stared at her, still unwilling to believe.

"How did you, we, not see this before?" he asked when her words became truth in his mind.

She shook her head. "I do not know. Perhaps the events of tonight brought it to the forefront. But I should have known there was more to this. I have been both blind and stupid. Why did I not pursue their dream connection that spanned such great distances?" she asked.

He rubbed his chin. "We all, Phrynia included, assumed it was nothing. Do you think Regnaryn sensed it?"

"She probably felt something, but not knowing any better assumed it was friendship."

"What do we do now?"

She looked directly into his eyes. "Nothing."

She thought he might explode.

"What do you mean, nothing?" he cried.

She shook her head. "For the moment, there is nothing we can do. You know we cannot tell them. They must find each other and the bond on their own."

"Yes, I know, but..."

"There is more." she said. "I sense great pain and hardship ahead for them. I think it is connected to their bond and Karaleena's prophecy."

"You mean they will try to deny their bond?" he asked in utter disbelief.

"That is my fear. The future is always uncertain, but..."

"Breaking a soulbond, or even attempting to, will drive them mad if it does not kill them outright," he said.

Trebeh sighed. Both knew the truth of his words.

"There must be something we can do to help," Ayirak pleaded.

"You know better. We cannot interfere. They must work this out on their own. The only thing we can do is wait."

"Are you going to tell Phrynia of this?"

"I am not sure," she replied. "I do not know what good would come of others knowing."

Ayirak walked to her and wrapped his arms around her shoulders. "This is Phrynia we are talking about. If nothing else, she can help with your fears about what you saw in a way I never could."

She stroked his hand and nodded. "I will see if she is still awake. Go up to bed. I will join you shortly."

He kissed the top of her head and left the room. He smiled, knowing full well it would be hours before she and Phrynia stopped discussing this.

### 

Trebeh called to Phrynia, trying to sound calm and nonchalant even at this late hour. Naturally, such tricks did not work.

Trebeh related the incident in the stable and was relieved to find Phrynia had no knowledge of it.

She told the drageal what she had seen within the children's minds. Both women were upset that they had not recognized the signs. Trebeh then disclosed what she had encountered hidden deep within Graeden's mind.

:*That is almost more disturbing than what you saw of their bond.*: Phrynia said. :*I fear this means there are outside forces at work here that also know of the prophecy and more. Even things we are not yet aware.*:

Trebeh reluctantly agreed. Both knew that, at this point, the only thing they could do was wait and hope for the best. For now, Regnaryn and Graeden remained safe within the confines of Reissue Grove.

# CHAPTER TWENTY-SEVEN

TREBEH CLIMBED the stairs to check on Regnaryn and Graeden. She was not surprised to see Neshya lurking outside Regnaryn's door.

"Good morning. I had not realized you had returned from your brother's house," she lied. "Is Ennales with you?"

"No, I came alone. I wanted to check on Regg."

Trebeh nodded. "I see. Is she still asleep?"

"Yes. Mama, I want to apologize for my actions last night. I was out of line. I know you would never do anything to hurt her." Neshya looked away and shook his head. "It is just that, well..."

"I know." She smiled, reached over and tousled his hair. "She is your little sister."

When he neither pulled away nor scowled, she realized how concerned he was for Regnaryn. "She *will* be alright, son. I promise."

He nodded.

"Did you check in on Graeden, too?"

Neshya made a low growl.

"It sounds like he is still asleep," he said, "and a bit too comfortably, if you ask me."

Trebeh shook her head. "There is more to this than you know," she said.

Neshya glared at her. "You said that last night. What more is there to say than what happened? Tell me."

"Not now."

Neshya rolled his eyes.

She quietly opened Regnaryn's door and peeked in at the sleeping girl. She closed the door and turned back to Neshya. "Please bring me the vial of the healing potion. And the pitcher of tea and glasses. I will be with Graeden."

"Yes, Mama." He headed downstairs.

She unlocked the door to Graeden's room and saw he was just waking. "Do not move too quickly," she said.

Her words came too late.

Graeden fell back onto the pillow, wincing. "How is Regnaryn?" he asked in measured breaths.

"She is fine." Trebeh settled herself in the chair by the bed.

Neshya entered, carrying a tray. He put it on the table beside Trebeh. The young yeckal glared at Graeden, quickly turned, and left the room.

Trebeh poured a small quantity of the healing potion into one of the glasses of tea, stirred it, and held it out to Graeden.

"Drink this," she said. "It will make you feel better."

He turned his face to her and scowled through eyes that were nearly swollen shut.

"I do not want to feel better," he said somberly, flinching from the discomfort speaking caused. "You should have let Ayirak kill me."

"Oh, please, not that again," she said, extending the glass.

Graeden slowly sat up and accepted the glass. Pain showed on his face as the glass touched his lips. He turned to put the emptied glass on the table and doubled over, barely able to breathe. Trebeh held him and discovered several cracked ribs. She went into the bathroom and returned with the basket of bandages.

"Why are you doing this?" he asked softly as Trebeh finished.

"Because your ribs are injured," she answered.

"No, that is not what I mean," he said, his frustration obvious.

"What happened last night was not your fault," she told him again.

"But," he began but was immediately cut off by her glower.

There was silence until Graeden yawned.

"It is about time that took effect," she said, standing up. "Now lie back and get some more rest."

With the effects of the potion taking hold, he obeyed. Trebeh straightened the covers and leaned over him. She kissed his forehead. "Rest, my son, all will work out for the best."

He barely heard her last remark before he fell asleep.

### 

*:How is she doing?:* she mindcalled to Neshya as she left Graeden's room.

*:She is still asleep.:*

*:Good,:* Trebeh answered. *:I am going downstairs. Do you want something to eat?:*

*:No, I am fine.:*

She went to the kitchen and filled the pitcher with tea, then placed it and a plate of honeycakes on a tray. As she climbed the stairs, she heard Neshya trying to comfort Regnaryn. Trebeh entered the room and poured tea. One look from Trebeh told Regnaryn her refusal to take the tea would not be tolerated.

She offered the plate to Regnaryn, who reluctantly took a cake. Trebeh handed the plate to Neshya, who eagerly crammed a cake into his mouth as if he had not eaten in weeks. Trebeh shook her head.

"How are you this morning, child?"

Regnaryn shrugged.

"You really need to eat that, dear," Trebeh said, pointing to the cake in the girl's hand.

Regnaryn took a small bite and then another.

"How is Graeden?" She put the empty glass on the side table. "Neshya will not tell me anything."

"I told you," Neshya said, trying to contain his anger, "you should not be worrying about him after what he did. He is not worth it."

Trebeh glared at Neshya. The young yekcal stormed out of the room.

"Graeden is doing as well as can be expected," Trebeh said, turning her attention back to Regnaryn. "The worst injuries are a few broken bones, nothing too serious. He will be fine in a few days."

"I am glad he is not hurt too badly," Regnaryn answered, holding back her sobs. "I would have never forgiven myself if it would have been, well... Mama, I am so sorry. It was all my fault."

"Child, I told you last night and I will tell you again, it is not your fault. Nor was it his."

Trebeh toyed with the idea of forcing the girl to get up, but thought it better to give her some time to work things out on her own.

"Mama," Regnaryn sobbed. The child looked as if she had something on her mind, but said no more.

"I understand, child."

Regnaryn nodded and slid under the covers.

# CHAPTER TWENTY-EIGHT

REGNARYN DID NOT leave her room that day or the next morning, nor would she allow anyone to visit her. On the second afternoon, Trebeh knocked on the locked bedroom door and was met with silence.

*:You will open this door, young lady, or you will have me to deal with,:* she said sternly.

Trebeh heard the key turn in the lock. The door slowly opened. Head bowed, Regnaryn stood for a moment, then turned, crossed the room to her bed and crawled back under the covers.

Under other circumstances, Trebeh might have been moved by the swollen red eyes and tear-streaked face, but Regnaryn had wallowed far too long in self-pity. Trebeh's hardened expression took Regnaryn by surprise.

Trebeh crossed to the large wardrobe. She reached in, grabbed several items of clothing, and threw them toward the bed. They landed at Regnaryn's feet.

"Bathe and get dressed," Trebeh ordered.

"I do not want to," Regnaryn sobbed.

"It was not a request," Trebeh snapped. "You will either get up and get yourself bathed and dressed, or I shall do it for you."

Regnaryn did not argue. She stripped off the nightclothes she had been in for the last two days and entered the bath chamber.

A few minutes later a half-dry Regnaryn emerged, towels haphazardly wrapped around her hair and body. She was surprised to see Trebeh had made the bed. Her mother did not often clean up after the older children. Regnaryn knew this was Trebeh's way of telling her, in no uncertain terms, she would not be returning to the confines of her bed.

Regnaryn slowly dressed. As she finished buttoning her tunic, Trebeh said, "Come here, let me fix your hair."

Regnaryn sat at her mother's feet. Trebeh unwrapped the towel and vigorously rubbed the long strands of red hair to remove the excess water.

"For as long as I can remember," Trebeh said as she dropped the towel on the floor, "you never were very good at drying your hair."

Regnaryn smiled faintly. Trebeh ran the comb through the long silky hair. Regnaryn purred and Trebeh rejoiced at her child's reaction. She hoped it meant the girl would snap out of her depression.

"Done," Trebeh said, putting the tie at the end of the long braid, "now let us get something to eat downstairs."

"I would rather stay in my room," she answered, showing her mood had not changed.

"Yes, I am sure you would." Trebeh sighed. "But you see, *I* want you to come downstairs, so you will."

Trebeh put her arm around Regnaryn and nudged her out of the room. The house was empty, except for the sound of Graeden's gentle snoring.

"Where is everyone?" Regnaryn asked as they entered the kitchen.

"It is mid-afternoon," Trebeh answered.

"Oh, of course," Regnaryn replied.

Trebeh put a chunk of bread along with meat and fruit on a

plate and placed it in front of Regnaryn. The yekcal filled a glass with tea and set it beside the plate. As much as the girl had protested, she now ate and drank all she was given.

"Would you like more?" Trebeh asked as Regnaryn took the last bit from her plate.

"Yes, please," she replied, her voice muffled by the food that still filled her mouth.

Regnaryn sipped her tea and finished the second helping almost as quickly as the first.

The silence was shattered by the squeals of the twins bounding through the door ahead of the others. The twins shrieked with delight when they saw Regnaryn and ran to her.

"Enough," Trebeh said to the twins. "Leave your sister alone."

The youngsters reluctantly obeyed.

"It is still a beautiful afternoon, a bit chilly, but beautiful. I think we should sit in the garden for a bit," Trebeh said. She turned to Nelluc. "Please get Regnaryn's coat."

"I would rather go back to my room," Regnaryn answered so softly that even Trebeh's cat-like ears strained to hear.

"No," Trebeh answered.

Regnaryn stubbornly remained seated. Nelluc tried to give her the coat.

"In a war of wills, young lady, you will find yourself on the losing side," Trebeh said, walking toward the garden door. She opened it and stepped outside. "Now, put on your coat and join me."

Regnaryn immediately rose from her chair and walked to the door. She knew, though Trebeh's demeanor was calm, the yekcal would tolerate neither defiance nor disobedience.

### 

A week passed. Graeden's injuries healed faster than expected. But all was not back to normal. Neshya and the other siblings, except the young twins, found him hard to accept.

The bigger problem was Regnaryn and Graeden. The two could barely be in the same house, never mind the same room. Each would turn and run in the opposite direction at the sight of the other. The mere mention of the other's name would result in a fit of crying or an onslaught of apologies. Their behavior kept everyone in the house frazzled and tense. Ayirak, still struggling to fully forgive the boy, found himself having to tread gingerly whenever either was around.

"What are we going to do about those two?" Ayirak asked. "No one can tolerate their behavior much longer."

"Yes, something must be done."

"Why not just sit them both down at the table and force them to talk to each other?" he asked.

"Forcing them to meet, to speak, will only make things worse. We must find another way."

Ayirak nodded and crawled into bed beside Trebeh.

"It is the soulbond that is causing this extreme tension. It is pushing within them; it wants to be acknowledged, to show itself. So it is elevating their emotions to levels neither has ever experienced, trying to get them together, but they are resisting. And the more they resist, the harder the bond pushes and the more emotional they become. And the more the rest of us suffer."

Ayirak shook his head. "I had not thought of it like that."

"And there is something else," she said.

"What more could there be?"

"What will happen when they finally do acknowledge it."

Ayirak did not understand.

She shook her head. "Has it been so long that you have forgotten?"

Ayirak drew in a breath. "Oh, of course. I could never forget that, my love. I guess I just was not prepared for anything like that to happen to Regnaryn."

Trebeh smiled at the obvious distress he felt at the prospect she presented.

"Do you have something in mind?"

162

"Yes, I do," she answered.

"I guess you had better tell me about it."

She laid out her plan. He shook his head once or twice in disbelief, but he did not interrupt.

"Are you sure there is no other way?"

"None that I can think of. But if you have a better idea, I am willing to listen."

He thought a moment and shook his head, "I would still prefer a face-to-face confrontation. I do not like all of this sneaking around." He saw the resolute look in her face, confirming the inevitable. "But I guess you are right. When?"

"Tomorrow. But it must look like a coincidence and not something forced on them."

"Hmm, that will not be easy. Those two are edgy about everything around them."

"I know."

# CHAPTER TWENTY-NINE

REGNARYN RUMMAGED through the baskets at the back of the storage building, looking for the last item Mama had sent her to retrieve. Why Mama needed all of this, when there was plenty of food at the house was beyond her. She brushed by a basket of apples and it toppled over, spilling its contents. She cursed aloud.

"Who is there?" a familiar voice from the open doorway asked.

Regnaryn jumped in surprise, hitting her head on the shelf. "Damn it!"

"Regnaryn? Are you alright?" Graeden rushed into the room, knocking the crate in the doorway out of his path.

Regnaryn rushed past him, trying to reach the door before it closed.

"No!" she screamed as the door slammed just beyond her fingertips.

"What?"

"You let the door close," she screamed, pointing at it. Her emotions ran out of control and rage burst to life within her.

"And?" Graeden asked.

"We are locked in!" she shouted. "We are stuck here until

someone comes looking for us. What are you doing here, anyway?"
She stormed across the room.

"Trebeh told me to come down here because she needed some
spices," he answered with more than just a hint of annoyance,
unsure why she was so angry.

Regnaryn mumbled under her breath.

"As for the door, who makes a door that does not open from
the inside?" Graeden snarled, his own emotions inexplicably out of
control.

"It is broken, you idiot, it was not made like that!"

"And just how was I supposed to know that?" he shouted back.
"Just mindspeak for help. If I remember correctly, you are good at
that."

He rubbed his shoulder.

She ignored his comment. "There *is* a sign."

Graeden looked toward the door and pointed to the floor. "You
mean *that* sign? I guess I did not realize I was supposed to read THE
FLOOR!"

The two faced each other. She scowled and raised her hand to
slap him. He grabbed her wrist.

She tried to pull her hand away, but he would not release her.
Their eyes were locked with such intensity, their gazes stayed
unbroken until she struck him with her free hand. She went to strike
again, but he caught her wrist. She cursed and struggled to break
free, but he would not release her. The battle of wills continued for
several moments.

When she finally ceased struggling, he said, "I will release you, if
you promise not to hit me again."

Regnaryn nodded but did not soften her glare.

Graeden slowly let her go and jumped back.

"I said I would not hit you again." She scowled. "You did not
have to move."

He searched for the right words. "I know you are still angry
with me for what happened in the stable." He looked into her eyes

then turned away. "And you have every right to be. What I did was unforgivable."

Her eyes welled with tears. "I am not angry with you, I never was. I thought you hated me for what Papa did to you."

He looked at her. "I could never hate you."

They stood in tense silence. He took a step towards her. She quickly stepped back and turned away. He feared he had once again angered her.

"Do you want some cider?" she asked, breaking the awkward silence. Without waiting for his reply, she headed for the back wall.

"Um, yes, that sounds fine," he replied, again confused by her actions.

She reached for a bottle. It slipped from her grasp and crashed to the floor. She bent to pick up the pieces.

"Damn!" she cried.

Graeden saw the blood trickling down her hand as she raised the fingers to her mouth. He raced across the room to her and gently took her hand in his.

"Let me look at it," he said as she tried to pull away. "Please."

"It is nothing, just a little cut," she said.

"I would feel better if you would let me look at it."

She nodded and stopped struggling.

"There is a sliver of glass in your finger."

He pulled the shard from her finger without waiting for permission. Once out, the blood flowed more freely. He reached into his pocket and withdrew a handkerchief. He wrapped the cloth around the fingers and held it tightly.

She winced.

"I have to apply pressure to stop the bleeding."

"I know."

He lifted his free hand to her face and caressed her cheek. "I am so sorry, Regnaryn."

"It is alright, it does not hurt," she said.

"I was not talking about your finger," he said, looking deeply into her eyes. "I am sorry about the night in the stable, about everything that happened."

Her face darkened. She looked away at the mention of the incident. Graeden feared he had once again offended her.

"No," she said softly, not looking at him. "I should apologize to you. I am the reason you were hurt."

"It was not your fault," he said more sternly. "No, do not look away. Listen to me, I am serious. I should have known better. I knew down deep that you... you did not..." He struggled to find the right words. "It is just, well, just know I am to blame for all that transpired."

"I do not know what you mean." She pressed the palm of her hand to his cheek.

He pulled free of her.

"See, you do believe it is my fault."

"No, no, that is not it," he said. "Please believe me, it is just... Oh damn, how can I explain this to you?"

He shook his head. "I want you, Regnaryn. Want you in ways you do not know exist. I want you more than I have ever wanted anyone in my life. That is wrong. You are an innocent, a child."

She resented his remark. "I am not a child. We are almost the same age."

Graeden turned his gaze to her. "Yes, that is true, but there are many things you are unaware of. Things that happen between a man and a woman. Things you have never experienced, because of how you were raised." He saw her face cloud with confusion. "As the only human."

She looked at him. And for the first time, she understood. She clasped his face with her hands. This time, he did not pull away. They looked deeply into each other's eyes. And at that moment, they knew; knew each other's every thought, every desire, everything. Knew they were meant to be together.

She kissed him on the lips. He returned her kiss, pressing his lips hard against hers. She did not protest. He pulled her close, slowly running his hand from her shoulder to the small of her back. He moaned slightly as his sex responded to his desire for her.

She seemed to know what he wanted, as if she were in his mind. She pressed her hips ever so slightly toward him.

She held his head in her hands and brought her slightly open mouth to his. She purred in a deep guttural tone. They removed each other's clothes, gently caressing newly bared skin. They eagerly removed each piece of clothing on this intimate journey of discovery.

When both were naked, they stretched out upon the pile of discarded clothes, facing each other. He tenderly caressed her breasts then kissed them as his hand passed lightly over her belly and then dipped lower to her thighs. She trembled as he continued to touch her.

She purred and caressed his manhood. He moaned. She released him and rolled onto her back. He gently pushed her legs open and knelt between them. He leaned over to again kiss her breasts, and she sighed as the hardness of his sex nudged against her body. He gently bit her nipple. She held her breath as wave after wave of sensations she had never before experienced coursed through her body. He looked into her eyes and gently entered her. She let out a small cry of pain. He stopped, but she drew him down on her.

Their passion reached a height Graeden had never experienced. It was as if they were feeling each other's desires, which made their every movement, every action, perfect. He could not explain it and did not care how it happened. He only knew he wanted this feeling to go on forever, wanted time to stop at this moment with the two of them joined together like this. He did not want this to end.

But it did. They lay with their bodies still entwined, neither wanting to part.

Regnaryn stared into his eyes. "I understand now," she said.

"I am glad," he whispered.

She pulled him closer. She kissed him so passionately, it took his breath away. Their bodies again responded. The lovemaking that followed exceeded description, far surpassing their first time of just a few moments earlier. They fed off of each other's thoughts and desires, reaching even higher levels of ecstasy.

Their lovemaking concluded, both exhausted but unwilling to part. They just lay there on the dirt floor content to be with each other.

"Get dressed, both of you," Trebeh said from the other side of the door.

Regnaryn and Graeden were wrenched back to reality.

"I need to talk to you," Trebeh continued.

The couple looked at each other. On one hand, they thought they should feel shame, but they did not. They dressed quickly.

The door opened as Regnaryn finished buttoning her tunic.

"Well, I am glad that is over with," Trebeh said.

Graeden and Regnaryn stared at her, unsure of her meaning. She smiled and motioned Graeden to prop the door open with the nearby crate. Trebeh walked slowly into the room and sat on a box against the wall. Graeden looked toward the door, waiting for Ayirak to appear once again to beat him. But the yekcal was nowhere to be seen. Graeden returned to Regnaryn and grabbed her hand.

"Relax, children," she said as she watched their eyes, which only momentarily left each other. "What occurred here today is the culmination of something far greater than both of you, than any of us. Something we have been expecting since that night in the stable."

"I do not understand," Graeden said.

"I expect not."

Trebeh smiled, then told them of their soulbond. Her face lit up when she spoke of the heights of pleasure, passion and happiness being with one's soulbound partner offered. Regnaryn accepted Trebeh's words as truth. Graeden appeared doubtful.

"Seriously? One person bound to another by some thread of fate such that they are blind to everything around them?" Graeden asked, still unwilling to release his hold on Regnaryn.

Trebeh laughed softly. "So, I suppose you have another

explanation for being unable to let loose of Regnaryn even though you fully expect Ayirak to appear and throttle you."

Graeden blushed, but he held fast to Regnaryn, and she to him.

"That is what I thought," Trebeh said. "Did you not think it odd she did not mindcall someone when you got locked in here?"

Graeden shook his head. "I guess I did not think about it. We were arguing and..."

Trebeh smiled broadly.

Graeden looked at her. "Why are you smiling?"

"I am sorry, child, I was just remembering something from long ago." She stared dreamily into the distance.

"What?" Regnaryn asked.

Trebeh looked at Regnaryn. "How Ayirak and I discovered our bond. When we first met, we could not stand being around each other for even a moment." Trebeh smiled at the distant memory. "Until... Well, I do not think you need to hear the details. Let me just say, I understand what went on here."

Graeden and Regnaryn said nothing.

"Regnaryn, I think we could all do with something to drink," Trebeh said.

Regnaryn hesitated.

"Oh, dear girl, he is not going anywhere. You can release him for a moment."

Regnaryn reluctantly withdrew her hand and walked to the cider bottles.

*:Be careful of the broken glass,:* Graeden warned. *:I do not want you to get hurt again.:*

Regnaryn nodded then stopped.

"You did it, Graeden!" she said excitedly.

"Did what?"

"You mindspoke to me, and more than just a single word! Mama, he did it. He mindspoke. Is that not wonderful?"

Trebeh nodded. Regnaryn almost danced to the shelves and grabbed three small bottles.

"Does this mean I have mastered mindspeech?" Graeden asked.

*:I do not know, mindspeak to me.:*

*:What do you want me to say?:*

*:Whatever you would like, son.:*

Regnaryn watched as first Trebeh and then Graeden smiled.

"I did it, Regnaryn, I mindspoke to her."

The yekcal nodded.

"But why did it take so long? Why did I have such trouble with it?"

"Look at all that was going on around you. So much has happened to you in the last few months – that place you were held when Regnaryn first met you and whatever went on there, your reluctance to believe what you saw here, and the battle within yourself to explain the intense desire for Regnaryn when you felt it forbidden." Trebeh could see he did not really understand. "We can discuss this at home where we will all be far more comfortable."

They started to leave, but Regnaryn hesitated. "I need to clean up and get the things you needed."

"I will have Neshya come and do that." Trebeh motioned Regnaryn toward the door. "As for those items, I do not really need them now. I changed my mind on what we will be having for dinner."

"Trebeh!" Graeden said with a hint of shock. "Do you mean you sent us down here to get us together?"

Trebeh's eyes twinkled, but she said nothing.

*:Ayirak, we are on our way.:*

*:And?:* he asked.

*:And what?:* She knew full well what he meant.

*:What happened?:*

*:Are you asking for details? Why you dirty old cat!:* she said, playing with him.

*:No!:* he said with shock and embarrassment. *:How did you lock them in the storeroom without them suspecting?:*

Trebeh laughed, *:I did not have to do anything, seems that old,*

171

broken door did all the work for me. So, in a manner of speaking, it really was coincidence that they got trapped in there. Or their soulbond was tired of being ignored.:

    :Is Regnaryn alright?:

    :They are fine, both of them.:

# CHAPTER THIRTY

REGNARYN RAN to the door and kissed the waiting Ayirak. She turned and motioned Graeden to follow. Less eager, he cautiously climbed the porch stairs. He jumped back when Ayirak moved toward him. The yekcal pretended not to notice and patted him on the back.

"Where is everyone?" Regnaryn asked.

"They have all gone to stay elsewhere tonight. Your father and I wanted to be alone with you two," Trebeh said, stifling a laugh at the expression on Graeden's face. "There is much to discuss."

They entered the kitchen and saw the table already laid out with food.

"I thought you both might be hungry when you returned," Trebeh said.

Graeden nodded and sat beside Regnaryn. Ayirak and Trebeh sat across from them.

"So tell me more about the soulbond," Graeden said between bites of food. "It still sounds pretty farfetched to me."

Trebeh smiled. "Enjoy dinner first, then we will talk."

When the last of the meal was done, Regnaryn stood and

reached for the plates. Trebeh stopped her.

"Not now, child," she said. "That can be taken care of later."

In the other room, Ayirak and Trebeh sat in their usual chairs and, not surprisingly, Graeden and Regnaryn sat close beside each other on the couch. Graeden still half-expected Ayirak to object as he had in the past.

"This soulbond thing sounds a bit unbelievable," Graeden said once again.

Ayirak shook his head and Trebeh took his hand.

"Perhaps." She smiled. "After all that you have been through in the last few months, I would think you would be used to unbelievable by now."

Graeden nodded.

"I am not convinced soulbonds are unique to Reissem Grove. I think they occur everywhere," Trebeh said.

"Well, I never heard of any such thing before."

"Perhaps not, but your people do not cultivate their innate abilities. You believe only what you see, only what is in the physical realm."

"You are not trying to say that everyone could do some of the things you do here, are you?"

"I cannot discount the possibility. After all, you and Regnaryn connected well before you entered this place, remember?"

Graeden nodded.

"And what about the place you were held prisoner? How did you escape? And what of the time you feel you lost?" Trebeh asked.

Graeden stood. He walked to the window and peered out. Regnaryn wanted to follow him, but Trebeh stopped her with a shake of her head. He stared into the night for several moments, then turned back to them.

"I am not sure what happened during that time," he said quietly. "You are right. There are times when something sounds or feels familiar or horrifying but, try as I might, I have no explanation why. I glimpse names or faces, but then they disappear, as if I have been made to forget them."

Ayirak and Regnaryn looked surprised at Graeden's answer. Trebeh did not.

"I sense someone has locked things away in your mind," she said.

Graeden walked back to the couch and sat down beside Regnaryn. "But, why?"

Trebeh shrugged.

"That will need to wait for another time," Ayirak said as he felt the emotions within the two youngsters mounting once again. "Right now, we must discuss how you two are going to deal with all of this."

"What do you mean, Papa?" Regnaryn asked.

Trebeh felt the awkwardness in Ayirak. He did not like discussing personal matters, especially with his daughters. He looked at Trebeh.

"What your father means is, how will you control your desires?"

Their expression showed they did not understand.

Trebeh sighed. "You need to shield your passion from the outside world."

"I thought we had shieldings," Graeden said.

"Yes, for your thoughts, not for the emotions you now feel for each other. They are breaking through those shieldings like floodwaters over a dam."

Graeden blushed. "You do not mean that everyone knows what went on?"

"No. I made sure the storage room was shielded before you went there, allowing whatever occurred to be contained within. No one knows."

"But you knew," Graeden said.

Trebeh laughed. "To a point. I knew what was going on, not the details."

"But your, um, timing was..." Graeden did not know how to put his thoughts into words.

Trebeh smiled. "Yes. Well, when I arrived, the pressure against the shielding was considerably less than just a few moments before."

Graeden and Regnaryn looked at each other and flushed. Ayirak looked away.

"What must we do?" Regnaryn asked.

"Tonight your father and I will ensure your room is properly shielded," Trebeh began. She almost laughed at the look of relief that crossed the young lovers' faces. "Tomorrow, we will help you learn to create your own shielding. After all, I do not think you want to have us around you all the time."

The young couple nodded shyly.

"I do not think I will be much help in that," Graeden said. "I cannot create a shielding adequate enough to contain my own thoughts."

Trebeh smiled. "I think you will find your abilities have changed. After all, look how easily you can now mindspeak. But you will not be trying to shield an entire room, unless you want to. More than likely, you will create the shielding to only surround the two of you."

Regnaryn looked puzzled.

"The shielding is not actually to keep others out, but rather to keep your energy in."

"Energy?" Graeden asked.

Trebeh nodded. "Your passion. The smaller area you shield, the more you will benefit from it."

Graeden and Regnaryn glanced at each other and smiled as Trebeh's words became clear.

"But, I still do not understand how you knew of this bond before we did?" Graeden asked.

"The night in the stable, when both of your emotions were laid out raw, I saw the golden thread of a soulbond between you."

"So that is how you knew what to expect today," Graeden said.

Trebeh nodded. "Yes. And once a couple has been bound, when they have physically acknowledged it, as you two did this afternoon, it is something that lasts a lifetime. Some say even beyond. Be warned that, as I told you earlier, if separated, the consequences can be horrible. It can cause a depression so deep, madness or even death can follow."

"Whoa, wait a minute," Graeden said. "Even if I can accept the concept of this tie between us, you are saying if we are separated we will go mad? You and Ayirak are not always at each other's side, and I see no madness here."

"I am sorry, I did not make myself clear. I meant more permanent separations – the death of one of the pair or the deliberate severing of the relationship. Separation that would involve great time or distance."

Graeden tried to digest her words. The more she spoke, the more fantastical it sounded, yet the more he believed her every word.

"But, what of the others – especially Neshya?" Graeden asked, changing the subject. "How are they going to react to our new relationship? I know they are aware of what went on before." Graeden looked away. "And I am sure you two are the only reason I was never punished for my actions."

Trebeh walked over to the young man. She knelt in front of him and took his face in her hands. "You must get over what happened that night, it was not your fault. Surely you see that now."

He nodded.

"I have already explained the situation to them," Ayirak said. "They understand."

Graeden was surprised to see there was no longer any trace of anger in Ayirak's voice.

"Do not worry, Graeden, all will be fine now," Trebeh said.

Graeden was still not certain how he would be able to face the others or how they could so easily accept this change. He doubted he could do the same if it were his sister in Regnaryn's place, even if there was a soulbond involved. Still he had no reason not to believe the two yekcals.

"It has been a long day for all of us," Trebeh said, "and I am sure we could all use a good night's sleep."

###

Regnaryn and Graeden had no sooner closed the door to her room when their passions once again overtook them. Their fervor reached levels neither had known nor imagined. They did not want to miss one moment of experiencing the sight and feel of the other, but eventually both succumbed to exhaustion and fell asleep in each other's arms.

###

Regnaryn awoke to the sunshine to see Graeden leaning on his elbow, staring and smiling at her. She touched his face. He took her hand and gently kissed it. He pulled her towards him.

*:Children, breakfast is ready,:* Trebeh's voice sounded in their minds, pulling them away from their developing passion.

They kissed once more then rose, dressed and went downstairs.

After the morning meal, the task of teaching the youngsters to build their cooperative shielding began. Ayirak still held reservations as to Graeden's ability to learn. To his surprise, the young man showed impressive skill.

*:Trebeh, how is it that Graeden is doing so well when he struggled so in the past?:*

*:Do you not think the stress he was under before yesterday played some part in his problems?:*

Ayirak finally understood and watched with awe at the ability displayed by both Regnaryn and Graeden.

"I thought there was only one kind of shielding," Graeden said, "the one you built on my first day here. But this is completely different."

Trebeh smiled. "There are as many types of shieldings as there are reasons to create them. The purpose of the shielding determines how it is built."

"Of course. That makes perfect sense."

Late in the afternoon the couple constructed a shielding that the yekcals could not easily penetrate.

"You both have made astonishing progress today," Trebeh said. "I am very impressed."

Regnaryn and Graeden beamed.

Graeden said, "I think Regnaryn did most of the work."

"No matter. You both did very well. Now, it is time to think about dinner."

Regnaryn followed Trebeh into the kitchen and saw far more food there than required for the four of them.

"Are the others are coming back tonight?" she asked.

Trebeh nodded and Regnaryn ran to tell Graeden. He felt less enthusiastic. Graeden continued to fear the others would still harbor at least some shred of anger toward him. Neshya had warned him on the first day what would happen if he ever hurt Regnaryn.

Just before dinner, the others returned. Regnaryn ran and hugged each of them. She picked the twins up and danced around the room, making them squeal with delight. Graeden warily approached Neshya, unsure of the young yekcal's response.

Neshya smiled, *:Do not fear, brother, I understand now.:*
*:But how? How can you so easily change your mind?:*

Neshya shrugged, then blurted out, "Wait, you can mindspeak now? When did that happen?"

Graeden flushed, and Neshya laughed. "Oh, ho, I see! So what you needed was..."

"That is enough, young man," Trebeh called from the other room. "Dinner is ready."

# CHAPTER THIRTY-ONE

AT SOME POINT during the long winter's confinement, talk turned to Regnaryn and Graeden having a home of their own. It was decided that Regnaryn's childhood home would be perfect – close enough for visits, but far enough away for privacy.

After several weeks of Regnaryn changing her mind from wanting to go to wanting to stay, the couple agreed that a home of their own would be a good idea.

To everyone's surprise, even after all these years of abandonment, the house required only a good cleaning and a few minor repairs to make it habitable again.

A few weeks later, the couple moved in.

### 

Graeden brought Merlona back to the stable after a leisurely summer ride. Regnaryn came up behind him, wrapped her arms around his waist, stood on tip-toe and kissed his neck.

"I think we should visit your family," she whispered into his ear.

He turned to her in surprise. "My family?"

"Yes, we should go to Hammarsh Keep."

He was speechless.

"You have been here almost a year and on the road for almost as long, right?"

He nodded.

"You try to hide it, but I know how much you miss them, and I am sure they miss you, as well. I can only imagine how terribly I would miss Mama and Papa and all the others, even Neshya," she said, rolling her eyes, "if I were gone that long. Your family really has no idea where you are, so we should visit them."

"You realize that would mean we would not be able to return to Reissem Grove for near on a year."

"I know."

"And you realize we will be out of contact with everyone here for that time."

She nodded.

He hugged her.

"Thank you, my love. Thank you so much."

She smiled as he chattered about the various members of his family. She had heard most of it before, but let him speak.

"I think we should leave next week," she said when he finally stopped to take a breath.

"Really? Next week? Do you think we could be ready that quickly? There is so much we would need to do. And we would need to get another horse for you... and..."

She put her finger to his lips.

"We could be ready. Arrangements can be made."

He took her in his arms once again and kissed her. Suddenly, he looked concerned.

"What is it?"

"What will Ayirak think?" Graeden asked. "And Trebeh? I mean, I think she enjoys having us within a stone's throw. What will she say about our going so far away and for so long?"

"They will just have to accept it. I am sure they understand how much you miss your family," Regnaryn replied. After a moment of thought, she added, "I think we should tell them right now."

"Now?" Graeden gulped. "Face to face?"

Regnaryn smiled. "You are not afraid, are you?"

Graeden nodded. "Maybe just a little, after all, Ayirak can be, well, Ayirak. Why not just mindspeak it to them?"

She put her hands on her hips and stared at him.

"Alright, alright," he said, smiling at her scowl, "face to face it will be. But..."

"But, what?"

"I will need a kiss to bolster my courage."

He kissed her, first softly then with more passion.

She pulled away, laughing. "Oh, no. We are going to talk to Mama and Papa now."

"What?" He feigned ignorance at her unspoken accusation. "I just wanted a kiss, that is all. You did not think I was going to try to... I would never..."

"Uh, huh."

"Alright, perhaps the thought did cross my mind."

"Anyway, it is after lunch so Papa will be in a good mood."

Graeden was not sure a mere meal would be enough to soften the blow of their news.

### 

"So, to what do we owe this visit? Do you miss us that much already?" Trebeh asked as Regnaryn and Graeden entered their home.

"No. I mean, we miss you," Regnaryn sputtered and Trebeh laughed. "We have something to tell you both."

"You are not? Not already," Trebeh asked, sounding both excited and concerned.

Ayirak agreed. "It is too soon."

Regnaryn did not understand.

"No, no. That is not it," Graeden replied. "She is not with child."

Trebeh looked both relieved and disappointed at Graeden's

words.

Regnaryn shook her head. "We came to tell you we are going to Graeden's homeland."

Regnaryn saw Ayirak glare at Graeden.

"Papa, stop that. It was my idea, not his."

"Well, that is a surprise. When did this all come about?" Trebeh asked.

"I have been thinking about it for some time now. But I just told Graeden a little while ago," Regnaryn answered

"Oh," Ayirak said, "and I am sure he agreed instantly. Are you aware how long you will be away? Did you give any thought to that?"

"Yes, I have," Regnaryn replied. "In fact, that was Graeden's first concern."

Ayirak harrumphed. "Well, have you thought about the journey itself? It is not going to be easy."

"Papa," Regnaryn said. "Remember, it is not as if I will be alone. Graeden will be with me."

"You have been quiet, Graeden," Trebeh said. "Surely you have an opinion on this."

Graeden coughed. "Well, it would be nice to see my family. And even though we have gotten word to them, I am sure my mother still worries."

"Yes, I am sure she does," she said, her voice cracking just a bit. "When do you plan to leave?"

"Next week," Regnaryn said.

"Surely you will need more time to prepare," Ayirak said.

"If we wait too long, we will have to deal with the weather," Graeden replied. "Even leaving immediately, it will be winter when we get to Hammarsh."

"True," Trebeh said and then the reality struck her, "and you will be gone until well past next summer."

Graeden nodded.

"It is not fair for us to keep you away from your family," Trebeh said, trying to hide her fear that once gone, they would not return. "What can we do to help?"

# CHAPTER THIRTY-TWO

"THERE IS FAR less preparation needed for the journey than I expected," Regnaryn said.

"I left on a moment's notice with just the clothes on my back."

"Yes. And, I remember the state you were in when you arrived. I certainly do not want to look like that when I meet your family."

"But you still loved me." He smiled, recalling how raggedy he had looked.

"Imagine that!"

"Seriously, if this is all we need, I think we can leave much sooner than next week. Maybe tomorrow or the next day."

Graeden shook his head. "I do not think that would be such a good idea."

"Really?" she asked. "I would have thought you would be thrilled to be able to get on the road sooner."

"Oh, I would love to. I am concerned about Trebeh and Ayirak's reaction to this change in plans."

"I will talk to Mama."

"If that is what we are going to do, then I will go upstairs and begin packing right now."

"Wonderful. I will join you in a bit."

###

Graeden's mind turned to Hammarsh Keep as he packed his clothes. He envisioned Regnaryn meeting his family. He knew everyone, especially Taaryn, would instantly adore her, just as he did. Suddenly, his joy screeched to a halt.

The others! The ones who put on airs and puffed themselves up in deluded self-importance would deride Regnaryn's naiveté and ignorance of their world. They would attack her with whispers and innuendo and snide remarks behind her back.

He would tell Regnaryn to ignore them. But eventually, she would crumble under the weight of their cruelty.

No, he could not take Regnaryn to Hammarsh Keep.

As soon as that thought crossed his mind, Graeden felt Regnaryn's hand on his shoulder. She jumped back, stunned.

"You do not want me to go to Hammarsh," she cried. "You are ashamed of me."

Graeden, startled by her sudden outburst, asked, "What do you mean? I am not ashamed of you. Why would you say such a thing?"

"You lie! You do not want me to meet your friends, your people." She was almost in tears, screeching at him.

"I do not understand what you are talking about?"

"You were just thinking that. I saw it. Felt it in your mind."

"You were in my mind?" Now it was his turn to be angry. "How dare you!"

"That is not the point. You are ashamed of me!"

"I am not ashamed of you. I would never be ashamed of you," he insisted, trying to calm her. "You misunderstood."

He reached for her. She pulled away. He reached out to her mind and, for the first time since they had bonded, found it sealed off to him. He blocked her path and grabbed her by the shoulders. She squirmed to get free, but he would not let go. The look in her eyes held a steely coldness he had never seen before and it sent a chill down his spine. Still, he would not release his grip.

"Regnaryn," he said. "Please listen."

Her rigid posture told him his words were not getting through. He pulled her closer and pressed his lips against hers. She sank her teeth into his lip hard enough to draw blood. He released her and jumped back.

She licked the blood from her lips and stared at him like a wild animal preparing to strike the death blow to its prey. She strode past him, challenging him to stop her.

Graeden stood motionless. He wanted to chase after her, but the throbbing pain in his lip gave him second thoughts. Yet, he could not let her think he was ashamed of her. He reached out to her mind only to be blocked once again. Perhaps some time alone; time to calm down. Then she would allow him to explain.

### 

Graeden sat in the garden until the cool night breeze roused him from his inner numbness. He climbed the stairs, oblivious to the darkness. For the first time, he found the bedroom door locked.

"Regnaryn," he said, knocking lightly.

No response.

He rapped harder. "Please let me in."

Nothing.

He called to her again, even considered breaking down the door. What good would that do? Dejected, he left.

### 

He stared into the darkness, trying to fathom why she would not listen, why she failed to understand he only wanted to protect her. In the short time they had been together, they had always thought and acted as one. Now, she had blocked him from her mind. He drifted off to sleep and felt more alone than ever before.

"Graeden."

The whispered word echoed through his mind, shattering his lonely silence.

"Regnaryn," he answered like an excited child. He turned and saw her standing in the doorway, the morning sun reflecting off her hair. He ran to her. "Let me explain."

She did not answer.

"What you saw in my mind is not what you think," he said. "You misunderstood."

"I know what I saw. You are ashamed to bring me to your home, to your friends."

"I am not ashamed of you. I am afraid for you."

"Afraid? Am I to fear your friends?"

"No, not my friends."

"Then, who? Your family?" Her words sounded clipped, her voice emotionless, her eyes cold.

"No. My family will love you. My friends will love you, but there are others. Others who will not understand you, how you act."

"How I act?" She raged. "That makes no sense."

"Regnaryn, the outside world is not like Reissem. There are people out there that are vicious for no reason."

"You are just making excuses. I know what you were thinking,"

She walked out the door before he had a chance to answer. He had never seen this side of his beloved before.

He ran after her and again tried to explain. Hoping she would listen. Wanting her to believe.

She glared at him. "Your words sound like excuses, lies. If so many of your people are like that, what kind of place is this Hammarsh Keep? It sounds horrific."

He shook his head. "No, it is a beautiful place with beautiful people, but there are a few who will dislike you."

"Why?" she asked.

He shook his head. "For any number of reasons, or for no reason at all. Because they are petty and revel in causing misery and pain to others."

"That is gibberish," she said. "People do not do such things without cause."

"In the world beyond Reissem Grove, they do. There are people who do not need a reason to be cruel. They just are. And there will be nothing I can do to stop them."

Regnaryn took a step back. Angry, she twisted his every word to fit the scenario her mind created.

"So, you will allow these horrible people to hurt me."

"No! No! That is not what I meant. You are not listening."

He continued, repeating the same things over and over until his voice grew hoarse. Still, she refused to understand.

He reminded her how he had reacted when he first arrived in Reissem Grove — how difficult it had been for him to accept the others in this place, how hard it had been for him to fit in, even though everyone immediately accepted him. He explained that, unlike Reissem Grove, where everyone had affection, love, for everyone else, the same was not true outside of this place. He pleaded with her to believe his concerns were for her well-being. Nothing more.

Their eyes were locked as he spoke. He searched for any glimmer of understanding, but saw only her steely glare. He tried to convince her, but her expression did not change.

Finally, after he had exhausted every argument, every explanation he could think of, he said, "I am deeply hurt that you refuse to believe me. You have closed your mind to reason and hear only what you want. What you have chosen as the truth, no matter what I say. I have tried and failed with all at my disposal to convince you otherwise. My only recourse is to ask you to look within my heart, within my soul. You know all that I am is open to you, now and forever. Look inside of me and when you have done so, tell me truthfully if you still hold to your belief that I am ashamed of you."

He looked into her dark green eyes, searching for the warmth that had been there before; for the sparkle that made him want to lose himself in them from the first time he saw her. He found neither.

"Please, please, believe me."

She turned from him. "I do not."

Those three words, spoken with no trace of emotion, tore out his heart. She had taken the life from him. He was empty, dead.

He could not breathe, could not speak. His only hope was this would pass. But deep within, he sensed it would not.

Hours drifted by. Night fell. Graeden called to Regnaryn more times than he could count, only to be met with silence. Finally, he gave up. She had barred him from her mind. His well of emptiness deepened.

He waited, but she did not return. He called to her, aware that she could hear him and deliberately chose to ignore him. He could do nothing more than wait. He sat, oblivious to the tears that streamed from his eyes.

### 

Graeden awoke to see Regnaryn standing in front of him, the sunlight in sharp contrast to the darkness of her glare.

"Regnaryn," he said.

She did not answer.

"I have missed you so much," he continued.

She said nothing, did nothing more than stare.

The silence was unbearable. He took her hand. She did not resist.

"I heard you calling me," she said, her voice flat.

His heart soared.

"I was thinking about what you said about leaving now for Hammarsh Keep. That would allow us to arrive well before the cold of winter sets in. Though you may not think it severe after living here. We could either arrive unannounced, or send a messenger from one of the villages. If we do not alert them, they will be not be expecting us, so there will be nothing special planned."

He knew he was babbling, but could not stop himself.

"If we send a messenger, I am sure they will have a huge celebration in your honor. Or, if you prefer, we could wait until next spring to leave and then we could..."

She closed her eyes and sighed, exhausted by his chatter.

"I am not going." The calm coldness of her voice sent a shiver through him.

"But you wanted to go," he said. "Surely you do not still believe I do not wish you to go. Have I not explained that?"

She turned away.

"No, no, that is fine," he began. "We do not need to go if you do not wish to. We can stay here in the Grove. I do love it here."

"No." She turned to him. "I want you to go, to leave. Leave this house, this place. Go to your precious little Hammarsh Keep or wherever, I do not care. Go and never return."

He stood dumbstruck, her words cut him to the core. A part of him wanted to take her in his arms and smother her with kisses so she would once again feel the love he felt for her. But she already knew he loved her. Knew it and chose to ignore it. Chose to disregard his love. She turned away.

"With all you know of the link that binds us, the consequences of your request, is this what you truly want?" he asked. "Will this make you happy?"

"Yes," she replied, her voice still icy.

He bowed his head. "Then I will leave immediately," he said, his voice dead.

Graeden climbed the stairs to the bedroom that had once held such heated passion but now felt cold and empty. He grabbed the bag that he had begun to pack a few days earlier and haphazardly threw the rest of his belongings into it.

He entered the kitchen and found Regnaryn standing where he had left her.

"If you have no objection," he said flatly, "I would like to take enough supplies for Merlona and myself to keep us until we reach a village."

She waved her hand but did not look at him, did not speak. He took some food and stuffed it in his bag. Then, he turned and walked out.

Merlona raised her head as he entered the stable. Moments

later, the two followed the path that led out of Reissem Grove. Graeden did not look back. No reason to. There was no longer anything for him here – here or anywhere else.

# CHAPTER THIRTY-THREE

*:TREBEH!:* Phrynia gasped. *:Did you...:*
*:What was that?:*
*:I am not sure, but it is not good.:*
*:Oh, no!:* Trebeh cried. *:It cannot be. They would not. Surely they know better.:*
*:What?:* Phrynia asked and then realized Trebeh's meaning.
*:No. You are not thinking Regnaryn and Graeden...:*
Both women called to the two young people, but received no reply. They sensed Regnaryn but could not find Graeden anywhere in the Grove.
*:This is bad,:* Trebeh said.
Phrynia agreed.
*:I need to go to her, Phrynia, something is terribly wrong and if... No, I do not even want to think that.:*
Both women raced to Regnaryn's house. They arrived to find her alone in the garden.
"Did you not hear us calling?" Trebeh asked.
"Yes, I guess so," Regnaryn said without looking at them.
"Is something wrong?"

"No, I am fine. Why are you here?"

"We felt something, something disturbing."

"And you immediately thought of me?" Regnaryn asked, turning to face her visitors.

Trebeh and Phrynia were stunned by the look in the young girl's eyes.

"Where is Graeden?" Trebeh asked.

Regnaryn stood and walked away from the two women. "Gone."

"Gone? What do you mean gone?"

"It is not a difficult concept," Regnaryn said. "I sent him away."

The women were shocked by Regnaryn's revelation and, even more so, by her cold apathy.

"Surely you are joking, child," Phrynia said.

The glare Regnaryn shot the drageal made it clear she was not. Phrynia shook her head. "Why would you do such a thing?"

"I do not believe it is any of your business what I do."

Trebeh walked over to the girl. "I am your mother," Trebeh said calmly. "I am concerned with everything you do."

"You are not my mother! My mother is dead."

Regnaryn's rage surprised Trebeh. The young girl started to storm away, but the yekcal grabbed her arm.

"Let go of me!" She slapped the yekcal.

Trebeh released her hold on the girl. Regnaryn took a step back.

"Now get out of my house, both of you, and do not come back. You are not welcome here."

### 

"This is my fault."

"Why?" Phrynia asked.

Trebeh shook her head. "I saw the impending strife in their relationship from the very beginning. I should have warned them or watched them more closely. I should not have let them move away from the family."

Phrynia stopped and blocked the yekcal's path. "You are not to blame for this. This was her decision, not yours."

"But she is just a child," Trebeh stated.

"No, she is not."

Trebeh knew the drageal spoke the truth, but it did not alleviate any of the guilt the yekcal felt.

"What will happen to her? And poor Graeden, he is alone."

"We will look for him and bring him back," Phrynia said.

Trebeh nodded.

### 

For days the drageals took to the sky in search of Graeden, but they found no trace of him anywhere. They called to him and searched for his mind. They found and heard nothing. Finally, Phrynia summoned them back.

# CHAPTER THIRTY-FOUR

GRAEDEN WANDERED aimlessly, his thoughts always on Regnaryn. What had caused her to change? He still could not understand why she refused to listen or to believe anything he said.

During the first few days, or was it weeks, he heard distant voices. But his mind was so clouded with pain and sorrow, he could not respond.

Only Merlona kept him from rolling up into a ball to die. He tried to set her free, but she would have none of it. So, he tended to her even if he chose not to do the same for himself.

Soon enough, the weather changed from the warmth of summer to the chill of autumn. It was not until the first snow began to fall that Graeden realized they were only several days ride from the Keep. He then understood that Merlona had once again dictated their course, this time the one that carried them home.

### 

The snow fell heavily until it almost touched Graeden's heels as he rode, but Merlona refused to stop. The snow finally ceased, and through the trees, Graeden saw the outer walls of the Keep. For the first time in many months, he felt something other than emptiness and loss.

They emerged from the wood and crossed toward the Keep's entrance. Within an hour's ride of the gates, they were confronted by a party of riders. Graeden immediately recognized the leader of the group as his brother, Gantell. He dismounted and approached the men.

"Stand your ground, sir," Gantell barked, "and state your business."

Graeden laughed at his brother's authoritative demeanor.

Gantell bristled. "You think there is humor here, stranger?" Gantell raged at the hooded man.

Graeden smiled. "As a matter of fact, I do."

Gantell sensed there was something familiar about this dirty, road-worn stranger and his scraggly horse.

"I was not aware this was the way visitors to Hammarsh were greeted. And even more so, I am hurt that you would have forgotten me in the short time I have been away..." Graeden paused. "...brother."

Graeden pushed the hood from his head and watched with amusement as Gantell's expression changed from anger to acknowledgement and then joy.

"Graeden? Graeden!" Gantell shouted and leapt from his horse. He ran to his brother. "Is it really you?"

He wrapped his arms around the nodding Graeden and effortlessly lifted him off the ground. Several of the other men dismounted and circled the brothers.

"Where have you been? What have you been up to? Look at you! Thin. Very thin." Gantell stroked his chin and nodded. "Ah, but that may work in your favor, little brother."

"Work in my favor?"

"Think about it," Gantell answered, tapping the side of his head. "When Mother sees her little lost babe so thin and frail, she will forget how angry she has been at your vanishing and want to do nothing but fatten you up!"

Everyone laughed.

"Sir, should I ride ahead to inform the Lord and Lady of your brother's return?" asked a man Graeden did not recognize.

"No! Definitely not!" Gantell roared with laughter. "I think Mother and Father should see what winter's first storm has brought us. The looks on their faces will be priceless. What do you say, brother?"

"I am not sure that is a good idea, Gant."

"Ha!" Gantell said, ignoring Graeden's opinion.

Graeden shook his head and mounted Merlona.

"A warm fire and a decent meal will do you some good." Gantell climbed back into his saddle.

"Yes, I am sure it will." Graeden patted his mare's neck. "And Merlona will certainly appreciate the comfort of a stable and a decent grooming. Is that not so, girl?"

The horse nodded her agreement though Graeden doubted any of the others noticed.

"I cannot remember how long it has been since I have had a hot bath or slept in a real bed."

The men rode directly to the stables. Only when Graeden was satisfied Merlona, his savior, was properly settled in would he follow the impatient Gantell.

"I really think I should clean up a little before I see Mother and Father. You know how they feel about appearance, and mine is nowhere near acceptable," Graeden said.

Gantell laughed as he looked his younger brother over. "No, I want them to see you as I did. I want to see the expressions on their faces when they realize it is you."

"I still do not think this is a good idea."

###

The group approached the Great Hall. Gantell covered most of Graeden's face with his hood. The others positioned themselves to hide the intruder. The group stormed into the Hall, disrupting the conversation the Lord and Lady were having with Matteus.

"How dare you enter this Hall like a bunch of hooligans, unkempt and unwashed? This is not the local tavern, you know," Emmaus roared.

"My apologies, Father," Gantell said, bowing. "We found this stranger approaching the Keep, and he refuses to identify himself."

"And you bring him into my Hall?"

"He would only tell us that he had to see you on a matter of utmost importance," Gantell lied. "I felt it best to bring him to you, under guard, of course, in case he did indeed have important matters to discuss."

"Fine, bring him here and let us be done with this," Emmaus said.

The group approached and positioned themselves so the intruder could now be seen.

"Well," Emmaus said, "you wanted to see me?"

Graeden raised his head slightly. Prescia let out a shriek of delight as she ran to the stranger.

"Graeden!" she shouted and threw her arms around him. "It is you!"

He laughed at the disappointment on Gantell's face.

"Yes, Mother. I have returned."

Gantell shook his head. "But how did she know it was him?"

Matteus chuckled. "Will you never learn, Gant? His eyes are a dead giveaway, especially to Mother."

Prescia wept with joy as she hugged Graeden, then stroked his face to make sure he was real. When she was sure he was neither ghost nor dream, she released him and allowed Emmaus and Matteus to welcome him.

Prescia wagged her finger at Gantell. "You could not just enter and nicely announce that your brother had returned, could you? No, you once again had to play games and torment your mother."

Gantell bowed his head and meekly replied, "Sorry, Mother."

"Over and over he tries to fool her, even though she sees

through every one of his schemes," Matteus said to Graeden.

Gantell turned and dismissed his now snickering men.

Prescia, content that Gantell was duly contrite, turned her attention back to Graeden. "Take off that cloak and let me have a good look at you."

He did as told, and she sighed. "Oh, it is worse than I thought. Emmaus, look at him, he is so thin. If he were any thinner, he would be invisible. When was the last time you had a good meal?" She stroked his hair and looked disapprovingly at his scruffy beard and dirty clothes. "Or a hot bath?"

Emmaus laughed." If you want answers, love, you will need to give the boy a chance to speak."

She waved her hand at her husband to dismiss him. "And where in the name of all that is holy have you been for all this time? Just two notes in near on two years, both of which barely said anything more than you were alive. Do you have any idea how worried I was about you?" Her expression conveyed the depths of her sadness, disappointment and anger.

"Mother, I am sorry," he said, holding both of her hands in his and kissing them. "My actions were inexcusable."

Her face changed immediately to love. Matteus laughed quietly and said in a half whisper to his father, "How can he make her melt like that? If it were anyone else, she would have already skinned them alive."

Emmaus nodded. "He has always had that effect on her."

"Now to answer your questions," Graeden said. "I have eaten, in a manner of speaking, every day. But as for a good meal or a bath, I would say that would have to be before I left Rei...," he hesitated on the word, not ready to tell anyone, not even his mother about Reissem Grove or any of its residents. "Er, before I began my journey home."

Prescia and Emmaus noticed his slip of the tongue, but neither pressed him. For now. When he was comfortable, they felt certain he would tell them of his journey.

"Well, the first order of business will be to get rid of some of that road dirt," Emmaus said.

"And that horrid beard," Prescia added.

"Or at least clean it up," Emmaus said with a grin.

Graeden rubbed his chin and nodded.

"After that, we will need to fatten you up so your mother can stop going on about how thin you are. And as luck would have it, you have arrived just in time for the evening meal. Have you been away so long that you require an escort to your room and the dining hall," Emmaus continued, still grinning, "or do you think you can find your own way?"

"Unless you have altered the Keep, Father, I can find my way," Graeden answered, "but I would not object to company."

Gantell and Matteus both slapped their younger brother on the back, nearly knocking him over, and maneuvered him to the corridor that led to his room.

### 

"He has changed, Prescia." Emmaus put his arm around her shoulder and drew her close to him. "Matured."

She nodded. "But something is not right. I sense a deep sadness within him, as if he left something behind. Left it or lost it. Something very dear to him."

Emmaus wrapped his other arm around her and hugged her tightly. "And just how do you know this, my love?"

"I saw it in his eyes," she answered.

"Ah, yes, of course, his eyes."

"Scoff if you will," she said, "but Graeden's eyes have always been an open door to his soul. And did you hear the way he tripped over his words. For some reason, he does not want to tell us where he has been."

"Oh, could you not see a map in his eyes as well?" Emmaus winced as she rapped him the back of his head. He pulled her close and kissed her. "I believe you, love. But there is nothing we can do about it right now."

"Oh!" she said and pulled away. "I must tell Cook there will be an additional mouth to feed, and we must inform the rest of the family that Graeden has returned."

"I will inform the family. I do not want to be the one to tell Cook at this late hour," he said.

"Coward," she replied and laughed. "Normally I would not either, but it is Graeden. I think I could tell her midway through dinner, and she would whip him up his own seven course meal that would far surpass what she had spent hours preparing for the rest of us. Oh, and just wait until she gets a look at how thin he is. She will be feeding him every minute of the day to fatten him up."

They laughed at the image of Cook chasing Graeden with a shovel full of food.

# CHAPTER THIRTY-FIVE

THE RAGE THAT sustained Regnaryn in the days following
Graeden's departure soon cooled. As the gravity of her actions and
loss became clear, she felt consumed by a melancholy so
overwhelming, she neither ate nor slept. She paced, day and night,
through the empty house, refusing all offers of comfort or company.

Near autumn's end, Regnaryn suddenly appeared at Trebeh's
door.

"May I come in, Mama?" Regnaryn asked quietly and waited for
permission.

The yekcal was shocked by the girl's appearance – face drawn
and haggard, eyes sunken and dull. And so thin, Trebeh feared she
had not eaten in weeks. "Of course, dear, this is still your home."

Regnaryn followed Trebeh, looking around as if she had never
seen the place before.

Trebeh motioned her to sit. "Keep me company while I prepare
dinner."

The girl mechanically obeyed and murmured a muffled thank
you when Trebeh put a glass of tea before her.

"It has been quite some time since we have seen you, dear,"

Trebeh said. "I hope all is well."

Regnaryn ran her fingers along the sides of the glass.

"Mama." The pain in her voice tore through the air like a scream.

Trebeh sat down beside her. Regnaryn broke down and cried. Trebeh put her arm around her suffering child. Regnaryn felt so frail, Trebeh feared she would break.

Regnaryn buried her face in the yekcal's shoulder and sobbed. Trebeh held her.

Regnaryn slowly pulled away. "He is gone," she said.

"Yes, child, he has been gone for some time now. You sent him away."

Regnaryn nodded. "I was angry, because he was ashamed of me."

"Surely you were mistaken."

"He said I was wrong and tried to explain, but I did not believe him. I blocked him from my mind and would not answer him. Then I told him to leave." Regnaryn paused and looked into the distance. "But he should have known I did not really mean it. Mama," she continued, her voice cracking. "He was supposed to come back."

"And how was he supposed to know that?"

Regnaryn shrugged. "He just should have."

Trebeh felt anger rise within. She stood, walked away, and took a deep breath to calm herself.

"Why did you not call him back?" Trebeh asked, her voice quiet and controlled, but with an edge that surprised Regnaryn.

"I do not know."

"You have absolutely no idea what you put that boy through when you sent him away. Or do you?"

Regnaryn stared at Trebeh.

"You shut him out of your mind and your heart, but you could still feel him. You could feel his pain."

Regnaryn shook her head. "He is gone. I can no longer find him."

"Now you feel the same emptiness, the same agony, he has endured since the moment you shut him out."

"You do not understand..."

Trebeh shook her head. "No, it is you that did not understand, not until now."

Regnaryn stared open mouthed at her mother. Trebeh had not raised her voice, yet her tone and the anger in her eyes screamed the yekcal's rage. Regnaryn had never seen Trebeh like this.

"But," Regnaryn tried to interrupt.

"You put that boy through misery. I do not know exactly what you said or did to make him leave, but..."

"I just told him to go," Regnaryn said softly, tears streaming down her face once again.

Silence. Trebeh took a steadying breath to control the anger she felt at Regnaryn's selfish stupidity.

"You told him to go," she said in a near whisper. "With all you knew about the consequences of what would happen, you chose to send him away."

"But he was not supposed to really leave. I thought he would come to you. Or just come back a little while later."

"No!" Trebeh roared, then took another breath. "You saw into his mind, saw he was not coming back. Still, you chose not to call to him. Not to tell us where he was so we could go after him. Only now, now that he is beyond your reach, do you regret your actions, because now you are experiencing the same pain."

"This is not my fault!" Regnaryn shouted. "You are my mother. You should have told me! You should have stopped me! You are to blame! You should have done something to stop this from happening."

Last straw. Trebeh flew across the room and loomed over Regnaryn.

"We *did* tell you. *You* refused to listen." Trebeh's eyes flamed with rage, Her whispered words, spoken through gritted teeth, were controlled.

For the first time in her life, Regnaryn feared the yekcal. The look in Trebeh's eyes, her breath hot across the girl's face as she stood nose to nose, terrified her.

"There is only one person responsible for this situation. You!" Trebeh walked out of the room.

Regnaryn sat motionless for what seemed to be an eternity. She had never seen Trebeh in such a state. Not ever.

Regnaryn walked into the room. "Mama?"

Trebeh remained silent.

"I... I did not see what I had done. Honestly, Mama, I did not realize. I know everyone told me but I just did not understand. Maybe some part of me did not believe. I am so sorry."

"I am not the one who deserves your apology," Trebeh said without anger.

"This is the true realization of my nightmares. I am indeed the evil being that the voice called me."

"Not evil, child, just foolish."

"What can I do to put things right?"

Trebeh shook her head. "I am not sure."

"Mama," Regnaryn said in a small pained voice, "can I come back home? For good, I mean. I cannot stand being alone another moment."

Trebeh looked beyond the anguish on Regnaryn's face and deep into her mind. She was dismayed at the extent of the pain Regnaryn harbored.

"If that is what you want, child," Trebeh said.

"Thank you, Mama," Regnaryn replied.

### 

The front door opened. The air filled with the sounds of shouting children. They raced noisily through the house, but immediately quieted when they saw Regnaryn.

As soon as the surprise of her presence wore off, the twins raced in and pounced upon her.

"So, you just could not stand being away from me any longer, could you?" Neshya jibed, trying to mask his shock at her appearance. "As it should be." He kissed her on the cheek.

*:Mama,:* Neshya said, *:is she alright? She looks so... so...:*

*:She is fine, child. Nothing a good meal will not cure.:*

Neshya knew his mother was lying, but he said no more. He was just glad to see Regnaryn.

"Regnaryn is coming back home to stay," Trebeh announced.

The twins cheered and bounced on Regnaryn's lap, causing her to wince.

"Did I hear correctly?" the booming voice came from the doorway.

Regnaryn gently nudged the twins from her lap and rose slowly from her chair. Ayirak motioned for her to sit. She obeyed. He cast a concerned look at Trebeh as he quickly crossed the room and kissed the young girl's upraised cheek.

Trebeh motioned to Nelluc and Neshya. They gathered up the protesting twins and left the room.

"Well, child, " Ayirak said, "I am glad you have decided to come home."

# CHAPTER THIRTY-SIX

FALL BECAME winter and Regnaryn settled back into life with the family. She hid her pain, now coupled with guilt, from the family though she felt sure Trebeh understood the depth of her sorrow.

On an unseasonably mild winter's evening, the family was pleasantly surprised by the arrival of Javis and his family.

"It is good to see you, son," Ayirak said as the group entered, "Laiana. Children." The kitlings bounded for Ayirak, and he scooped them up in his arms.

Trebeh ushered the group to the couches by the fireplace. "We were about to have tea, would you like some?"

Laiana sat down and nodded.

"Just tea?" Javis asked. "Surely you have something more substantial to offer. Cakes? Bread? I am hungry."

Trebeh turned to Laiana. "He never changes, does he?"

Laiana shook her head. "No matter how much I feed him, he is always hungry. And his sons have inherited his appetite."

Regnaryn entered the room with a tray of tea and cakes, and she placed it on the table.

*:Mama,:* Javis started.

*:My goodness, Mama, she looks terrible,:* Laiana finished her mate's thought.

*:She is doing as well as can be expected,:* Trebeh responded, making it clear there would be no further discussion.

"So, to what do we owe the pleasure of your company, children?" Trebeh asked.

"Can we not just come to visit?" Javis asked with a wry smile.

Trebeh laughed. "Not in the middle of winter. You are more bear than yekcal when it comes to cold weather," she said. "If you had your way, you would hibernate from the first leaf changing color until midsummer."

"That does sound like the perfect winter to me." Javis laughed. "Yes, it is true. We did come here tonight for a reason." He stopped and took a sip of his tea while the others waited. After several moments of silence, he continued, "Laiana is going to have another child."

Everyone in the room expressed their delight, everyone but Regnaryn. Javis' announcement, made with such joy, released something within Regnaryn. Something ugly.

Her insides lurched as the bile rose in her throat. She ran from the room, barely reaching the bathroom before she became sick. But that was only the physical manifestation of whatever now possessed her. She hated her brother, Laiana and their unborn kitling. Hated them so intensely, she could barely breathe.

The family sat in stunned silence at her reaction. Even more unsettling was the loathing she exuded and the darkness that passed over the entire room. A collective shiver went down everyone's spine as they tried to understand what had just occurred.

"I will go to her," Trebeh said .

Trebeh reached the hall as Regnaryn closed the door. She heard the young girl crying as she vomited. She probed Regnaryn's mind, shocked at the intense anger and hatred there.

"Are you all right, child?" Trebeh asked quietly.

The door opened. Regnaryn looked nothing like the creature

who had left the room.

"Yes, Mama. I do not know what came over me. Please apologize to the others and tell Javis and Laiana how very happy I am for them." She turned and ran up the stairs.

### 

Regnaryn tried to mask the dark moods that now occupied more and more of her waking hours. Even sleep offered no relief. At every turn, she felt increasingly bitter and resentful of all around her. She cursed their happiness. She knew her escalating despair was her own doing, but that knowledge only made her mood bleaker.

One day Regnaryn abruptly announced, "I am going home."

"You are home, dear." Trebeh knew what Regnaryn meant.

Regnaryn shook her head. "No, I am going back to my house."

Trebeh nodded.

"I did not think it would come as a surprise. Perhaps it is even welcome. "

"Not unexpected, child, but certainly not welcome," Trebeh said honestly. "I do not like the idea of you being all alone."

Regnaryn smirked. "Oh, yes, because I am so very pleasant to be around. Mama, I see what I am doing to the family and to you, in particular. But... but, I just cannot seem to do... act... feel any other way. I have tried, Mama, please believe me. I have tried, but I cannot."

Trebeh put her arm around the young woman. She felt Regnaryn stiffen before she slipped away from the embrace.

"When will you leave?" Trebeh asked.

"Now. I just wanted to let you know, so you would not worry."

"I always worry, dear. Always."

The darkness of Regnaryn's gaze lightened for just a moment, then returned.

"And the others? Will you tell your father? Neshya and Nelluc? Ennales and the twins?" Trebeh asked.

"No," Regnaryn rasped.

She hated herself for the way she was acting, but she could not help it. The more she felt the loss of Graeden, the more she lashed out at all around her.

### 

Regnaryn again spent her days aimlessly wandering through the empty house. She rarely ate and gave no attention whatsoever to her appearance. Even in the dead of winter, she barely warmed the house.

Ayirak wanted to forcibly bring Regnaryn home. Trebeh gently reminded him that such an action would be futile. Though Regnaryn was not his natural child, she had inherited most, if not all, of his obstinacy.

# CHAPTER THIRTY-SEVEN

MUCH TO HIS brothers' chagrin, Graeden stopped to drink in the sight of every nook and cranny of the Keep. He behaved as if he had never seen the place before.

Gantell and Matteus buzzed around Graeden like bees at a hive. They bombarded him with questions.

"I will answer all of your questions when everyone is gathered together. Right now, all I want is a bath. Preferably hot, but any would do."

Matteus grinned. "I guess that can be arranged, and I suppose we can wait until dinner to hear all about your adventure."

If they noticed, neither brother acknowledged Graeden's look of dread at the prospect.

"Oh, just wait until the girls hear you are back," Gantell said. "What do you think, Matteus? Will he need the guard's protection to keep him safe from his many female admirers?"

"Perhaps. And we may need to keep him under lock and key to let him get any sleep," Matteus added.

Graeden opened the door to his room to find Harold, a servant who had been with the family since before Emmaus had been a boy.

Harold stepped forward and bowed.

"It is wonderful to have you home, Master Graeden."

"Thank you, Harold." Graeden answered. "How did you know I was back?"

Harold smiled. "Surely you have not been away so long that you have forgotten how quickly news spreads through this household."

"I guess I had."

"Well, young sir, I have drawn a hot bath and laid out clothes for you. Although," Harold said, looking Graeden up and down, "now that I see what is left of you, I fear they will be too large. No matter, if you can make due this night, we can have something better for you tomorrow."

"No need, Harold, I have clothes in my bag."

"I will see to them, young sir." He took the bag from Graeden and excused himself.

Graeden entered the bath chamber followed by his brothers. They rattled on about all that had happened during his absence. Graeden, half-listening, stripped off his dirty clothes. He had no sooner slid into the hot, soapy water when the door burst open and he was besieged by a wall of chatter coming from a passel of siblings.

In the next moment, he was splashed in the face.

Taaryn glared down at him. "You leave without telling me, and you return the same way," she accused. "I thought we shared everything?"

Matteus and Gantell burst into laughter. "Everything?"

Taaryn's outrage only fueled their mirth.

Graeden took her hand. "I am sorry, Taaryn. I should have told you."

She looked into his eyes. She saw and then felt the sorrow he concealed. "If you ever do anything like that again, you will have more to worry about than Mother's wrath. You will have mine!"

"Now that I have been duly scolded, let me get a look at everyone. You have all grown so much," he said, directing his comment more to the younger children who so wanted to be grown up. "Why, if I met most of you on the street, I would hardly recognize you."

"Nor we you," Taaryn added. "Even in the bath we can see you are nothing more than skin and bones."

Graeden nodded. "So I have been told." He turned his attention to the two babies being held by his sisters. "And I see there are additions to the family."

"Yes," Taaryn said "these little lovelies were born this past spring."

"So," Graeden said, "what have you all been doing in my absence."

Immediately, everyone began to talk. Graeden raised his hand for silence. "Whoa, whoa. One at a time, starting with the littles... the youngest."

Taaryn noted Graeden's odd reference.

The youngsters squealed with joy at the chance to speak first. Taaryn and Matteus watched Graeden's genuine interest in the children's words with confused surprise. Before his departure, Graeden had had little time and even less patience for his youngest siblings.

After all had spoken, Graeden raised his hand. "Alright now, this bath is getting very cold." He shivered. The children giggled. "Not to mention that Mother will have our hides if we are late to dinner, so I think it is time for all of you to get cleaned up and for me to get dressed."

A collective sigh of disappointment filled the room. "I will still be here tomorrow, I promise," Graeden assured them.

Taaryn and Gantell herded everyone out of the room.

Matteus, still in the doorway, turned to Graeden. "We will meet you in the dining hall. Just know that you will not be able to put everyone's questions off much longer. I wonder, are you avoiding answering questions to buy time to conjure up your tale of this past year?"

Graeden stepped out of the tub and wrapped himself in a towel.

"Would I do that?" Graeden answered. "You give me too much credit. You know I am not bright enough to be that devious."

Matteus laughed. "And you seem to have mistaken me for Gantell, because I do know you. I also know a great deal can happen in a year."

Graeden threw the wet cloth at Matteus, hitting him squarely in the face. "Yes, my aim has improved."

Matteus smiled and left.

Graeden dressed and tried to decide what he would say to the family's questions. He trimmed his beard and tied his hair back to please his Mother. He paused for a moment, trying to remember how long it had been since he had been this well-groomed. He smiled at his own vanity.

Then, he walked down the hallway to face his family.

# CHAPTER THIRTY-EIGHT

THE CLAMOR in the dining hall ceased with Graeden's arrival. Emmaus motioned Graeden to sit beside him, in the seat reserved for honored guests.

He crossed the room and apologized, first to his parents and then to the others, for his tardiness. He saw his mother's look of disapproval, more at his still unshaven face than his lateness. Almost immediately everyone began to fire questions at Graeden. Emmaus raised his hand, and the room quieted.

"If you give your brother the chance to fill his empty belly," Emmaus said, "he will be more inclined to answer your questions."

"Graeden, it is so good to have you with us again," Jereth said, heartily patting him on the back.

"It is good to be home. Where is Kyra?"

Jereth started nervously. "We... well, she..."

"What he is trying to say, son," Prescia broke in from across the table, "is that your sister is heavy with child and not having an easy time of it. She has been confined to her bed."

"Kyra confined to bed? Have you had to tie her down or knock her out?" Graeden asked.

Jereth grinned. "It has not quite come to that point, yet."

Prescia smiled. "Yes, Kyra has been, well, less than congenial to poor Jereth of late."

Graeden commiserated, "I can only imagine."

"She really does want to see you. If you could find the time to see her tonight, I would greatly appreciate it," Jereth said.

"I will go to her after dinner."

Jereth returned to his seat. Emmaus rang the bell to summon the servants. As always, it seemed the bell barely quieted before enormous platters of food were placed on the table, and goblets and tankards were filled with drink. And just as quickly, the servants disappeared, only reappearing to refill a glass or remove an empty plate.

Graeden shoveled the delicious food into his mouth.

"Slow down, boy," Emmaus said with a laugh, "This is not a race. Your food is not going anywhere."

"Yeah, all we need is for you to choke on your food on your first night back," Matteus said.

"Your concern moves me, big brother," Graeden mumbled through a mouthful of food.

"Do not flatter yourself. Our only concern is that you might choke before you have told us all about your grand adventures," Gantell added, making everyone at the table, except Prescia, laugh.

Graeden winced but did not reply, preferring to concentrate on the delicious fare.

At meal's end servants cleared the table then placed clean plates and silver in front of all seated. Graeden glanced at his father.

Emmaus leaned over and said, "I do believe Cook has something special for you."

The words had no sooner left Emmaus' mouth before Graeden heard a familiar voice.

"If ye drop that, I will be stewing yer bones for tomorrow night's supper!"

The doors swung open and four very large servants entered. They carried the biggest cake Graeden had ever seen. Cook scampered around them, shouting orders. The men placed the cake on the table along the wall to the delight of all.

Cook turned toward Graeden's seat only to find it empty. Suddenly, he grabbed her from behind, picked her up and swung her around. The old woman, already scarlet from the heat of her kitchen, reddened even more as she squealed like a schoolgirl.

Graeden set her down as she scolded him for being so brash. Family and servants alike roared with laughter.

"So how has my best girl been?" Graeden gave her a peck on the cheek. "Did you miss me, or have you found someone else to replace me in your heart?"

"Pshaw, ye always were a silver-tongued scamp," she said, failing to hold back both her laughter and tears. "Now let go of me so I can get a proper look at ye."

Graeden carefully set her down. But before he could get out of the way, she smacked the back of his head and tweaked his ear. He pretended to be hurt and whimpered, which reignited the laughter. Graeden took two steps back and danced in a circle so the old woman could get a good look at him.

She shook her head. "Old Harold said ye were a bag of bones, and from the looks of ye, he were not exaggerating." Turning to Prescia, she said, "I have my work cut out for me, m'lady, fattening this young 'un up."

"And it looks like you are trying to do it all at once," Graeden teased, "between the meal and now this magnificent cake. If you keep this up I will not fatten, I will explode. But really, Cook, this is unbelievable! How did you get it done so fast? Did you have spies to let you know I was coming?"

She smiled shyly and turned to leave the room. Graeden caught her by the arm and guided her to his chair. "Come sit here with me and enjoy your labors. Then you can tell me just how much you missed me."

She looked to Emmaus.

"I am in the seat of honor so if I wish you to stay, you must," Graeden reminded her.

The flustered Cook sat in the chair Graeden held for her.

"In fact," Graeden said, "I think we should have everyone in to share Cook's masterpiece. There is certainly enough for all."

The servants hesitated until Emmaus nodded.

"That is a fine idea, son. However, all cannot fit in this room, so let us retire to the Great Hall to enjoy Cook's fine cake and hear of Graeden's adventures."

A cheer went up all around as the servants milled around the room. Graeden knew it would take very little time for the rest of the household to appear.

"Let me serve everyone," Cook started.

"No, mum," said a servant Graeden recognized as Cook's daughter. "Master Graeden has made you a guest at the table and guests do not serve."

Cook reluctantly agreed as the younger woman motioned to the others. She approached Emmaus, curtsied, and spoke softly to him. Emmaus nodded in agreement.

"Good idea," Emmaus said. "Everyone come get a piece of cake and proceed to the Great Hall."

"Master Graeden," someone called from across the room, "you are to get the first piece."

Graeden made his way to the cake with Cook in tow. He took the plate with the first piece and handed it to her.

"You, as my guest, will have the first piece," he said with a slight bow and took another plate.

Graeden put his arm around Cook. "Now, dear lady, you have yet to tell me just how much you have missed me and how truly happy you are to have me back."

She reached up and tweaked his ear again, sending yet another howl of laughter through the room. Graeden winced playfully as he escorted the rotund woman out of the dining hall.

They reached the Great Hall, already prepared for the impending crowd. Trays of wine, beer and cider sat on the many tables that lined the walls of the large room. Floor pillows and chairs had been brought in to accommodate all.

As more family and staff bustled in and began to mingle, Graeden took his untouched piece of cake and slipped away. He took a deep breath and tried to push down the pain he felt welling up inside.

### 

Graeden climbed the stairs. He tapped lightly on the door at the opposite end of the hall from his room.

A little wisp of a girl opened it. She licked her lips at the sight of the cake on his plate. Graeden told her to go to the dining hall, assuring her he would tend to her mistress. She curtsied and scampered down the hall. Graeden quietly crossed the small antechamber into the bedroom.

"Well, they certainly were not lying when they said you were *heavy* with child," he said as he saw Kyra fidgeting in her bed.

"Graeden!" she squealed.

He crossed the room, put the plate on the nightstand and sat beside her. She threw her arms around him and hugged him so tightly, he could barely breathe. A kick from her belly nearly threw Graeden off the bed.

"Have you got a mule in there?" he asked.

"It certainly feels like one at times," she said, smiling broadly at him. "Now..."

"I know, I know," he interrupted.

"Stand up and let me take a look at you."

He stood and did his little twirling dance. "And yes, I have already been told, I am too thin."

She laughed and rubbed her stomach. "Ah, to be told such a thing must be nice. I remember when I was thin."

He picked up the plate.

"Here, I brought you some cake."

"You need it more than I do."

"All right, I will eat it," he said, picking up the fork.

"Oh, no, you will not." She playfully grabbed for it. "Eating is about the only thing I am allowed to do."

"That is why I brought it." He handed her the plate and watched her take a bite.

"Oh my, Cook has certainly outdone herself this time. But then again, you always were her favorite. So tell me, little brother, what have you been up to since you have been gone?" she asked as she put the last bite of cake in her mouth.

"Not much," he answered nonchalantly.

She nearly spit out her cake. "What do you mean, not much? You are gone for over a year then suddenly turn up unannounced, looking like this and all you can say is not much!" She pointed her fork at him and shook her head. "Even if that *is* the truth, you had better think of something more interesting because no one is going to believe you."

He grimaced, thinking of what he had actually done during the time he had been away. Not much might not be believable, but neither would a tale of drageals and yekcal.

"Graeden?" she said, bringing him back from his thoughts. "I see your time away has not cured you of your tendency to daydream."

"I guess not."

"So, you are not going to tell me. Fine, I will just force it out of Taaryn." She laughed at Graeden's expression. "Oh, come now, everyone knows you two tell each other everything. You always have. It is really annoying."

Graeden looked down at his lap. "Uh, yeah, I guess that is true."

Kyra became more serious. "Graeden, you know Mother was very distraught after you left. It was bad enough you were gone, but the way you left, like a thief in the night just sending her a note. After a while, with no word from you, people said you were dead or worse, but Mother would have none of that. Let me just, say it was very difficult to be around her for quite some time."

He looked away from his sister and nodded.

"Please, promise me if you plan on leaving again do not just steal away. Tell Mother."

"I promise," he said softly. "But Kyra, how are you doing? You look well, but Jereth and Mother said you were…"

She laughed. "Having difficulties. Yes, that is the polite way to say I have gotten so fat, I can barely move." Heartened by his thoughtfulness, so out of character from the Graeden of just a year or so ago, she reached for his hand. "Do not worry, brother. I am just frustrated. You know how I hate being stuck in one room, never mind in this bed. I am all right, really."

"Are you sure?" His concern caught her off guard.

She hugged him again. "Yes."

They chatted about everything and nothing until they were interrupted by a commotion in the hall and a knock on the door.

"Aha, I told you he was hiding up here," Gantell said as he, Matteus and Jereth entered the room.

"Right! The only reason you knew was because Kyra's servant told you he sent her down for cake." Matteus laughed.

"But I was right."

"Really, Graeden, you need to come downstairs. Everyone is waiting." Matteus said.

"Excuse me," Kyra said sternly. "I am in this room, too."

The two brothers shrugged. She tossed her bed pillows, hitting each of them squarely on the head.

Graeden kissed his sister on the cheek and joined his brothers, leaving Jereth alone with Kyra.

# CHAPTER THIRTY-NINE

REGNARYN RACED down the path that led away from Reissem Grove, the only home she had ever known. She wiped her tear-streaked cheeks and ran until her lungs burned and her legs gave out. Exhausted, she dropped to her knees. She could see nothing in the darkness. She cursed herself for leaving on a moonless night. She found a tree to lean against, pulled her cloak closely around her, and fell asleep.

### 

The light of day revealed to Regnaryn the true depth of her actions – first toward Graeden and now her departure from the protection of Reissem Grove, her family and her friends. For a fleeting moment, she considered returning. She doubted anyone had even noticed her absence.

She shook her head. No. Leaving had been the right choice. Returning now, maybe ever, would be both selfish and childish. Without Graeden, the darkness within her would only deepen until she might actually strike out at someone with more than words. She had treated everyone so badly of late, they would probably welcome her absence.

Regnaryn nibbled on a chunk of bread to quiet her growling stomach. Again reality struck at the realization that she had no idea where she was going or even where she was. She just needed to get away, far away from home and family. Somewhere she could be alone, somewhere she would not be forced to endure the joy and happiness of others.

Regnaryn looked around and saw the path she had taken the night before widened ahead, meaning it probably led to a village. That would not do.

She recalled tales of northern wild lands populated by beasts of indescribable ferocity and horror, but no people. At this moment she feared people more than beasts, so she headed north.

### 

Each day, Regnaryn walked until her legs would take her no further. Though she never saw other creatures, she felt watched. She shook the thought off as silly, but it did not go away.

The first few nights she cried herself to sleep. She ached for Trebeh's comforting touch and Neshya's annoying teasing and all the other things she had left behind. But with each tear, Regnaryn reminded herself there was no other way. She had brought this upon herself, and she intended to deal with the consequences alone.

At the end of another full day of walking, Regnaryn set up camp, built a small fire and sat mesmerized by its dancing flames. Somewhere in the distant reaches of her mind, she heard a friendly familiar laugh, but she dismissed the sound.

She ate a bit of cheese and bread, and then succumbed to fatigue. She crawled between her blankets and quickly fell asleep.

### 

Regnaryn wakened, choking and gasping for air. She immediately realized she was no longer in the clearing. She was in a cave with slimy green walls and an acrid stench that hung so heavy in the air, it made her retch. She heard muffled voices in the distance.

She tried to get up, but she could not. Panic swelled within her as she struggled to move.

Suddenly she heard the laugh from her dreams. She tried to call out but found she had no voice. The more she silently screamed, the louder the laughter became and the harder it was to breathe. Finally she gave up.

"That is better," the voice said. "Surrender to me, and I will make your end come quickly."

Regnaryn gathered all of her strength, unwilling to be silent. "I will never surrender to you."

He laughed again. "You are as stubborn as your father. As you wish, but know that your suffering will be far worse than his." Then the voice disappeared.

As the air grew thicker, Regnaryn feared she would suffocate. She briefly wondered if that might be a better fate than facing the monster of her dreams.

*:Wake up,:* a tender voice called. *:They are coming. You must flee.:*

Regnaryn bolted upright. She breathed in the clear, crisp air of her camp and sighed with relief.

*:Did you not hear me, girl? Leave. They are coming!:* the tender voice cried.

"Who is coming? Who are you?"

*:That is of little consequence. Go. Now!:*

The urgent tone made Regnaryn rise and gather her belongings. She kicked dirt on the near dead fire to ensure it was out.

*:Hurry.:*

"Where?"

*:Over the ridge to your left. I will be waiting.:*

Regnaryn raced to the top of the ridge, but saw no one. She continued down the other side, certain she would find the owner of the voice at the bottom. She did not.

A cold gust of wind made her shiver. Regnaryn looked up, saw storm clouds and hoped they would not bring snow.

*:Silly girl, you did not prepare very well for this journey. Follow the path, I am not far ahead.:*

"Who are you?"

The voice laughed. *:Find me and I will tell you.:*

For some reason, Regnaryn trusted the vaguely familiar voice and continued along the trail. Still, she found no one there.

Atop the next ridge she halted at the sight of a being unlike anything she had ever seen. It was as if someone had sewn bits of several animals together – a horse's head, moose's antlers and long grey hair that hung like thick ropes from its back to the ground. It gave a slight nod of its massive head, then turned and slowly lumbered away.

Regnaryn raced up the path, calling out. Neither it nor the voice responded. At the top of the second ridge the being was nowhere to be found. Regnaryn wondered if she had imagined it.

She continued down the slope and cautiously approached a small stand of trees, behind which were half-hidden openings to several caves. Still, no sign of the being.

Regnaryn cautiously surveyed each of the cave openings. None showed signs of recent entry — no tracks or disturbance to the snow on the low branches. Still, something compelled her to go forward. Sword in hand, she entered the left-most cave and walked slowly into its depths, allowing her eyes to adjust to the darkness.

*:Very good, child.:* the voice said.

Regnaryn bristled at being addressed so by a stranger, but said nothing. At the back of the cave, she saw the odd-looking being.

*:You chose well. Now, do put that sword away. If I were of a mind to harm you, I could have easily done so without you ever being aware of my presence.:*

Regnaryn knew the being spoke the truth. She sheathed her sword but did not approach.

*:Come.:*

Regnaryn stood her ground. "Who are you?"

*:Such a deep question,:* it answered with a chuckle. *:Each of us is*

*so many things, it is difficult to say with certainty who one truly is.:*
Regnaryn rolled her eyes. It laughed.

*:To some I am friend and confidant, to others mortal enemy. I am by birth, an emuranda and held the position of herd-queen. But that time has long since passed.:*
Regnaryn listened, her sense of familiarity returning. She could not quite place it, but the more she spoke, the more familiar she felt.

*:For those who call me by name, I am...:*
"Jucara!" Regnaryn shouted. "I knew I recognized your voice. You... you..." Regnaryn walked closer to Jucara and stared into the emuranda's eyes. "You were the one, the voice in my dreams when I was sick so long ago. You comforted me. Eased my pain. You helped me hold on when I wanted to let go, telling me of the bright future that lay ahead for me."

Jucara nodded.

"I thought you a dream, a product of my imagination."

Jucara smiled. *:I was a dream, or at least a part of your dream. Much like you were to Graeden at your first meeting.:*

Regnaryn flinched. "How do you know about that?"

Jucara did not answer.

"But surely, you know now that you were wrong about my life. I have no bright future, no greater destiny. You should have let me die."

Jucara laughed. *:I see you have gained quite a flair for the melodramatic. I am sure Trebeh has not enjoyed that.:*

"How do you know of Trebeh and of Graeden?"

*:I know many things past and future - about you and your recent actions, about the world - many things, indeed.:*

Regnaryn's face reddened. She turned and stormed out of the cave.

*:Do not stay outside too long, child. It is terribly cold,:* Jucara called as she nestled onto a pile of soft leaves and breathed an ever so rare sigh of relief.

Within mere moments, Regnaryn returned, shivering but

silent.

*:Wood is by the entrance, build a fire to warm yourself. There are rabbits in the corner, take one and give me the others.:*

Regnaryn nodded, brought the rabbits to Jucara, then built a fire and placed the rabbit over it. In no time at all, the aroma of the roasting meat filled the cave. Regnaryn's stomach growled ferociously, reminding her how long it had been since she had eaten anything more than berries and bread.

After she ate, Regnaryn stifled a yawn and tried to stay awake.

*:Sleep, child. You are safe.:*

Jucara had no sooner spoken than Regnaryn's eyes closed as she slid to the ground, curling up under her cloak.

*Safe for the moment,* Jucara thought.

# CHAPTER FORTY

*:GOOD MORNING, DEAR,:* Jucara said, dragging a deer carcass into the cave.

Regnaryn nodded and rubbed the sleep from her eyes.

*:This should feed us for a few days.:*

"No, I must be on my way."

*:Is there somewhere you need to be?:*

Regnaryn shook her head.

*:It is just as well. My old bones are telling me the weather is about to take a turn for the worse. I fear snow will be upon us before this day is over.:*

"Should it not be spring by now?" Regnaryn asked.

*:Have you forgotten where you are?:*

Regnaryn looked away. "Can you not alter the weather like Vilera and the others in the Grove?"

*:No.:*

"Not even a little?"

*:Not even a little. Can you?:*

"Of course not. Why would you think that? I have no such power."

*:Nor do I.:*

It took a moment, but Regnaryn understood, "Oh, I assumed since you can do so many other things, you could do that as well."

*:Did you sleep well?:* Jucara asked, changing the subject.

"Hmm." Regnaryn yawned and stretched. Jucara smiled at how yekcal-like the girl's movements were. "That was the best sleep I have had since..."

*:Graeden left,:* Jucara finished her thought.

Regnaryn nodded. "Yes. You seem to know everything about me, and I know nothing of you."

*:There is not much more to say than what I said last evening.:*

"Oh, yes, that is all there is to tell." Regnaryn laughed. "And what was it you had me running from yesterday?"

*:A herd of wild boar. I did not want to see you trampled.:*

Regnaryn was not sure the emuranda spoke the truth, but was not certain she wanted to know.

"There is something else I am curious about," Regnaryn said. "You say you are aged, but you look no older than Trebeh. How old are you?"

*:If a human lives seventy winters, I have lived well over seven human lifetimes.:*

Regnaryn looked astonished as she calculated the emuranda's age.

*:My stay in this world is coming to an end. It is nearly time for me to move on to the next. This winter will be my last.:*

"Now, who is being melodramatic?"

*:Neither drama nor despair come into play here. It is a fact, plain and simple,:* Jucara answered, *:beings are born, live and eventually die. It is the cycle of life.:*

Regnaryn did not respond.

*:But enough of this, I am hungry and if you do not cut some of this meat off for yourself, I might just eat it all,:* Jucara said, again changing the subject.

###

Late that afternoon, a light snow began to fall. It continued over the next eight days, leaving the two unable to venture very far. Luckily, the cave's entrance was protected by a rock overhang that allowed some light and fresh air into the cave.

The weather proved relentless, as if winter refused to give way to spring. Soon there was no game to be found, not even a single mouse or insect, and all that could be foraged nearby was buried by deep snow. The food stores they had gathered were gone. There was no more wood for a fire. Their future did not look promising as winter continued to rage.

At the start of yet another blizzard, Jucara approached Regnaryn. *:The time has come, child, we must face the inevitable. We cannot both survive another storm.:*

"What are you saying? Of course, we will survive. Winter is almost over."

Jucara shook her head, *:You know that is not true. I am old and have lived my life. But there is much left for you to do.:*

"What do you mean?"

*:You have a destiny, and death by cold and starvation is not it.:*

"I am so tired of hearing of destiny and prophecy. You and the others tell me of this, yet I see none of it. I possess no great power to do anything but hurt others – first Graeden and then my family. Perhaps my destiny is to die here, and relieve them of their pain."

*:Ah, the drama of youth,:* Jucara said with a smirk.

Regnaryn glared at her.

*:You do indeed possess a destiny and great power, whether you believe or not.:*

Regnaryn wanted to interrupt, but Jucara continued. *:And this winter marks the end of a life that was long and filled with sacrifice and reward. I am prepared to make one final sacrifice to receive the ultimate honor, but I need your help.:*

"What do you wish of me?" Regnaryn asked, unsure she wanted to know.

*:I wish you to kill me then use my body for food and my pelt for*

*warmth,:* Jucara said without emotion.

Regnaryn gasped. "What! You cannot be serious? I cannot do that!"

*:It is the natural way, the emuranda way.:*

"NO!" Regnaryn shouted. Tears streamed down her face. "I cannot. I will not. I do not care if it is the emuranda way. It is not my way."

*:There is no greater gift my people can give than to be able to help another live. Under other circumstances, I would just go off, lie down in a field and wait for death. But that would not help you.:*

Regnaryn's expression changed from disbelief to horror.

Jucara continued, *:You have barely begun your life.:*

Regnaryn shook her head, not wanting to hear any more.

*:It will serve no one if we both die here. Allow me to do this one last thing for you... for myself, my peace of mind.:*

Regnaryn sobbed hysterically.

*:All right, child. We will speak no more of this. I did not mean to upset you so. Come, sit by me.:*

### 

The temperature remained bitter and the snowdrifts impassible. The food supply was gone. One evening, Jucara suddenly stiffened, leapt to her feet and ran to the cave entrance.

*:Something is coming. Get your sword. Now!:*

Regnaryn ran to the cave entrance. Jucara appeared unsettled, frightening the young girl.

Regnaryn stepped into the entrance, sword in hand. Jucara immediately charged, impaling herself on the blade so quickly, Regnaryn could not react. She stared into the eyes of her friend dying at the end of her sword.

Regnaryn pulled the blade from Jucara's body, but it was too late. The emuranda slumped to the ground, blood flowing like a river. Regnaryn fell to her knees and cradled Jucara's head.

"Why!" Regnaryn wailed. "Why did you do that?"

*:Because you could not, my little one,:* Jucara said tenderly. *:Do*

*not mourn for me, I go to a better place where my Goddess will shower me with all her blessings and love. Now is not the time for tears. There is much to be done so that I may find my spirit's path.:*

Regnaryn muffled her sobs and nodded.

*:You must use this body to sustain yourself – the meat for sustenance, the pelt for warmth. Promise, child. If you do not and you, too, die, I will be damned to walk the paths of eternity alone, in darkness without Her light or guidance.:*

"But I know nothing of how to tend to meat or hides," Regnaryn cried. "It will all go to waste, your sacrifice will be in vain. You will be cursed, and it will be my fault."

*:None will go to waste,:* Jucara replied. *:I have enough energy to cast one final spell, my death spell. When my spirit leaves this body, the pelt will come off as if it had been prepared by the best tanner and the meat will stay fresh until eaten. Whatever you cannot use, you must scatter outside for others to find, thus allowing me to help them cheat death a bit longer.:*

Jucara's life-force rapidly slipped away. *:There is one more thing I ask of you.:*

"Anything," Regnaryn replied.

*:Take the amulet from my neck and wear it always. It will bring you focus and strength through the ordeals you have yet to face.:*

Regnaryn nodded and removed the chain of tiny blood-red stones that held the large red amulet, about the size of a newborn yekcal's hand, from around the emuranda's neck.

*:Thank you, my dearest child,:* Jucara said. *:There are many trials that await you; many decisions to make. Be strong and choose wisely. And know there will be another you will meet who will help you on your path. Trust her as you have me.:*

With that, Jucara closed her eyes and entered the spirit world.

Regnaryn cradled Jucara's lifeless head in her arms. She cried until neither voice nor tears remained.

Then, as if in a trance, she placed the chain around her neck and went about the business of carrying out Jucara's last wishes. She worked well into the night. And when she slept, her dreams were filled with nightmares of butchery – of Jucara and of everyone she had ever known or loved.

# CHAPTER FORTY-ONE

AFTER MORE THAN a week of Graeden avoiding her, Taaryn knew it was time to confront him.

She sat near his bed and waited for her twin to awaken. As midday approached, she walked to the bedside and shook him.

"Stop it, Regnaryn, it is too early to get up. Just come back to bed," he murmured.

Regnaryn? Taaryn shook him again. He opened his eyes.

"Get up." She grabbed the corner of the blanket and gave it a tug, Graeden, now fully awake, held it fast over his body.

"I would not do that if I were you, Taaryn." He motioned toward the nightclothes tossed over the other chair.

Taaryn blushed, retrieved his clothes, and threw them at him. "Get dressed. There is much we need to discuss."

"What is on your mind?" He finished buttoning his shirt and sat on the bed.

She walked up to him and demanded, "Who is Regnaryn?"

He looked at her in shock. He tried to recover his composure. "I do not know what you are talking about?"

"Liar! One does not usually invite someone he does not know

to just come back to bed."

"Where did you hear such words?" he sputtered.

"What are you hiding, brother? You know you can tell me anything."

He hung his head. "I know, Taar. I know."

"Then, please do. Whatever you are holding within is tearing you apart. Tell me and together we will fix it."

"There is nothing you or anyone else can do to help."

He smiled weakly. As always Taaryn saw through the false smile to the pain. She threw her arms around him and fiercely hugged him.

"I should not have come back," he whispered not really meaning her to hear. "I must leave."

"Of course you should be here. Now please, talk to me. Let me help."

He stared at the wall as if gathering his thoughts. Taaryn waited, knowing he would now tell her what weighed so heavily on his mind.

When he finally began, the floodgates opened. At times his words did not make sense, but she did not interrupt. He spoke of dreams and nightmares and other terrors, of feelings that time – days or weeks – had vanished from his memory. He was visibly distressed until he began to speak of the place called Reissem Grove.

He paused, not sure how much to tell Taaryn. He worried that even she would think him mad if he told all, but he held nothing back. He told her first of the yekcal. He expected disbelief, but saw none. He talked of the drageals and the others. And while she gasped in amazement at his descriptions of these beings, she believed him.

"But what of Regnaryn?" she asked.

His eyes showed both great love and sorrow at the mention of her name.

"I fear my words are inadequate to describe all that is Regnaryn. She is like you, sister. Inside, in her soul. I could never lie to her, either." He smiled, but his eyes still spoke of the most profound sadness.

He described their first meeting at the edge of the Grove and his uncontrollable desire for her. He spoke of the incident in the stable, of Ayirak's reaction and his own shame. His words faltered when he tried to convey the details of the soulbond, but he told Taaryn all he knew. He told her of the joy he felt when they were together, and his despair when Regnaryn sent him away.

"There were times I did not care whether I lived or died."

Taaryn knew she could do little to ease his pain.

"Do you still feel the same? Even now, now that you are home among friends and family?" Taaryn asked. "Do you still wish to die?"

He looked at her with both shock and acknowledgement. "You know my thoughts almost as well as I do. My response to anyone else would be all is fine. However, I will not insult you with such lies. I honestly do not know. At times I do feel fine, as if all will work out. But then..."

"There is a darkness that enshrouds every fiber of your being," Taaryn finished his thought. "The very sight of other people's happiness makes your blood boil. And when it passes, you are guilt-ridden and ashamed. The only thing that keeps you from ending your life is the fear that the darkness holds something far worse."

Graeden looked at her in awe, nodding his head slowly.

"Yes! How did you know?"

"When I look into your eyes, that is what I see. What I feel." She tried to swallow the lump forming in her throat. "I am terrified for you and with you."

"What can I do, sister?"

Now it was her turn to shake her head. "I have no answers. Those can only come, I fear, from you. From you and Regnaryn."

"When did you become so insightful?" he asked with just a hint of a smile.

"All twin sisters are," she answered, trying to lighten his mood "You have just recently gotten smart enough to see it."

He winced as if hurt, and she tousled his hair.

"Now, I do not know about you," she said, "but I am hungry. It is already well past the midday meal, but I am *sure* Cook will be willing to find something for you to eat and you can share your food with me."

Both laughed.

### 

Spring brought the usual hustle and bustle around the Keep. While everyone else rejoiced in the change of season, Graeden's mood darkened. Taaryn was the first, but not the only one, to notice how he withdrew deeper into himself with each day.

From the day of his return, Prescia watched the change in her son. She saw the forced smile he presented to others as he tried to engage in their joviality. It saddened her to watch him retreat to places she could not follow. Prescia wanted to confront him, to find out what troubled him so, but she knew in her heart he was not yet ready to tell her. Her only comfort was her certainty that he had confided in Taaryn.

But there were things Graeden had not told even Taaryn. He was silent about the unsettling dreams that came as his mood became increasingly oppressive. He could never recall the details of the dreams upon waking, just the intense feeling that something was desperately wrong.

### 

Graeden returned to his room one late spring morning and was thrown to the floor by an unseen force. He raised his head to see the very air around him pouring forth blood. Unable to move, he gagged on the blood-filled air and was overwhelmed by anguish and self-condemnation.

After what seemed an eternity, the room returned to normal. He gasped for breath and saw Taaryn in the doorway, looking terrified.

"What was that?" She ran to him.

"You saw it, too?" he asked, still trying to catch his breath.

"I saw nothing, but I was overwhelmed by a devastating sense of distress and self-loathing. You were writhing on the floor, pounding your fists and screaming Regnaryn's name. I tried to enter, but until this moment, it seemed as if the doorway was blocked by an invisible barrier."

She helped him to the chair and went to get a cloth to wipe his bloodied hands.

"What is going on, brother? Does this have something to do with you breaking that, that..."

"Soulbond," Graeden said.

"You left behind a soulbound mate?" Prescia cried from the doorway.

Taaryn and Graeden both jumped, neither one aware of their mother's approach.

"Why in all that is holy would you do such a thing? Were you not warned of the consequences?"

"You know of soulbonds, Mother?" Graeden asked in wonder.

"Intimately," was her reply.

"Intimately?" the twins asked in unison.

"Your father and I are soulbound," she answered as the twins stared at her, mouths agape. "We felt it the first time we met. Now I understand your behavior since your return, son. You must be going through agony. Once the bond is consummated, separation is virtually unbearable."

Graeden nodded. "So I am learning."

"Now tell me more of this Regnaryn. I take it she is your beloved."

Graeden nodded, and he shared with his mother all that he had already told Taaryn of his journey and of Regnaryn.

"Can you not contact her with your mind?" Prescia asked.

"No, my ability is not that strong. Even when we were on opposite ends of the Grove, I could just barely reach her," Graeden answered then realized what his mother had asked. "You know of mindspeech, as well?"

"Is that what it is called? Your father and I have always been able to talk to each other without saying a word."

Taaryn and Graeden glanced at each other in surprise,

"Well, that explains a lot," Taaryn said wryly. "I always wondered how you two always knew what the other had seen."

Prescia smiled coyly, then her expression became more serious. "Your father will need to know of this. I have called him."

At that moment, Emmaus entered. The expression on his face told the children he had heard all that had been said.

Emmaus asked about the incident, and Graeden described the experience.

"Is this the first time?" Emmaus asked.

Graeden nodded. Then his expression turned to one of horror. "Something terrible has happened to her, I know it."

"Possibly," Emmaus replied. "but I am certain she is alive. If she were not, you would be..." He thought a moment, trying to find the right words. "Well, let me just say you would not be this calm."

"But what was it?" Graeden asked. "I felt such horror."

Emmaus shook his head.

"I must go to her," Graeden said, rising from the chair and then falling back in exhaustion.

"You are in no shape to leave right now." Prescia stroked Graeden's head.

"And even if you were, all the roads are impassible due to the rains and the spring thaw." Emmaus added.

"But she needs me," Graeden said, almost overcome by emotion.

"As soon as it is safe, we will make arrangements for your departure, son," Emmaus said. "It will do neither of you any good if you get hurt or worse on your return journey."

Graeden reluctantly agreed.

"I think we should keep Graeden away from the others until he is ready to leave," Taaryn, who had been quiet since her father's arrival, suggested.

"Do you wish us to shut your brother up like a prisoner?" Emmaus snapped.

Taaryn quickly shook her head. "No, that is not it. The family would be fine. It is just that, it is so hard on him when he is around people, and now with all of this. I just thought..."

Graeden reached his hand out to Taaryn. "That is a good idea."

"But what will we tell the others?" Prescia asked in a tone that hinted she already knew but wanted her children to complete their plan.

Both twins thought a moment, then Graeden spoke, "I do not think it wise to divulge the details of my journey or of Reissem Grove. Perhaps if we just tell them of Regnaryn, it might serve to explain my behavior."

They all agreed.

"We really need to tell Gantell first," Taaryn said with a smile. "Since you have spurned the attentions of all the girls since your return, he is beginning to think that you have changed your preference in partners."

Amused at the thought, Graeden agreed that Gantell would be the first to be told of Regnaryn.

# CHAPTER FORTY-TWO

REGNARYN SOBBED as the memories of the previous day overwhelmed her. She glanced toward the only food available and tried to ignore its source as she filled her empty belly.

She picked up Jucara's amulet which lay between her breasts. At her touch, the stone seemed to form a shape within itself. Yet, when she blinked, it again appeared clear and solid. She let it slip out of her fingers, wrapped her arms around her legs and rocked gently. Shivering, she pulled Jucara's pelt tightly around her and peered out at the weather that held her captive in the lonely cave.

### 

At last, winter surrendered. The nights remained frigid, but the days warmed enough to melt the drifted snow. Regnaryn could at last bid her prison farewell. Before leaving, she complied with Jucara's request and scattered the remainder of the meat outside for others to find.

Several days of wandering in the spring warmth brought Regnaryn to a dense forest. She knew immediately something was not right. She sensed no other living creature, neither mouse nor bird. Suddenly, a group of lizard-like creatures attacked.

The creatures punched and kicked at Regnaryn as they wrestled her to the ground. In the struggle, Jucara's amulet slipped from under Regnaryn's cloak. Her attackers panicked at the sight of it. They immobilized Regnaryn, using a spear to nudge the amulet back inside her cloak, then covered her head with a heavy hood that plunged her into total darkness. They wrenched her arms behind her back, ignoring her whimpers of pain and fear, and tied them with pieces of wood and rope to keep her hands from touching, then placed a rope around her neck.

Prodded to her feet, the creatures pulled the rope to make her walk. Each time she stumbled, they would drag, kick and poke at her to continue. Her fear exacerbated her intense pain.

*:Who are you, and why are you treating me like this?:* she cried in voice and mind but was met with emptiness and silence.

After a short distance, Regnaryn's captors pushed her into a kneeling position. As she knelt there, she sensed something approaching. It smelled musty, like mildewed wool. Overcome with terror, she felt an icy darkness envelop her mind.

Suddenly the hood was snatched from her head, and she found herself looking directly into the unmoving black eyes of one of her captors. The odd-looking lizard had legs so short, they looked barely able to support the stubby tree trunk-like body. Its sickly gray-green skin, cracked like a dried-up stream bed, was the source of the odor she had detected.

The creature's forked tongue darted in and out of its mouth as it fondled the handle of a silver whip hanging from a sash around its middle. Unlike the other creatures, this being was not devoid of emotion. It seethed evil. She shuddered as she stared into its dark eyes. The creature smirked at her reaction.

*:So, you can feel my power, eh, puny one,:* it said, its deep voice oozing vileness.

Regnaryn did not answer.

*:Do not ignore me, or I will make you regret it!:* He slapped her,

his sharp claws cutting deeply into her face.

She nodded.

*:That is better. I was told you possessed power, but to acquire not only the herd-queen's amulet but her pelt. I am impressed.:* He paused. *:Yet, you were so easily captured, could the Master be wrong in his assessment of you?:*

*:I found the pendant on a dead animal, so I took it. As for the pelt, well, one needs warmth,:* she replied.

He hit her again, shattering her cheek bone and his sharp claws gouging through her flesh. Still, Regnaryn remained calm.

*:Do not lie to me, human,:* he shouted then licked the blood streaming down her cheek. *:I have always enjoyed the taste of humans.:* His voice sounded calm but menacing. *:Their blood so salty, their meat so sweet. If you continue your lies, I will enjoy feasting on you while you scream in agony.:*

*:I tell the truth,:* she answered, masking her fear.

*:Perhaps.:* he said, pondering the possibility.

He moved closer and fondled her hair. Her terror grew. Then he jerked open her cloak and tore at her tunic. Her body tensed as he stared at her bare chest.

*:Do not flatter yourself. You repulse me. If I were attracted to your grotesqueness, your frail body could not physically accommodate my needs. I would tear your insides apart.:* He looked at her with a demented glare. *:I will remember that as an option, if you refuse to cooperate!:*

She trembled as he reached for her. He saw her reaction and moved slowly, relishing the fear his approach created. Then he snatched Jucara's amulet from around her neck.

Immediately, the amulet transformed from solid stone to molten liquid. The creature screamed in pain as the lava-like substance seared his flesh. He dropped the amulet, and the stone returned to normal.

Regnaryn snickered, enraging the creature. In a frenzy, he slashed at her face and body.

Regnaryn felt his tongue near her mouth as he again lapped at her flowing blood. She clamped it in her teeth and bit down as hard as she could, severing one side of its fork and spitting it onto the ground.

*:Your blood and meat are not tasty at all,:* she said.

*:You will regret that action, human.:*

*:Kill me and be done with it. I cannot help you with that pendant.:*

He stared, as if trying to read her mind. He sighed when he did not find the answers he sought. *:Alas, I cannot. The Master wants you alive. But heed my words, you will beg a thousand times over for your death.:* He moved closer. *:And the pain and agony you will endure will be delicious to witness.:*

He stepped back, stared into her eyes and waved his hands wildly in front of her, mumbling incomprehensible sounds as he cast his spell. As his words filled her ears, a shroud of darkness covered her eyes. Suddenly another voice in a distant corner of her mind shouted for her to shield herself. Regnaryn obeyed and felt a complete sense of calm. She let out a sigh and closed her eyes. The creature smiled and walked away, thinking her reaction surrender.

The others descended upon her, tearing away her clothes and slashing her body with claw and blade. They removed the restraints that kept her hands apart and broke her arms. She cried out in pain as they dragged her bleeding, naked body to their leader's feet.

A rope, attached to a hook in the roof of the cave, was fastened to the bindings reattached between her wrists. They raised her off the ground, putting unbearable strain on her broken arms. Regnaryn nearly passed out from the pain.

*:Oh, no,:* the leader said as he fondled the long silver whip, *:you will not escape my wrath that easily. You will remain conscious through every lovely bit of what is yet to come.:*

*:Why are you doing this to me? I have already told you, I cannot help you in what you seek from that pendant? I have no power.:*

*:You and I both know that is not true. The Master has seen it. I do*

*not know how you foiled his plans before, but you will not do so this time. And that boy you saved from the Master's grasp will not come to save you as you did him.:*

*:I do not know what you are talking about. I saved no boy.:*

*:Again you feign ignorance, but I know better. The Master said it was you who did so, and then later fended off his attack.:*

*:I do not know what you are talking about,:* she said, her mind trying to digest the creature's words.

The creature cracked the whip overhead. Sparks and flames exploded everywhere as it sliced through the air.

Regnaryn screamed in agony as the whip tore into her bare back, cutting deeply. Even when it no longer touched her, its fiery pain remained. Each lash spun Regnaryn around, exposing every part of her body to the whip's fury. The burning increased, and she feared she would burst into flames.

Suddenly, she felt a calm in her mind, and she stepped outside of herself. She watched the torture, as if it were not happening to her. Her body still screamed in response to the ordeal, but her spirit remained unaffected.

Eventually, the whipping ceased and her tormentor departed, leaving her suspended from the hook, her body bleeding and broken, her pain indescribable. After a time, she passed into unconsciousness.

### 

A barrage of icy water wrested Regnaryn awake and re-ignited the fiery pain from the previous beating.

The rope that suspended her was released. She dropped to the ground. As her feet touched the dirt floor, the pressure on her injured arms lessened and she sighed with relief. Immediately a club hit the back of her knees, forcing her to drop to the floor. She fell onto her arms. Her broken arms, unable to support her weight, forced her forward onto her face. She screamed. The creatures grabbed the ropes still tied around her wrists, and dragged her along the ground.

They stopped and pulled her to her knees. She once again faced the leader. Draped over a large throne-like chair, several creatures she assumed to be females fondled and caressed his body.

*:Well, pet,:* he said, *:I found our first evening together quite enjoyable. Did you?:* He laughed. *:I am anxious for you to experience some of my other talents. But, my pleasure at your pain will come soon enough. Right now, you will tell me what you know of the herd-queen and the powers of her talisman.:*

*:I know nothing of any herd-queen,:* she replied.

The leader leapt to his feet, sending his companions sprawling. *:Do not toy with me,:* he screamed. *:You handled the talisman without consequence.:* He held his blistered hands in front of her eyes.

*:I found it. I was not aware it held any kind of power.:*

*:Last night was just a small sampling of the pain I can inflict upon you. Do you wish even more torment?:*

*:I am not in control of what you choose to do to me,:* she said, surprised at her response.

He punched her in the face, effectively closing her left eye but she stood fast and did not falter. He beat her until he grew weary of it and returned to his eager companions.

*:I do not know if you are truly as stupid as you seem or if you are playing me for a fool? For your sake, I hope you are just stupid,:* he said, aware of his companions' increasingly erotic behavior. *:I grow bored with you, human, and I have better things to do,:* he eyed his companions. *:We will continue this later. I suggest you search your mind for the correct answers to my questions.:*

He waved his hand and she was once again dragged back to the other chamber. This time, they left her lying on the floor. To ensure she would stay put, they crushed her ankles.

### 

Regnaryn had no idea how long her ordeal with these monsters went on. She no longer knew day or night, only torture and pain. It was hard to believe that each successive torture session could be more horrific and agonizing than the previous one, but they were. She refused to beg him to kill her. She refused to give him that pleasure. She knew it would do her no good, because the Master he spoke of and feared wanted her alive.

In the quiet times, when the creatures left her alone, her mind pleaded with the powers that be to help her escape or die. The only answer she received — she would survive.

# CHAPTER FORTY-THREE

REGNARYN AWOKE to the sensation that another presence occupied the cave. She mindcalled to it and encountered shieldings of a strength beyond anything she had imagined. She painfully turned her head and saw a body covered in long white hair being dragged to the middle of the room. It was bound as she had been - hands trussed behind its back and head covered.

Almost immediately, the leader appeared. He removed the hood, but the body remained still. One of the others threw a bucket of water on it. The newcomer shook its head, tried to move but found it could not.

*:Well, Varlama, I finally have you. You are not as formidable an opponent without the herd-queen nearby, are you?:* he said. *:She is dead, you know.:*

Varlama answered to him alone. *:How do you know that? Certainly your meager powers did not defeat her.:*

*:As much as I would have enjoyed that, I did not have the pleasure,:* he answered, *:nor did I even see the body. Pity. That would have been a sight to be relished.:* He pointed to Regnaryn. *:She killed her.:*

*:And you believe her?:* Varlama asked flatly, now speaking to both. *:It is not like you to be so trusting, Kachurlak.:*

*:She possessed both Jucara's amulet and pelt,:* he replied with a sadistic laugh.

*:If she were a powerful enough magicker to kill Jucara, there is no way the gawara would have been able to capture her, dead or alive,:* Varlama said contemptuously.

*:We caught you. And, I am told, it was almost as easy as capturing her.:* He kicked Regnaryn in the belly, making her whimper in pain.

*:I never claimed to have any great power. Unlike you, I have never tried to deceive anyone, especially myself, into believing otherwise,:* she replied bluntly. *:If she merely came upon the carcass, she knows nothing of the powers she has in her possession nor how to use them. So, Kachurlak, although you now have the amulet within your reach, you still cannot control it. And, by the looks of your hands, I see you have already encountered some of the amulet's power. Even in death, Jucara has cheated you of your most sought after possession — her magic.:*

*:Your powers may not be as great as the herd-queen's,:* he sighed, *:but when I kill you, I will acquire them and your knowledge as you die. Do not believe for an instant that your death will come easily. Although I realize you will not allow me to feed on your pain, knowing you are experiencing it will bring me great pleasure.:*

Kachurlak barked commands. His minions suspended Varlama from the ceiling hook as they had Regnaryn. A large black enameled box was brought to him. He opened the cover and held it so both captives could see the sickly green aura emanating from it and the variety of blades, one more sinister looking than the next, contained within.

*:Oh, I am going to enjoy this immensely, Varlama,:* he remarked as he stroked one of the long narrow bladed knives as if it were a lover. *:I am sure you know what these are. With them, I can remove every bit of your skin, disembowel you and carve the meat from your bones while you still live.:*

He turned to Regnaryn. *:Watch closely, pet. This may be the end* *that also awaits you.:*

He slowly approached Varlama, relishing the fear emanating from Regnaryn. He placed the point of the knife just under Varlama's chin. She did not react.

Regnaryn felt a strange force welling up inside – a wrath, hot and red, reminiscent of Jucara's amulet in Kachurlak's hands.

Kachurlak and Varlama sensed the change in the girl. Varlama smiled, but Kachurlak showed an expression of terror that Regnaryn had never seen on the gawara's face. Before he could react, Regnaryn's fury erupted like a volcano, filling the cave and all of its tunnels with molten lava. Regnaryn took no pleasure in the destruction and death she caused.

*:I am sorry I could not save you, but at least our deaths will be quick and painless,:* she told Varlama.

Regnaryn thought of Graeden, how much she loved him and the regret she bore for hurting him. Then, she fell into unconsciousness, welcoming the end of her torment.

# CHAPTER FORTY-FOUR

A SENSE OF HORROR tore Taaryn from her slumber as she sat slumped in the chair beside Graeden's bed. Her breathing became hampered by a stifling heat. When she opened her eyes, she saw red everywhere, as if she were immersed in lava.

Graeden writhed on the floor. She tried to go to him, but became immobilized by a pain far worse than she had ever thought existed. Helpless, she could only imagine the magnitude of Graeden's experience.

Finally, the room returned to normal. The pain slowly subsided, but neither twin could move. Emmaus and Prescia rushed in and gently cradled the twins in their arms.

"We awoke to your screams in our minds. What happened?" Emmaus asked.

"I do not know. I was sleeping, but I awakened to a sense of terror and pain," Taaryn said. "It was as if we were in a river of molten rock. It was horrific."

"It is Regnaryn," Graeden whispered, struggling to speak. "Something has happened to her, something worse than the last time. I must go to her. Now!"

"Yes, you must go to her," Emmaus said. "But you are in no condition to leave tonight." He put his hand on his son's shoulder. "Rest now. Tomorrow we will prepare for your departure."

Emmaus carried him to the bed.

"Sleep, son, I fear the journey ahead will be long and perilous. You will need all of your strength."

Graeden closed his eyes.

Emmaus turned to Taaryn, still on the floor beside Prescia.

"Now, young lady, it is time for you to return to your bed and rest as well."

Taaryn shook her head, nearly overcome by pain. "No, I need to stay with Graeden."

Ignoring her protest, Emmaus picked her up and carried her out of the room. He called back to Prescia, "I will send Matteus to stay with Graeden."

Taaryn had just been settled in her bed as Prescia entered.

"I need to be with Graeden."

"Matteus is with him. He will be alright," Prescia said.

"You are not really going to let him go, are you?"

Emmaus looked at her. "We have no choice. He must."

Taaryn pounded her fist on the bed. "Must? What if he has another of these episodes? I will go with him."

"You are in no shape for that kind of journey," Prescia began.

"Then neither is Graeden," Taaryn interrupted. "He suffered far more than I did."

"That may be, but I do not believe we could keep him here, save locking him in a dungeon," Emmaus replied.

"And even then he would claw his way through the walls," Prescia added.

"We will send Matteus with him," Emmaus said.

"But I must go, I need to help him," Taaryn insisted. "He is a part of me."

Prescia stroked her head. "Yes, dear, but this is not your journey. Now rest."

Taaryn glared, but did not protest further.

###

"Are you serious about sending Matteus?" Prescia asked, settling into the chair across from him.

Emmaus nodded. "Graeden cannot travel alone, and Matteus is the one who can best handle any situation he will encounter both on the road and in that place." He took her hand. "It will be fine, I promise."

Before she could reply, a knock sounded at the chamber door. An elderly male servant entered to announce a visitor.

"At this hour? Who would be so discourteous?" Emmaus asked.

"He would not give his name, my lord, only that he brings news of someone called Regnaryn. He asked for young master Graeden," the servant replied. "When I told him the young master was not receiving visitors, he asked for you, sir."

Emmaus and Prescia looked at each other. No one in the Keep, save the immediate family, knew the name Regnaryn.

"Bring him here," Emmaus said.

"Sir, if you ask me, he looks suspicious," the servant said. "I would be careful around him, my lord. I do not trust him. He does not look you in the eye. A man cannot be trusted if he cannot look you in the eye."

"I will keep that in mind."

Within a few moments the stranger was escorted into the sitting room. He bowed deeply to the Lord and Lady of the Keep, but he said nothing until the servant departed.

"I am sorry to arrive at such an unholy hour, my Lord. My Lady," he said, bowing his head to them. "I am here to see Graeden."

"He is not receiving visitors at this hour. What business do you have with him? You mentioned Regnaryn."

"Ah, so he has told you of her. That is good," the stranger said. "How is he?"

"He has seen better times," Prescia replied but offered no further explanation. Emmaus was surprised she had said that much to this stranger.

The stranger bowed again. "My apologies, Lady Prescia, I am Ellyss. I met your son on his trip to Reissem Grove."

"And you are here for what reason?" Emmaus asked with more than a little suspicion in his voice. "He made no mention of you."

Ellyss turned to Emmaus. "It is good you are cautious, Lord Emmaus. There are forces at work here that even I am not fully aware of."

"That is not an answer."

"I have come to escort Graeden back to Reissem Grove. His presence will be required there in the very near future."

"Do you claim to see the future?" Prescia asked.

"Not I, good Lady, but I know others who can indeed do so. Graeden needs to return. He and Regnaryn must be together. You know the consequences of breaking a soulbond, and I know you have experienced some disturbing events since Graeden has been home."

Prescia and Emmaus knew the stranger, this so-called friend of Graeden's, was not asking for confirmation. He already knew.

"Tell me, sir," Prescia began.

"Please, my Lady, just call me Ellyss. I am far from sir to anyone."

Prescia nodded. "Ellyss, since you seem to know what has been happening within the Keep's walls, can you tell us what is causing these horrors that befall my son?"

Ellyss stared off into the distance. "I am sorry, I know no details, save that they involve Regnaryn."

"Yes, yes, we all know that," Emmaus interrupted. "You have still not convinced me that I should allow you to see my son, never mind taking him off into the wilderness."

Ellyss smiled faintly. "I understand, but I assure you I am not his foe."

He took their hands and closed his eyes, allowing them to see just a glimpse of their son's past and future. When Ellyss released them, Prescia and Emmaus looked at him and then at each other.

"What is this evil sorcery you wield?" Emmaus asked.

"It is neither evil nor sorcery," Prescia said in a whisper before Ellyss could reply. "It is truth."

Ellyss nodded. Emmaus was not convinced, but had learned long ago not to doubt Prescia.

"What is it you need?" she asked.

"Nothing more than to be allowed to accompany Graeden on his journey."

"He is in no condition to travel at this time. There was an incident earlier this evening," Emmaus said.

"Yes, I felt a disturbance. Was anyone else hurt?"

Prescia nodded. "His sister. She was in his room at the time."

"She must be quite close to him to share his experience," Ellyss said.

"They are twins."

"Ah, that would explain it. I am sure she will recover quickly. They are cut from the same sturdy cloth," Ellyss said, taking Prescia's hand in his. "May I see Graeden now?"

"He is asleep," Emmaus said, "and needs to rest this night. His brother is with him."

Ellyss nodded. "It is good someone is with him. I would not like to think of him sneaking out alone tonight."

Prescia nodded. "I will have someone escort you to the guest room and bring you some food. In the morning, you can see Graeden and prepare for your journey."

"That is kind of you, dear Lady. I will enjoy a good night's rest out of the elements."

# CHAPTER FORTY-FIVE

A SURPRISED REGNARYN found herself cradled in Varlama's arms. She felt none of the pain that had wracked her body since being taken captive by the gawara.

She looked into the soft violet eyes. *:I am sorry you had to die, but I could not allow him to torture you.:* A terrifying thought entered her mind. *:Why am I not alone? Oh no, please tell me I did not condemn you, too!:*

Varlama laughed and, in Reissem, said, "Do not fear, child, we are neither dead nor condemned, at least not yet. Look around, we have not left the gawara's cave."

Regnaryn lifted her head. They were indeed still in the cave, but it looked and felt different. Less ominous, less dark. She saw no sign of the molten substance she had created. Only black soot, everywhere. There was no sign of the gawara. All their devices of torture and pleasure were gone, the sickly green walls now whitewashed clean.

"But how? How did we survive? And how did I do this?" Regnaryn asked as she tried to sit up.

"Do not move, Regnaryn. Just lie there and relax. We will try to explain."

"How do you know my name? And who is we?" Regnaryn asked, trying to hold back her growing fear. "I cannot help you with Jucara's amulet any more than I could help him."

:*Do not fear, child. Varlama will not harm you.*:

Regnaryn was surprised to hear Jucara's voice.

:*She already knows the amulet's magic and is a force to be reckoned with in her own right. She is the one I told you to expect, the one who will help you understand your powers,*: she continued then turned her attention from Regnaryn. :*Where is Aloysius, Varlama? I thought he would be here.*:

"He is on his way. We thought it best he stay hidden until we saw what our young friend here would do."

"I do not understand. What do you mean?"

A white ball of light approached Regnaryn. She felt no fear, only comfort and love. It stopped and shaped itself into a semi-transparent form of Jucara.

Regnaryn's mind raced and words seemed to spill out of her. "Who is Aloysius? And where are the gawara? Why did you not help me? What..."

Jucara laughed, :*You are always so full of questions, dear one. Varlama will answer them in time. Right now, the healing process needs to begin. There is much for you to do and learn. Learn it you must, and quickly. If you do not, your newly awakened powers will destroy you and all around – be they friend or foe.*:

Jucara changed back to the ball of light and surrounded Regnaryn, inside and out. Regnaryn felt an overwhelming calmness. Varlama stroked Regnaryn's hair as she began to answer her questions.

"You know of your mother's prophecy, correct?" Varlama asked.

Regnaryn nodded.

"Jucara saw the same. She has watched over you since before you were in your mother's belly."

Regnaryn was stunned by this news. "How?"

Varlama smiled. "Those with great power have the ability to see across great distances and planes. In time, you too may develop such powers."

Regnaryn was too weak to protest, but Varlama sensed what she felt.

"Child, I realize you do not want to accept what you have been told, but surely after what transpired here today, you cannot deny it is true."

Regnaryn looked around and whispered, "But I do not want this."

"It does not always have to be destructive."

"Can you truthfully say I will never cause this kind of horror again?"

"We all have the potential for good and evil, and only time and circumstance reveal the path we will follow."

"I have been told I was evil, that I caused the illness that killed the humans in the Grove. Mama said it was not true." Regnaryn paused and looked beyond Varlama. "But now I am not so sure. Look what I have done."

"Yes, what you did here today was horrible," Varlama said.

"So it is true. The voice in the dreams was right. I am evil."

"No. The power you wield is not evil, just a bit wild and uncontrolled."

Regnaryn stared at Varlama.

"Tell me, what motivated you to do this? Did you release your power to inflict pain upon your tormenters? Did you revel in what you were about to do? Do you now enjoy the aftermath of the destruction?"

Regnaryn slowly shook her head. "No."

"Then why did you do it?"

Regnaryn looked up into Varlama's face and began to weep. "I am not sure. I only knew I could not bear to see you hurt as I had been."

"And you apologized to me for what you were about to do, did you not?"

Regnaryn nodded.

"But if you are as powerful as Jucara said, how could you have fallen captive?"

Varlama smiled. "Like so many who think themselves more important or powerful than those around them, Kachurlak was blind to all but what he wanted to see. If that were not so, he would have been far more suspicious of so many facets of what went on here."

"I do not understand."

"We knew Kachurlak would take you prisoner. I needed to be close to you after he did."

"You knew what he was going to do and you did not stop him!" Regnaryn railed. "Why? How could you allow him to hurt me so?"

Varlama bowed her head. "Alas, we could neither stop him nor ease your torment."

Regnaryn shook her head in disbelief.

"Jucara knew your magic would awaken under the stress of a violent ordeal. We hoped for the best, but had the worst occurred, if your powers had manifested otherwise or if Kachurlak was about to wrench them from you, I was to destroy you."

Regnaryn bolted upright. "What?" The sudden movement made her cry out in pain and she fell back into Varlama's arms. "You were going to kill me?"

Varlama nodded. "If the need arose, I would have done so without hesitation."

Regnaryn stared in disbelief.

Varlama continued. "I am very happy it did not come to that. Your magic is already much stronger than expected. I fear it would have taken all three of us to defeat you."

"And Varlama and I would now be in the spirit world with Jucara," a new voice chimed in, startling Regnaryn.

"I am sorry, my dear Regnaryn. I did not mean to surprise you," the voice apologized in the familiar coos of a chetoga. "I failed to realize that, in your weakened state, you might not sense my approach. I am Aloysius. Varlama and I often travel together." He paused when he saw the annoyed look in his friend's eyes. "Please, Varlama, continue. I only entered unannounced, because it is beginning to rain and you know how I hate my fur to get wet."

"Ever the vain one, eh, Aloysius," Varlama said.

"Yes, but is it not comforting to know some things remain constant?" He smirked and curled up beside them. "Please tell me exactly how this sweet young thing brought these vile, evil creatures to such an appropriate end." Aloysius spat at the thought of them.

"As I was saying, before my lout of a friend interrupted, had your intent been evil it would have taken all three of us to defeat you and we would have likely perished in the process."

"All I remember is a rage within me like a molten liquid, yet I do not know what happened next. Where are they?" Regnaryn asked.

Aloysius smiled and pointed to the ground. "That is what is left of them. Lovely black soot."

Regnaryn was disturbed as his meaning became clear – every gawara had been incinerated until only ash remained.

"Yes, the destruction of the gawara was extremely violent," Varlama said. "But, even after all they had done to you, all the pain they caused, their deaths were merciful. Even Kachurlak, who took such sadistic pleasure in the gruesome agony he inflicted, died quickly and painlessly. I would have dealt him a much worse punishment than you did."

"But..." Regnaryn interrupted.

"Let me finish," Varlama continued. "You did not use your power to avenge yourself. You invoked it to ease the pain of another, one you thought helpless. And, as you believed both you and I would die also in your fury, your last thoughts were of love. Those are not the actions of an evil person. I know you still have many questions, child, but right now you need to rest."

261

# CHAPTER FORTY-SIX

PRESCIA AND EMMAUS escorted the stranger into Graeden's chamber.

At the sight of the man, Graeden exclaimed, "Ellyss!"

The man nodded and shook Graeden's hand. Prescia and Emmaus, curious about this stranger, quickly realized no explanations would be forthcoming, so the pair left them alone.

"You remember me." Ellyss' smile hid the awe and concern he felt over the strength Graeden possessed to break the spell that had been cast upon him. "I had hoped to spare you those memories."

"I did not remember at first. Meeting Regnaryn…" His voice saddened at the mention of her name. "… opened many, but not all, memories to me. But seeing you has filled in the rest."

Ellyss smiled. "I have heard she is a very special young woman."

"Yes, and she is the one who helped me in that horrible place."

Ellyss could not hide his shock.

Graeden smiled. "So, you do not know all."

Ellyss did not respond.

Graeden motioned him to sit. "What brings you here? Now? Surely I am not in the same danger I was in at the inn?" Graeden asked, anxious for his family.

Ellyss shook his head. "None that I am aware of. I was just passing this way, sensed you were here, and thought I might stop in to visit."

"I do not believe you do anything by chance, that is not your way. No, there is more to your being here," he said with just the slightest edge to his voice. "Let us forego any attempt at deception, shall we? You know far too much about what has gone on since our last meeting." A thought crossed his mind. "What do you know of Regnaryn? I fear for her, yet I am not sure why."

"I know no more than you do."

Graeden jumped up, then winced at the lingering pain from the previous evening. He crossed the room and bent over Ellyss' chair until he was nose to nose with his visitor.

"NO! You know things before they happen," he snapped. "You knew where to find me, and yet you say you know nothing of Regnaryn."

Ellyss did not react.

Finally, Graeden staggered to the other chair. "How can that be?" he asked in a near whisper. He sat a few moments in silence "If you know nothing of her, why are you here?"

"I did not say I knew nothing, I said I know no more than you. We both sense something has befallen her, yet it is not within my power to see more than that."

"Then why have you come?"

"To accompany you to Reissem Grove, of course."

"How do you know of that place and that I plan to go?"

"That is a silly question. You sense Regnaryn is in trouble, and you are not by her side. What else would you do but go to her?" Ellyss replied.

Graeden looked embarrassed.

"You want to leave as soon as possible, right?."

"I had planned on leaving before sunrise tomorrow."

"And you were going to sneak away so no one would try to stop you."

Graeden nodded.

"Such subterfuge is no longer necessary, I believe your parents will feel better knowing you will have company on the road. And if you are up to it, we can leave this day."

### 

Later that morning, Prescia and Emmaus reluctantly saw the two men off.

"How can we be sure this Ellyss is friend?" Emmaus asked after the pair faded from sight.

"How can one be sure of anyone? There is something about him that assures me he will not harm our son. If Graeden accepts him as friend, then I do as well."

"I hope you are right," Emmaus said as they turned and walked into the Keep. "But why do you look so sad, my love?"

She shook her head. "Much danger awaits Graeden. I fear he may never return to us."

Emmaus was shocked at her revelation, but she would say no more.

### 

Taaryn awoke and raced to Graeden's room. His things were gone. She hurried to find her parents.

"Mother, Graeden, he is..." she cried as she burst into the dining hall.

Prescia nodded. "Yes, he left this morning."

"You let him leave alone?"

Prescia smiled. "I did not say he was alone."

Taaryn looked around. "The family is here. Who is with him?"

"A friend," Prescia replied. "Calm yourself, child. Graeden is in good hands. His friend arrived last evening while you slept. They left this morning."

"A friend? From out of nowhere someone arrives claiming to be a friend, and you just let Graeden go off with him?" Taaryn shouted.

"I do not appreciate your tone, young lady, nor do I feel the need to explain my actions."

The sharpness of her mother's voice took Taaryn by surprise. "What do you know of him?"

"I know Graeden greeted him as friend. That is sufficient for me, as it should be for you."

Taaryn reluctantly nodded. "But he left without saying goodbye to me... again."

# CHAPTER FORTY-SEVEN

GRAEDEN AND ELLYSS traveled fast. They set out before sunrise and rode well into the dark of night. They slept and ate very little, but always made sure their mounts were well-tended. At almost every village, they traded for new horses.

It was nearly midsummer when the pair arrived in what they knew to be the last village before Reissem Grove. They purchased two additional horses and alternated riding the two mounts from day to day to maintain their desired pace.

Within a day's ride of Reissem Grove, Graeden reached out to Regnaryn's mind. He could not sense her presence. Not surprising, since his mind talents remained weak. He hoped she would hear him and was disappointed to receive no response.

### 

Graeden and Ellyss slowed the horses as they approached the border of Reissem Grove. At the edge of the forest, Neshya met them. Graeden dismounted and walked toward his friend and brother, extending his hand in greeting.

"Why have you returned?" Neshya growled as he pushed aside

Graeden's hand. "And you brought an outsider with you. How much more damage do you wish to inflict upon us? You are no longer welcome here. Go! Now!"

Graeden was taken aback. "I do not understand."

"Nor do I," a voice boomed from just inside the trees.

Within a moment Ayirak and Trebeh stood behind Neshya.

"How dare you treat a member of our family in such a manner?" Trebeh demanded.

Neshya growled under his breath. "He is no longer a part of this family. Not after what he did to Regnaryn."

Graeden was at a loss. "What do you mean? I did nothing to her." He turned to Trebeh. "Where is she? Why has she not come to greet me? I do not understand."

"Do not play us for fools," Neshya snapped. "You deserted her, and it tore her apart."

"He did not desert her," Trebeh said softly. "She sent him away."

"What?" Neshya sputtered. "No one told me that."

"And when did the private affairs of others become your business?" Trebeh asked.

Ayirak raised his hand. "Be silent, boy, before you get yourself in more trouble." He turned and strode toward Ellyss. "It has been quite some time since you have crossed into our land."

"Yes, old friend. Far too long," Ellyss embraced Ayirak before he turned to Trebeh. He took her hand and kissed it.

"We have long wondered if we would ever see you again, dearest Ellyss. Welcome home."

Neshya and Graeden looked at each other in disbelief.

"Why did you never tell me that you had been to this place?" Graeden asked.

Ellyss smiled. "You never asked."

Trebeh and Ayirak stifled their laughter.

"Enough chatter," Trebeh said. "You are both little more than bones. Did you not eat on your journey?" Before either had a chance to answer, Trebeh grabbed Ellyss' arm and led him down the path. "Oh, Phrynia will be so thrilled to see you."

"Neshya, see to the horses." Ayirak put his arm around Graeden's shoulder. "Now, son, let us join the others."

Graeden nodded. The two followed Trebeh and Ellyss, leaving Neshya to scratch his head in confusion.

"But what of Regnaryn?" Graeden asked. "Where is she?"

"In good time, now I suggest we let Trebeh feed you. You know she has done nothing but cook since she first sensed your approach."

At the house, Graeden's questions about Regnaryn were again deflected. He wanted to shout to them that Regnaryn was in trouble and was about to interrupt.

*:Patience,:* Ellyss told him.

Graeden found he could do nothing more than comply with Ellyss' wishes. He ate in silence as the three old friends caught up. After all were sated, they retired to the other room. Ellyss nodded to Graeden.

"Where is Regnaryn? Surely she cannot still be angry with me for whatever transgression she perceived I committed," Graeden began. He received no response. "Why will you not answer my questions? What are you hiding from me?"

Trebeh shook her head. "Regnaryn is no longer angry with you, that much I know." Trebeh took a deep breath. "As for your other questions, we are not hiding anything from you, because we do not know."

Graeden stared at her. "That makes no sense."

Trebeh leaned forward and took Graeden's hands, "Regnaryn coped for some time after you left, but only until she could no longer feel you." She squeezed his hands, "When that happened, she changed. Her moods became dark and sullen and, on occasion, vicious. When she could no longer bear her loneliness, she left. One day she was here, the next she was gone and, try as we may, we could not find her. That was about this time last year."

"But how can that be?"

"We could not find you, either," Ayirak said. "Are you surprised we looked?"

Graeden nodded. "A little, I mean after all that happened." He stopped and thought a moment. "I remember voices calling to me, but my mind only wanted Regnaryn. Nothing else mattered."

Graeden gently pulled his hands from Trebeh's. "But if you know I am the cause of her sorrow, and yours, how can you welcome me back into your home and family?"

"Because," Ayirak replied, "we know she sent you away. You complied out of your love for her."

"But why have you come back in such a hurry?" Trebeh asked.

"And, if Ellyss is with you, I can only surmise there is more to this than just you wanting to be with her." He turned to Ellyss, "I am sorry, old friend, but more often than not, you are the harbinger of trouble."

Ellyss nodded. "Yes, the last time I was here was just before the illness."

"Regnaryn is in trouble," Graeden interrupted. "I have had horrible visions and dreams of terror and pain."

"Have you seen her in these visions?" Trebeh asked.

Graeden shook his head. "No, but I know she is their source."

"The boy is right," Ellyss said before Trebeh could question him further. "I have felt them, too."

Trebeh gasped and sank into her chair.

"She is safe for the moment," Graeden answered. "I know she is. I can feel it with every fiber of my being."

Ellyss agreed.

"What are we to do?" Ayirak asked.

Graeden walked to the window. He stared into the distance, "I had hoped she was here and all the dreams and visions were merely my imagination, but..." He paused and turned to them.

Before he could continue, the front door opened and voices filled the air.

"Children, come greet our guests," Trebeh called.

269

"Yes, Mama," two voices replied in unison. The next moment a pair of yellow and white yekcals bounced into the room. They looked at the stranger on the couch and nodded politely. They turned and saw the figure by the window, squealed with delight and ran across the room. They jumped up, grabbing Graeden around the waist and nearly knocking him over.

"Graeden!" they shouted in unison. "You are back!"

"I missed you so much."

"I missed you more."

Graeden laughed. "Norellan! Katalanar!" He carefully extricated himself from their grips and took a step back. "Let me have a good look at you. I cannot believe how much you have grown in so short a time."

The twins looked at each other and giggled.

Norellan turned to Trebeh. "Is Regnaryn coming home, too?"

"I would also like to know that," Neshya said from the doorway.

Graeden crossed the room. The young yekcal looked sheepish as Graeden approached. Graeden ignored Neshya's response and threw his arms around the yekcal.

"I have missed you, brother," he said in the yekcal's ear.

Neshya seemed at a loss. "I am sorry for how I treated you earlier."

"There is no need to apologize. I understand and would have reacted the same way had it been my sister." Graeden slapped Neshya on the back and drew him into the room. "Join us."

"Graeden, what about Regnaryn?" Katalanar asked.

"When is she coming back?" Norellan added.

Graeden shook his head and looked at the floor. "I am not sure," he whispered. He lifted his head. "We will just have to wait a little longer," he added, holding back his tears.

# CHAPTER FORTY-EIGHT

THE ROOM WAS unfamiliar and the snow against the window confused Regnaryn. She remembered being taken by the gawara in late spring. Another nightmare? Regnaryn shifted, the pain that coursed through her body told her it was not. She lifted the blankets and gasped at the sight of the scars that covered her body. Then, she began to cry.

"Do you cry out of pain or vanity?" Varlama asked.

"Both."

"Jucara healed you as well as she could. Kachurlak hurt you more than we thought, and it will take time for you to fully recover. The scars, I fear, are permanent."

Regnaryn wept openly at Varlama's revelation. "Then, I must remain alone forever, for no one will want to look upon me. Even Graeden would turn in disgust from such a sight."

"You think that little of your young man. That he only loved you for your physical beauty? Is he truly that shallow?" Varlama asked.

Regnaryn did not answer.

"If he came to you broken and scarred, would you turn him

away?"

"No," Regnaryn said, "but... but he is so beautiful."

"Yes, I am sure he is. And now you are not, so he will cast you aside?"

"No, that is not what I mean, that is not how I feel. You do not understand..."

Varlama sat beside her. "Tell me."

Regnaryn stared into the distance for several moments. When she finally spoke, she revealed feelings of inadequacy and insecurity, things she had never before admitted, not even to herself.

"Only now do I see that is the true reason I sent Graeden away. I feared that in the company of other human females, he would judge me inferior and grow to hate me and the bond between us." She shook her head. "I am the shallow one, shallow and selfish. How could I have done such a thing to him?"

Varlama gently stroked Regnaryn's back.

"Do you feel able to come to the dining room to eat?" Varlama asked, changing the subject.

Regnaryn nodded.

Varlama helped Regnaryn into a long robe. Regnaryn turned and caught a glimpse of herself in the mirror and gasped. Her face was still swollen and heavily bruised and her hair was chopped off close to her head.

"What did they do to my hair?" Regnaryn said in astonishment. "I expected my face to be a mess, but I do not remember them cutting off my hair!"

"I did that. It was so matted with blood and who knows what else, there was no other way to deal with it. Now, can you walk or shall I carry you?"

"I will walk." Regnaryn slowly started for the door.

"You are doing wonderfully. I did not think you would be even able to stand yet," Aloysius said as Regnaryn slowly entered. "Come, sit here, I have put extra cushions on the chair to make it more comfortable."

"Whatever you are cooking smells delicious." Regnaryn carefully lowered herself into the chair. "I did not realize how hungry I was until just this moment."

"That is not surprising, it has been quite some time since last you ate, child," Varlama said. "But, tonight you will have only broth and a bit of bread. The last thing you need is to upset your stomach."

Regnaryn nodded and ate. She sat quietly as the others finished their meal.

"You need to get back to bed. I do not want you up too long. You are still very weak," Varlama said as she and Aloysius cleared the dishes from the table.

"But I have so many questions," Regnaryn said.

Varlama nodded. "We can just as easily talk with you in your bed as at the table."

"And you will be far more comfortable," Aloysius added.

Regnaryn slowly rose and returned to her room. Varlama helped her into bed and pulled a chair close. Aloysius entered and sat on a large pillow at the foot of the bed.

"How long have I been here?" Regnaryn began. "It was late spring when the gawara captured me and now there is snow on the ground. It cannot possibly be winter again. Was I with the gawara that long, or have I slept through two seasons?"

"You were only with the gawara a matter of days," Varlama answered. "It is, in fact, still spring. However, we are high in the mountains, in the land of my people, where the snow never melts."

Varlama continued. "We traveled five days and have been here three."

"But how?" Regnaryn asked. "I do not remember leaving the cave."

"I am not surprised you do not recall the journey. You were unconscious most of the time. As to how you got here, you rode on Jucara's back," Aloysius said. "She was able to stay in solid form long enough to bring you here. And the constant physical contact with her sped the healing process dramatically."

"You call this healed?" Regnaryn asked with a wince.

"Compared to the condition you were in, you have made remarkable progress. Most beings would have perished the instant Kachurlak died, breaking the spell that kept you alive through his torture. That is why it was so crucial Jucara join with you so quickly. Nearly every bone in your body was crushed and your skin hung in ribbons from your bones. So, dear one, in just eight days you have indeed made a remarkable recovery."

"I am truly grateful to have your help," Regnaryn said.

Aloysius changed the subject. "I know you are acquainted with my people, since many chetoga reside in your lovely Reissem Grove, but would guess you have never seen nor heard of Varlama's kind, and have been too polite to ask."

Regnaryn blushed.

"I can tell my own story, thank you very much," Varlama said, playfully glaring at Aloysius. "I am a tazzamira, high mountain dwellers who have always kept to ourselves. That is why most people have neither seen nor heard of us. It is said that, in the early days at the dawn of time, we were nomads who settled in these mountains thousands upon thousands of years ago and have not left them since."

As Varlama described her people, Regnaryn looked closely at her for the first time. The tazzamira looked to be only slightly taller than Regnaryn but much broader at both shoulder and hip. Her body, except for her face, was covered with long, silky white hair. She appeared not quite human.

"That amulet," Regnaryn said, "you did not wear that in the cave."

"No," Varlama laughed, "it would not have suited our purpose for Kachurlak to know that I too possessed such a thing."

Regnaryn turned away. "You should both know I killed Jucara."

"No, child, you did not kill her. She impaled herself on your sword, a sword she tricked you into drawing. You had no way of stopping her. There was nothing you could have done," Aloysius interjected.

"How did you know?"

"She told us," Varlama answered.

"Why did Jucara not tell me of the amulet's power?"

"She could not take the chance of you knowing of its magic before we knew how your powers would manifest."

"Where is it now?" Regnaryn asked, stifling a yawn.

"It seems to have been destroyed in the cave, more than likely it returned to its fiery origins. That is enough for now, you need rest. We will talk again, later."

### 

Regnaryn woke to darkness. She heard Varlama and Aloysius in the other room, quietly talking. With great effort, she dressed and joined them.

"I was just about to wake you," Varlama said as Regnaryn slowly entered.

"I know you had no ill effects from last evening's meal, but I think it best for you to have the same fare tonight. Perhaps tomorrow we will try something a bit more substantial," Aloysius said.

"I have been wondering," Regnaryn said while the others finished the meal preparation. "Who is the Master that Kachurlak spoke of and feared?"

"Ah, the Master. So, that was how Kachurlak knew of you. I did not think he came upon you by chance," Varlama replied. "We know little of the Master save the whispered tales of cruelty and worse. What is consistent is his desire for power and that he will stop at nothing to obtain it," Varlama replied.

"And it seems he knows of you," Aloysius added.

"Kachurlak spoke of me saving a boy from his grasp." Regnaryn stopped, her eyes filled with tears and terror. "Oh, no!" she cried. "He meant Graeden. That also means the horrible being in my dreams, the one that nearly took me, is not only real, but is still after me."

Varlama and Aloysius tried to hide their surprise.

*:Ah, I see now, she is the one the boy spoke of when Ellyss freed him.:* Aloysius said.

*:So it seems. That makes it even more significant that you two rescued him at that moment. If he and Regnaryn already had some sort of connection, there is no telling what would have happened if that monster would have gotten control of the boy's mind.:*

"I was not aware of your dreams, but from the little we know of the Master, he is most adept at mind control so I must assume that he was, indeed, the one in your dreams."

As comforting as Varlama tried to be, Regnaryn's fear did not dissipate. "Then I am not safe from him. Here or anywhere."

"Calm yourself. There is no way he can penetrate the shieldings that protect this place."

"He breached the shieldings at Reissem Grove. How can you be sure he cannot do the same here?"

"I know," Varlama replied sternly. "The shieldings at Reissem Grove were not built to ward off attack. The shieldings here are as impenetrable as any could be. You are safe here. You have my word."

Varlama gently stroked Regnaryn's head. She felt bathed in a calming energy that immediately released her fear.

As they had the night before, the trio sat in Regnaryn's room after dinner.

"Even after all that has happened, and all you have told me about my power and magic, I still do not understand." Regnaryn shook her head slowly. "How did this happen? Before I met Jucara, I knew nothing of magic."

"You know more than you think, child, you always have." Aloysius smiled. "You grew up surrounded by it. You just never recognized it, because it was commonplace. Reissem Grove's very existence is magical. Do you not think the way it came to be, the mindspeech and all else that is Reissem Grove, is not magical?"

"Everyone in Reissem can do those things, so I guess I just never realized it was special," Regnaryn admitted.

"And what of your ability to speak to animals?"

Regnaryn nodded. "That is magic?"

"Yes, and an extremely rare talent."

"Oh."

"Remember how awestruck Graeden was?"

"Graeden... there were so many, er, other things happening..."

"Yes, dear, we know." Varlama smiled. "Passion and sex have a way of clouding one's perceptions of anything other than passion and sex."

Regnaryn blushed and changed the subject. "There is so much I do not understand."

"About?" Varlama asked.

"Well, for one thing," she began, "the way the gawara trussed me up when they captured me."

"Ah, that. Most magickers require their hands and eyes to perform magic or to spell cast," Varlama began.

Regnaryn looked confused.

"Do you remember how Kachurlak cast his spell upon you?"

"He stared into my eyes while he waved his arms and clapped his hands," Regnaryn said. "Oh, I see. He thought I could not perform magic if my hands were bound and my eyes were covered."

"Or swollen shut from beatings," Varlama added. "But as Kachurlak found out too late, your power does not require such menial trappings. Had he or his Master realized the true scope of your power, they would not have toyed with you as they did."

Regnaryn drew in a breath as the tazzamira's words became clear.

"What is it, child?" Varlama asked when the girl's expression turned pensive.

"You said you would teach me to how to use and control my power." Regnaryn said.

"Yes, but that will not begin until you are fully healed," Varlama replied. "Right now, you need rest."

# CHAPTER FORTY-NINE

"ALOYSIUS AND I have been talking," Varlama said as the last breakfast dish was put away. "We have decided it is time for you to learn to develop and control your powers."

"Really?" Regnaryn tried to hide her enthusiasm.

Aloysius nodded.

"In fact, tomorrow we will go to the place where you will train," Varlama added.

Regnaryn looked confused.

"You did not think we would do such things here in my house, did you?"

"I did not give it much thought."

"Our destination is about a day's journey, and we will be there for several weeks. So, we have some packing to do." Aloysius motioned her to follow.

Regnaryn eagerly complied.

### 

Immediately after they set out, Regnaryn's pent up questions, fueled by the magic tomes Varlama had given her to read, poured out. Varlama patiently listened.

"Except for recent events, I do not recall having any experience with magic," Regnaryn said. "At least, not real magic."

"All magic is real. From the most dramatic, like what you did in the cave, to that feeling in your gut telling you to beware," Aloysius said.

Regnaryn nodded. "I guess I still only think of magic as extraordinary things, and not what I grew up with. I forget not everyone has magic."

Varlama smiled. "Well, that is not wholly true. All creatures possess some magic, though it is often thought of more as instinct or luck."

"Like a hunter who seems to always find game?" Regnaryn asked.

Varlama nodded. "That is a form of earth magic. Those who possess it have a bond with the earth that they may not realize."

"And there are those who know of their powers, even if they are limited," Aloysius added. "Healers, weather witches, and such."

"Oh, yes, we have those in Reissem Grove." Regnaryn chuckled at the memory of her meeting with Jucara. "I was surprised Jucara could not alter the weather."

"Most magickers usually excel in only one or two of the primary elements – fire, water, earth, or air," Varlama continued.

"And some can control time and space or the minds of others," Aloysius added.

"Like the Master," Regnaryn said.

Varlama nodded. "There are also those who learn a bit of whatever they can and combine them in ways that best suit their purposes."

Regnaryn shook her head. "So I guess I will be the molten lava magicker, turning all in her path to ash and dust."

"Perhaps," Varlama replied.

Regnaryn looked shocked at the answer.

Varlama ignored her. "Only time and training will reveal if that is, indeed, your only talent."

:*Ha! The only limits she will have are those she puts on herself,:* Aloysius said to Varlama.

"What are your strengths?" Regnaryn asked her companions.

"We dabble in several areas," Aloysius said. "My main strength is earth. I speak to the land, and it to me. Varlama's, on the other hand, are wind and water. She can brew up an intense rain storm on even the clearest of days if she has a mind to."

"Some of your books spoke of blood magic, but did not go into detail. Is that what Kachurlak intended to use on you, Varlama?"

"Ha, as if that worthless creature could have," Aloysius snorted. "Sorry, do go on."

"When something dies," Varlama began, ignoring Aloysius, "its powers return to the earth. But one can choose to pass their power to someone close to them at their time of death. You have already experienced that."

"I did?"

"Jucara gave you her power to carry out her final wishes."

"Oh, yes, that."

"But there are dark rituals and spells, none of which are recounted in any of the volumes I care to possess," Varlama continued, "that allow someone to forcibly take another's power from them. That is what Kachurlak intended to do." When she saw the expression of fear that crossed Regnaryn's face, she asked, "What is it, child?"

"The voice in my dreams, the Master, said he would take my power from me," Regnaryn replied.

"That does not surprise me," Varlama said. "But we will take every precaution to make sure he cannot do that. Remember, your powers are no longer dormant. Now, you will learn to defend yourself against such things."

Regnaryn looked doubtful.

"You will learn protection spells to ensure your powers remain yours. It takes someone very powerful to break through even the weakest of these protections."

"And Kachurlak thought himself that powerful?"

Varlama nodded. "Apparently."

Regnaryn thought a moment. "But what if the Master is strong enough? What if he can do what he has threatened so many times?"

Varlama clasped Regnaryn's hand. "Child, we will see to it that he does not. I promise."

*:How long he has been infiltrating her dreams? I fear it was well before she made contact with Graeden in that inn,:* Varlama said to Aloysius.

*:Yes, it seems that way. But for him to have gotten to her mind within Reissem Grove means his powers are more than we first thought.:*

*:Reissem's shieldings were built for camouflage, not defense. Still, there could be another force at play here.:*

*:What do you mean?:* Aloysius asked.

*:Perhaps there is some link between them.:*

*:What possible link could that monster have with her?:*

*:I do not know. It is just a thought. Another avenue to investigate,:* Varlama answered.

### 

Just before sunset, the trio arrived at an almost invisible break in the trees. They walked down the narrow path until it opened into a large valley sheltered on all sides. The fading sunlight glistened off the sheer black cliffs, making them appear alive. Regnaryn turned, mouth agape as she took in the view before her.

"This is amazing."

"More than you know," Varlama said. "This valley, and others like it around the world, is fortified by all who have worked within its confines. Here we are secure; safe from the magic we use and the intrusion of outsiders. It is much like Reissem Grove, because only those who should be here can find it."

"These places have been used as training grounds longer than anyone can remember. We come here as novice or expert to hone our skills, new or old. And no matter what is done here, the magic cannot escape," Aloysius added.

"How can that be?"

"The shieldings laid into the surrounding cliffs absorb any stray magic and then use it to further strengthen themselves." Varlama said. "No one knows how or when the original spell was cast. We only know it is here and in all other such places."

Regnaryn nodded and Varlama continued, "Even if something goes wrong with one's magic, the damage would only be to the magicker and a few trees."

"And we come here because you fear this will happen with me?" Regnaryn asked.

"That is always a possibility with the untrained," Aloysius answered honestly.

"But, we really come to places like this more because they are hidden from the outside world. Thus, no innocents can stumble upon us and be inadvertently harmed," Varlama added.

Regnaryn felt only slightly reassured.

"Do not fear, child, I have never heard of a new magicker's powers going awry." Aloysius said. "It tends to occur only when experienced magickers, too full of themselves, fail to recognize their limitations or to take proper precautions for the work they are doing."

"Besides, it is a lovely spot. The weather is warm, the scenery beautiful and the water calming." Varlama pointed to a small lake on the far side of the ravine.

"Oh, my, I did not even notice that. And there is a cabin as well," Regnaryn said. "That is why we packed no shelter."

"Tonight we will relax and enjoy the evening air," Varlama said as she walked toward the cabin. "In the morning, we will begin."

"Good, I have been afraid something would occur and I would repeat what happened in the cave and hurt you."

"I thought as much," Varlama replied.

"Enough talk of what will come and what has passed," Aloysius said. "Right now, it is time to eat."

### 

"Surely it is not yet time to get up." Regnaryn tried to curl back under the covers as Varlama shook her.

The tazzamira pulled the blanket off the girl. "I told you this would be no picnic."

Regnaryn sat up and rubbed her eyes. "You did not say we would start in the middle of the night."

Varlama walked out of the room, waving her hand. "Be quick about it, or you will get nothing to eat. We start within the hour whether you are fed or not."

Regnaryn quickly dressed, ran outside to the fire, and found Varlama and Aloysius deep in conversation.

"So, when threatened with an empty belly, you move quickly," Varlama said with a laugh. "I will remember that."

She pointed to a pot of stew on the fire. Regnaryn filled her bowl and sat beside the others.

"We were discussing what to do today," Aloysius said.

"He thinks you should start by experiencing some of the elements and what they can do," Varlama said. "I, on the other hand, am of a mind to begin with creating shieldings."

"I already have shieldings," Regnaryn said between mouthfuls of stew and bread.

Varlama chuckled. "Oh, do you?"

"Of course. That is one of the first things I learned as a child."

"And you think them adequate?"

"Well, yes," Regnaryn said.

"Alright then," Varlama said with more than just a hint of sarcasm, "I guess we can move on to other things."

Regnaryn nodded.

Varlama continued, "You would not mind if I check just how good they are."

"No, of course not."

"Good, then that is where we will begin."

*:Please tell me you are not going to be too hard on her about this,:* Aloysius said.

*:No. Not too hard.:* Varlama laughed.

# CHAPTER FIFTY

"ARE YOUR SHIELDINGS up?" Varlama asked as the trio headed to the opposite side of the valley.

Regnaryn nodded. "Mama says to never drop them."

"That is good advice," Varlama replied. She promptly broke through the girl's meager sheildings and pushed her to the ground.

Regnaryn shook her head and looked up at Varlama. "What are you doing?"

"I thought you said your shieldings were up? I could have broken through that in my sleep. If that is the best you can do, it will take a lifetime to train you."

"But I was not expecting you to..."

"Oh, I am sorry. My mistake. I forgot, an enemy will always announce his plan to attack so you can prepare."

Regnaryn said nothing.

"Trebeh taught you well for Reissem Grove," Varlama said. "But the outside world is different. You must do more than shelter your thoughts and emotions."

The tazzamira extended her hand and helped Regnaryn to her feet. "When you met Jucara, you should have realized then that your shieldings were inadequate when she kept entering your mind," Varlama continued.

"I will not make that mistake again."

"Good, that is the first step," Aloysius said. "Now let us show you how to build more appropriate shieldings."

Regnaryn watched as they wove layer upon layer.

"Now you try."

Regnaryn began and suddenly stopped.

"What is it?" Aloysius asked.

Regnaryn smiled. "I have done this before."

"Really?" Varlama asked.

Regnaryn nodded. "In one of my dreams. I was accosted by something, probably the Master. He wanted to take over all of Reissem and somehow I stopped him. Mama and Phrynia told me the shielding I had built around my room was one of the strongest they had ever encountered. They had a hard time infiltrating it."

"Hmm, that is interesting," Varlama said. "If you did this instinctively, it should be even easier now. But, you say they infiltrated it. How?"

Regnaryn thought a moment. "They found tiny cracks and were able to send thought threads through them." She looked at Varlama. "But that is bad. I mean, then it was good, because I needed their help, but had they been an enemy, they would have destroyed me."

Varlama smiled. "Now you are thinking like a magicker."

Regnaryn created a new shielding, which Aloysius and Varlama easily broke through. She tried again and again, each time with the same result. Finally, after several attempts, Varlama stopped her.

"No," Regnaryn pleaded, "I am sure I can do this."

"Yes, I know you can, but not just now. You are making remarkable progress. It is getting harder and harder for us to break through. But there are other things to learn besides creating shieldings. Not to mention, it is near midday. We need sustenance to keep up our strength."

Regnaryn looked up to see the sun almost directly above her, "Oh, I had not realized it was so late." Her stomach growled. "Or that I was so hungry."

Varlama sat beside a rock and Regnaryn followed.

"Where is Aloysius?"

"He has gone off to catch his lunch and hopefully our dinner."

Both sat and leisurely ate.

"This afternoon we will see what areas you might have an affinity for."

"Oh."

"Does that idea not appeal to you?"

"Yes, of course, it is just that, well..."

Varlama smiled. "Are you nervous?"

Regnaryn nodded.

"Do not worry, nothing will go wrong. It is different here. You will not be under the same stress as before. And your conscious mind will be in control, not your instincts and emotions."

"Are we ready to begin?" Aloysius placed the kill that would be their dinner beside the rock.

Varlama nodded.

"Then, as usual, my timing is perfect."

Varlama walked to the water's edge. The others followed.

"You have already shown a talent with fire, I would like to see what you can do with its counterpart, water."

"Water?" Regnaryn questioned.

"Water can be as powerful as fire. And water is one of the most controllable elements," Varlama said. "So it is a good place to begin."

Varlama filled her cup and handed it to Regnaryn. "Besides drinking it or pouring it out, what can you do with that?"

"I could boil it."

"But that would be using fire. What can you do with just the water?"

Regnaryn thought for several moments. "I do not think you can do anything with just water alone."

"Why not?"

"If I heat it, I am using fire. If I freeze it, I am using cold which, being the opposite of hot, would somehow be related to fire. If I toss it up and out of the cup that uses air."

"Well done," Aloysius said. "You have just realized that all magic is related. Everything you do will encompass more than one element of magic to some degree."

"Why then do you refer to yourself by just one element?"

"Because, though a fire wizard knows he uses air to move the fire, his main focus is the fire. So, what can you do with the water in the cup besides boiling it and burning your hands?"

Regnaryn thought and then shrugged.

"Try using air to make it bubble out of the cup without heat," Aloysius offered as a suggestion.

"How would I do that?" Regnaryn asked after several moments.

"Just think about what you want to do and then send those thoughts to the water," Varlama replied.

Regnaryn stared intently at the cup but nothing happened. She let out a sigh, closed her eyes and tried again. Still nothing. After several more failed attempts, she threw the cup to the ground in frustration. "I cannot do this."

"Emotions will not help you master the task at hand. Try again. This time, calm your mind and concentrate," Varlama said, levitating the cup to Regnaryn's hands and drawing the spilled water from the ground and refilling the cup.

Varlama and Aloysius sat quietly in the shade as Regnaryn tried over and over to move the water. The more she tried and failed, the more frustrated she became.

"This is impossible!" She threw aside the cup and dropped to the ground.

In the next moment, a huge water spray washed over Regnaryn. "If you are going to act like a hot-headed, spoiled child, perhaps I need to cool you off," Varlama said without moving from her spot in the shade.

"I cannot do this. No matter how hard I try, I cannot move the water." Suddenly a look of recognition crossed her face.

"What is it?" Varlama asked.

Regnaryn smiled for the first time that afternoon. "Graeden said the same thing when I taught him to mindspeak."

"And what did you do? "

"I did not try to drown him. I encouraged him."

Varlama grinned. "Well, we all have our own methods. The bottom line is, you did not let him give up. Right?"

"Of course, not. I knew he could do it." She stopped and looked over at the others. "Alright, I understand."

For the rest of the day Regnaryn attempted to move the water. She kept her frustration at bay each time she failed to achieve her goal.

Just before sunset, she let out a yelp. "I did it. The water bubbled. It was just a little," she said, beaming, "but it moved."

"Wonderful. That is the first step," Varlama said, "and with that achievement under your belt, it is time to head back to the cabin."

Aloysius walked beside Regnaryn. "Just so you know," he whispered, "I am told it took Varlama near on a week to accomplish what you did this afternoon."

"I heard that," Varlama called back to him. "Would you like me to tell her how long you took to do the same, chetoga?"

Aloysius harrumphed and stifled a cough. "No, we do not need to go into that."

### 

It took only another day for Regnaryn to be able to get the water to bubble completely out of the cup. Once she did, all other water tasks came easily. Before long, she reached the same skill level as Varlama.

"Your talents are formidable, child. I cannot believe how far you have come in such a short time," Varlama said.

Regnaryn smiled. In the next moment, she felt something grip her shoulders and fling her to the ground. She looked around, but saw no one.

"You may have mastered the water techniques, but what good is that if you abandon your shieldings in the process?" Aloysius called from a distance. "Had I been an enemy, you would have been mine before you had a chance to realize what was happening."

Regnaryn stood up, rubbing her back. "I guess I thought that in this place..." Her voice trailed off.

Varlama gave her an exasperated look.

"It will not happen again," the young woman promised.

"It had better not," Varlama said. "Next time, it will be more than your pride that is hurt if we can so easily take you down."

Regnaryn nodded, knowing the words were no idle threat.

"Tomorrow, we shall begin work on the other elements. I believe you will master them more easily than water."

"Why?"

"You have confidence in yourself, and you now believe your powers are real."

###

"We have reached a crossroad, child," Varlama said as the group enjoyed their midday meal. Regnaryn looked at the tazzamira not sure what she meant. "In these few weeks, you have mastered the basics of all the elements. You have also laid down a decent foundation in time and space manipulation."

"Surely you cannot mean that this is all I have to learn?"

"Hardly," Aloysius replied.

"What you have just completed was the child's play portion of your training," Varlama added.

"Child's play?" Regnaryn asked, remembering the bumps, bruises, cuts and burns she had inflicted upon herself.

"Yes. Next you will learn how and when to combine what you have already mastered into new and more powerful techniques."

Regnaryn's face lit up. "That sounds exciting. Will we start tomorrow?"

Varlama smiled. "No, we need a day or so to rest and take stock of our supplies and such."

Suddenly, Regnaryn felt the sting of an attack, different from those of her teachers. The assault did not breach her shieldings and she quickly altered them to defend against the next strike. Whoever was behind this aggression was attacking more viciously than Varlama or Aloysius had ever done. Regnaryn fought off each attack. She looked to Varlama and Aloysius for assistance and saw both motionless on the ground. Her mind raced. What was going on? Varlama had said this place was safe.

Without further thought, Regnaryn took the offensive. She sent a surge of power, not the red molten lava she had used against the gawara, but a well-directed shove, in the general direction of her assailant. The attack instantly ceased. As it did, Regnaryn stopped and refortified her shieldings in anticipation of yet another attack.

She looked again toward her companions. They sat, grinning at her.

*:Enough,:* Jucara said from where Regnaryn had directed her counterattack, *:you have passed this trial, child.:*

"And far better than expected," Aloysius said as he and Varlama stood.

"How do I know, this is not just another ruse?" Regnaryn asked. "That you will not attack again."

"You do not, save for our word that the exercise is complete," Varlama said.

*:Regnaryn, you did remarkably well,:* Jucara said and appeared in a semi-transparent form. *:You repelled everything I threw at you with remarkable speed and ingenuity, altering your shieldings to not only accommodate but to anticipate the next strike. You have pushed me to the brink of exhaustion.:*

"I sensed your fatigue," Regnaryn said modestly, "and took the offensive."

*:Your attack showed exceptional control, sufficient to neutralize*

*but not destroy your attacker. And you did not lose focus even though you were tiring. Very well done.:*

Then, turning toward Varlama and Aloysius, *:I was not aware you had gotten her to the point of focused attacks yet.:*

Aloysius and Varlama shook their heads.

"We have not even discussed offensive tactics," Varlama replied *:Well, then, that is even more impressive,:* Jucara said, joining them. *:So I must surmise from what I saw here today, your charge's training is progressing well.:*

Varlama nodded. "Yes, exceptionally so. We were just discussing that it is now time for her to learn to create combinations."

Jucara turned to Regnaryn, *:I believe you already have a good start on that, as well. That attack combined the elements of wind, heat and lightning. Correct?:*

Regnaryn thought a moment. "Yes, I believe so."

*:And how did you come up with that combination?:*

"I am not sure. I wanted to stun and stop the attacker until I could determine the motive. I did not think of each part of the attack individually before I did it. There was not time," Regnaryn replied. "That is what you told me to do, Varlama, to think about what I wanted to do and act on it."

Varlama nodded. "Yes, and you did it perfectly."

*:Is this the first time you have tried just thinking of something to do and doing it, outside of the tasks set for you in your training?:* Jucara asked.

Regnaryn nodded. "Did I do something wrong?"

The others laughed. *:By no means. In fact, it is the goal we were working towards, and you just leapt right to it without instruction,:* Jucara said.

Regnaryn breathed a sigh of relief.

"However, your training is far from complete," Varlama said. "We need to verify that you can repeat what you did today with the same results each time."

"Or better," Aloysius added. "I would not be surprised if the next time you attempt that move, it will be far better than what we saw here today."

*:And we want to see what other techniques you might come up with,:* Jucara said.

Regnaryn nodded.

*:When Varlama and Aloysius feel you have finished your training, they will accompany you back to Reissem Grove.:*

Regnaryn was dismayed at that thought. She tried to hide it, but oftimes, especially at night, she ached for Graeden and had all she could do to keep her moods from spiraling into the same depths of darkness she had previously known. "I am not sure I really should go there," she said. "I think I would prefer to be on my own or stay with Varlama and Aloysius, if they will have me."

*:Really? I think that young man waiting there for you will be gravely disappointed to hear that,:* Jucara replied.

"Graeden? He is there? But how? When?" Regnaryn asked the nodding emuranda.

*:He arrived a day or so ago and was quite disappointed you were gone. Will you disappoint him further by not returning?:*

"No, no. How soon can we leave?" Regnaryn asked, her dismay now excitement.

"As soon as you show us you are ready," Varlama answered.

"Well then, what are we waiting for? We have work to do."

# CHAPTER FIFTY-ONE

REGNARYN DEVOURED each lesson like a starving animal, refusing to stop even when exhaustion threatened. Only when reminded that illness or injury would delay the trip to Reissem Grove did she relent.

In less than two weeks, she achieved results that should have taken several months. She felt absolutely ecstatic when told this portion of her training was complete.

The morning after her last training, Regnaryn was shown the ritual to return the magic they had used back to the land.

"Remember, child, these places bless us by augmenting our powers. We show our gratitude by returning what we have borrowed," Varlama told her. "And always add just a bit more of our own magic in appreciation for the protection afforded us."

With the ritual complete, the trio started back to Varlama's house.

### 

It took two days to prepare for the journey, days that were almost unbearable to Regnaryn. Impatient to leave, she could not sit still.

*:If I had the slightest knowledge of transcension,:* Aloysius told Varlama, *:I would teach it to her so she could instantly transport there. How long do you think it will take us to get to Reissem Grove?:*

*:Four or five weeks.:*

*:Really? Ugh, it will be torture to be with her in this state for that long.:*

*:And, the closer we get to Reissem, the more anxious she will become. I fear if we let her have her way, we will be traveling day and night without rest,:* Varlama replied. *:Perhaps we should bring a sleeping potion along, it might be easier to carry her than to have her awake.:*

The next morning, Regnaryn woke before sunrise and roused the others. They ate a hurried breakfast and left the house as the sun rose.

*:It is going to be a long journey.:* Aloysius sighed.

Varlama agreed.

### 

Graeden raced to find Trebeh and Phrynia.

He spoke, so excited his words sounded like gibberish.

"Slow down. We cannot understand what you are saying," Trebeh said.

*:She is coming back! Regnaryn is on her way home! Home to me! To you! To us!:* he mindspoke to them to get the words out.

"How do you know this, boy?" Phrynia asked.

Graeden had finally calmed down enough to speak. "She told me. Last night."

"Are you sure it was not just a dream?" Trebeh asked. "Wishful thinking?"

Graeden shook his head. "No, it was real. I know she was speaking to me."

*:Could that be possible?:* Trebeh asked Phrynia.

*:It would not surprise me after all they have been through both*

*together and apart.:*

"What did she say?" Trebeh asked.

"She is still very far away, somewhere to the far north. She knew I was here. They are on their way, but she does not know how long it will take to get here."

"Who is they?" Phrynia asked.

"I am not sure," he answered, "a chetoga and a tazza something."

"A tazzamira?" Trebeh asked.

"Yes," he answered. "A tazzamira and a chetoga. I know what a chetoga is. But, what is a tazzamira?"

Trebeh and Phrynia stared at each other in disbelief,.

"There is only one tazzamira I know of who travels beyond her own land," Phrynia said, ignoring Graeden's question.

"And with a chetoga," Trebeh added.

"Are you sure she did not mention their names, child?" Phrynia asked.

"No," he said. "I do not understand."

"Nor do we," Phrynia replied looking at Trebeh. "At least, not completely. As for answers to your other questions, they will need to wait until they arrive."

"Did she say anything else?" Trebeh asked.

Graeden shook his head. "Should I tell Ayirak and the others?"

Trebeh nodded and Graeden took off at a run to share his news.

"It does not surprise me that Regnaryn found her way to those two," Trebeh said.

"Or they to her," Phrynia added with a laugh.

"But where is Jucara?"

"I am not sure. But, you realize if she is, indeed, with Varlama and Aloysius," Phrynia replied, "she may be even more powerful than we thought."

Trebeh nodded. "But why have they not yet contacted us?"

"Perhaps they are still too far away," Phrynia said with a

chuckle. "The bond between Regnaryn and Graeden seems to allow them to reach each other across vast distances."

"Yes, he did say that he was able to feel her when he was in his homeland," Trebeh replied.

"I am sure Varlama or Aloysius will contact us when they can."

"Poor Graeden," Trebeh said. "His wait will feel like an eternity."

"It is you I feel sorry for, my dear. If memory serves me, the tazzamira homeland is more than a month's journey from here. How long do you think it will be before Graeden's excitement wears down Ayirak's last nerve?"

"I had not thought of that."

### 

Graeden immersed himself in anything he could do to keep his mind busy, anything to make the day go by faster so he could get to the night and his dreams with Regnaryn.

It was just shy of a month after Regnaryn's first message when Trebeh and Phrynia approached Graeden.

Phrynia began, "If we tell you something, can you keep it from Regnaryn when she contacts you?"

"I do not know," Graeden answered. "Why? What is it? Is something wrong?"

"Nothing is wrong."

Graeden looked relieved.

"Varlama, the tazzamira Regnaryn travels with, has a request to ask of you," Phrynia answered. "She did not wish to intrude upon your mind uninvited. She wishes us to meet them before they get to the Grove. But wants to keep it secret from Regnaryn."

"Why?" Graeden asked.

Phrynia smiled. "Varlama and Aloysius want to surprise her."

"Wait, did you say Aloysius? I believe I have met him."

"You did? When? Are you sure?"

"He was traveling with Ellyss when we met after the incident at that inn. But I am not sure he liked me."

"Really? Why not?" Trebeh asked.

"Well, when we first met, I called him a ferret," Graeden replied sheepishly.

Trebeh and Phrynia tried to stifle their amusement, but could not control their laughter.

"It was not my fault. I knew nothing of chetoga or of any of you then," Graeden added in his own defense.

"I am sorry, we do not mean to laugh. It is just that, well, we know Aloysius and can imagine how he reacted," Phrynia said.

"I am sure he will not hold that against you," Trebeh added.

"Now, go gather your things together," Phrynia said. "We leave in an hour and will be gone for several days."

The trio left Reissem Grove. Trebeh and Graeden traveled on foot. Phrynia flew on ahead to scout their path and look for campsites. They traveled about two hours and then camped for the night. As expected, Graeden did not want to stop.

The next morning they rose with the sun and set out again. Just before midday, Phrynia returned.

"Have you sighted them yet?" Graeden asked.

"Yes, they are about two hours foot travel to the northwest," Phrynia answered. "They too have stopped for their midday meal."

"That close? I did not expect to meet them for another day or so," Trebeh said.

"Nor did I. Regnaryn must be pushing them even harder than Graeden is pushing you," Phrynia said with a smile. "I alerted Varlama that we were here. We shall meet in the clearing by the river. It should take you about an hour to get there."

"Why are we just sitting here if they are that close?" Graeden asked excitely. "We need to go to them."

"Relax," Trebeh said. "How does she look, Phrynia?"

"Well, but something about her feels different," Phrynia said. "I fear she is no longer the innocent she was when we saw her last."

Both mother and mate looked worried. Neither consciously

thought of that, neither wanted to. Now, they needed to face it.

### 

"We can eat while we walk," Regnaryn said when Varlama and Aloysius insisted on stopping for the midday meal. "We are so close to Reissem Grove. If we just keep moving, we can be there well before nightfall."

"Child, sit and relax a moment," Aloysius said. "You have been pushing us very hard on this trip, and we are tired."

"Besides, we are not going to Reissem Grove tonight. We probably will not be going there for a few days," Varlama said.

"What do you mean? Why are we not going there for a few days? That is ridiculous! We are less than a half day's walk away, and you say we are not going? If you two are tired, I will go on by myself. I left alone, I can return the same way."

"Calm down," Varlama said.

"Do not tell me to calm down," Regnaryn shot back at her.

"Fine. Do as you please. But, if you take off on your own, you will miss Graeden."

"Graeden?" Regnaryn asked.

"It is our gift to you," Varlama said. "We felt it might be easier for you two to become reacquainted away from the Grove and all your well-meaning friends and family."

"But, how?" Regnaryn asked, now smiling from ear to ear.

"We contacted Phrynia and your mother. They are with him," Aloysius answered.

"Where?" Regnaryn cried.

Varlama stated. "Less than an hour's walk I think. Then we will meet this Graeden we have heard so much about."

Regnaryn swallowed her meal so fast, she almost choked. Varlama and Aloysius seemed to take hours to finish theirs. Finally, they resumed their trek, Regnaryn so excited she nearly burst.

### 

Graeden devoured his meal in the blink of an eye. He nervously paced until the two women finished theirs. Phrynia took to the air, and Graeden set out at a near run. Trebeh hurried to catch up.

Within the hour, Graeden and Trebeh met Phrynia near some large trees.

"Where is she?" Graeden asked.

"They should be coming into view shortly," Phrynia answered. "If you keep going along this path, you will arrive at a clearing…"

Graeden did not wait for her to finish. He sprinted down the path, leaving the two women behind.

"It is my guess that is where we will meet them," Phrynia finished to his back. Turning to Trebeh, she said, "I would bet Varlama and Aloysius are dealing with the same excitement on the other side of the clearing."

Trebeh laughed. "Knowing Regnaryn, it is likely far worse. You know, I would love to run with him to meet her. But, as much as I know she loves me, I am not the one she most wants to see."

Phrynia chuckled. "Remember when we were the center of our children's universe?"

### 

Graeden ran so fast toward the clearing ahead that, had the terrain not been flat, Trebeh and Phrynia would have lost sight of him.

Regnaryn and Graeden reached the clearing at the same moment. They ran to each other, tears of joy streaming down their cheeks. As the lovers met, they embraced and kissed passionately. Regnaryn immediately threw up a shielding to envelop them.

The four old friends entered the clearing, staring in awe as their charges embraced and then disappeared.

"By all that is holy," Trebeh began as she and the others stood together, "is that what I think it is?"

"It does seem to be an invisibility shielding," Varlama answered.

"Did you teach her that?"

Varlama and Aloysius shook their heads. "No. Neither of us can do that."

"How did she manage?"

Aloysius scratched his head. "She does have a knack for being able to envision something and then make it happen."

"And she has been devouring every book on magic I own, so she could have read of it in one of those," Varlama added. "Nothing that child does surprises me. She is quite remarkable. And over the last few months, she has done things we never imagined."

Phrynia and Trebeh were speechless.

"After traveling with those two," Aloysius said, "we deserve a rest for our weary old bones."

"I am sure they will be occupied for some time," Varlama said. "And, there is much that needs to be discussed."

The four old friends sat and chatted, catching up on each other's lives. Trebeh avoided the topic of what Regnaryn had gone through and the others allowed her this brief respite from the truth.

"Where is Jucara?" Phrynia asked as their reminiscing wound down.

*:Here I am, old friend,:* Jucara answered, watching the surprise on their faces.

Trebeh finally asked about Regnaryn's ordeals. Varlama and Aloysius told of the events that had befallen Regnaryn since her departure from the Grove. Trebeh barely managed not to wail in sorrow as her worst fears came to fruition.

"They seem to coincide with the visions Graeden had in Hammarsh," Trebeh said after regaining some semblance of composure.

A look of bewilderment came over Varlama and Aloysius.

Trebeh continued, "You were not aware of that?"

Trebeh related what Graeden had told her of the visions, about their horror and how certain other members of his family not only felt but saw the events, as well.

*:There is far more to their powers than any of us have even begun to comprehend,:* Jucara said.

"But what of the one you call the Master?" Phrynia asked.

"Ellyss mentioned him, as well," Trebeh added.

"Ellyss is here?" Aloysius asked

"Yes, he escorted Graeden from his homeland to Reissem Grove."

"It will be good to see him again," Aloysius said. "But if anyone tells him I said that, I will emphatically deny it."

Everyone laughed as Varlama turned back to Phrynia. "You wanted to know of the Master?"

"Is he the one who haunted Regnaryn's dreams?" Phrynia asked.

"That is what we believe."

Phrynia and Trebeh glanced at each other.

"Can she defeat him?" Trebeh asked unsure if she wanted to hear the answer.

"I hope so, but we do not know enough about him to say for certain."

"What now? There is a training site on the north side of the Grove, but after hearing and seeing what she is now capable of," Trebeh said, "I am not sure it will be sufficient."

Varlama clasped her hand on her friend's shoulder. "It will be fine. After all, look at the group we have to keep it fortified. Other than practice, I am not sure there is much more that any of us can actually teach her."

*:Do not dismiss Graeden. His powers have yet to emerge. And that young man just may surprise everyone. You will be wise to use him, as well.:* Jucara paused to allow the others to digest her words. *:And he will require your assistance, even more so than Regnaryn did.:*

They looked at each other in amazement. Not one of them had ever associated Graeden with power.

# CHAPTER FIFTY-TWO

AS SOON AS Graeden's fingers touched Regnaryn's face, he felt a surge of energy surround them.

"What is that?" he asked.

"I am shielding us from the outside world," she answered as they began to caress each other. "I have created an invisibility shielding. No one can see us. More importantly, no one can feel any of our passion. It will all stay within the shielding's boundaries for us alone to experience."

He reached to remove her tunic, but she grabbed his hand.

"What is it, my love?" He took her hand and gently kissed it. "Do not tell me you have become shy around me. Or that you do not feel the same desire I do."

"I want you more than you can imagine, but there is something you must know before we go any further," she concentrated on holding her passion, and his, at bay. "Much has happened since last we were together. I am not the same person I was then. I have done things, seen things, and had things happen that have changed me forever."

"No matter what has or will happen, I love you," he said. "And I will never leave you. I will never again allow you to send me away. I am not whole without you. If you do not want me, strike me down here and now, for I will have no reason to live. Life without you, my love, is too hard to bear."

"I have no intention of sending you away," she replied. "But, after you see what I am now, you may turn away in horror and disgust. I will not fault you for that nor will I bind you to the words you have just spoken. You, my love, are so beautiful. I am ugly."

She opened her tunic. Graeden gasped at the sight of the horrible blood-red and purple scars that covered her from neck to waist. She was prepared for him to bolt. But Graeden did not run. He did not even turn away. Rather, tears ran down his cheeks. He fell to his knees, dragging her with him. He softly kissed each scar as if hoping his love would heal them.

Regnaryn openly wept at his actions, knowing he truly loved her for who, not what, she was.

"My dearest Regnaryn," he murmured as he removed the rest of her clothing and continued to kiss her scarred body. "What horrors you have been through without me there by your side to help you. But more so, I am saddened that you thought I loved you only for your physical beauty."

"I am sorry," she said. "I thought I had conquered my doubts and insecurities, but a part of me still feared I would disappoint you. Never you to me. I am glad I was wrong."

With that, there were no more words, no thoughts, just pure unbridled love, physical and emotional. Their passion brought them to heights neither had ever dreamed of. Once again they became one, body and soul. Both now knew they would never again allow themselves to be separated.

### 

Well into the next morning, Regnaryn and Graeden were finally too exhausted to make love another time but neither closed their eyes to sleep. After being separated for so long they could not bear to lose sight of each other for more than the time it took to blink. Neither could they stop touching each other – gently stroking one another's face or arm or whatever was within reach.

"What brought you back to Reissem Grove?" she asked.

"I knew you were in trouble. I felt compelled to help you. I had no idea you were not there."

She stared at him in confusion. "How did you know that?"

"Did you not reach out to me across your dreams?" he asked. "Like at the inn?"

She shook her head.

Graeden scratched his chin, then told her of what he had seen and felt while in Hammarsh Keep. He watched her as he spoke and saw the glint of recognition in his words.

"But it was not just me," he said. "The night of the second vision, Ellyss, the one who saved me at the inn, arrived in Hammarsh Keep having experienced, to a much lesser degree, the same feeling."

She nodded. "I think I know when each of your visions occurred, though like you at the inn, I did not consciously call to you but..."

They stared at each other in awe over what had transpired between them.

"What does this all mean?" Graeden asked.

"I am not sure."

"And what of your companions?" Graeden said.

Regnaryn smiled, the same smile that had so captivated Graeden upon their first meeting. She told him all about her magical training, of the mishaps and triumphs, and of all she had learned.

At last sleep overtook them. They slumbered in each other's arms. When they awoke, they made love again with the same passion they had previously shared.

Deep into the night Regnaryn lowered the shielding that surrounded them.

For the first time since they had reunited, they looked for the others and saw them sleeping near a waning fire. The couple chose not to disturb them.

Instead, Graeden and Regnaryn strolled to the nearby stream to bathe. As they basked in the warmth of the stream, Graeden once again kissed her. As his hands moved over her body, he jumped back.

"What is it, my love," she asked, fearing that he had changed his mind now that the initial fires of their rekindled passion were quenched.

"Your scars," he cried, "they are completely gone!"

She felt her skin and discovered he was right. All had disappeared. They stepped out of the stream and examined her body in the moonlight. No sign of any of the scars, no hint they had ever been there.

*:That is my gift to you, dearest one,:* Jucara said as she appeared beside them.

"But how?" Regnaryn asked in amazement.

Graeden understood. "Had she done it before you came back to me, you would have always harbored the doubt that I loved you only for your outward appearance. But since I cared nothing about what you called your ugliness, you now know the truth. Is that not right, old friend?"

*:I am glad to see you still remember me after all this time.:*

"How could I forget the one that came night after night into my childhood dreams to tell me of the wonders I would someday encounter? Until I came to this place, I thought you were only a child's way of making a glass window come to life. I beg your forgiveness for not believing."

She nodded. *:I am extremely happy for you both. Remember to always keep each other close and let your love guide you through the trying times ahead.:*

"You say that as if we will not see you again," Regnaryn said.

*:I have completed the tasks set for me. What happens in this world's future is up to you - the living. Say my farewells to the others, I could not bear to tell them myself.:*

The couple nodded. Jucara faded from sight.

Regnaryn buried her head in Graeden's chest and sobbed. He

held her close, allowing her to release the emotion and pain. After a few moments, she looked up at him. "I will never forget her."

"She knows that." He ran his fingers through her hair as he held her. "You are shivering. We need to get you dressed and over to the fire. After all you have been through, I will not have you catching your death from the night air."

### 

Graeden added wood to the fire. He and Regnaryn sat wrapped in each other's arms as the others slept nearby. They did not speak, not even with their minds. Holding each other was all that was needed.

Just after sunrise, Aloysius and Varlama began to stir. Regnaryn ran to them.

"Look," she cried. "The scars! They are gone! Jucara healed them all! Look!"

"That is wonderful, Regnaryn," Varlama said, yawning.

"Yes, child, it is wonderful," Aloysius said then added wryly, "but they did not matter to Graeden, did they?"

Regnaryn shook her head.

The sound of Regnaryn's voice woke the others. Trebeh stretched and rubbed the sleep from her eyes as Phrynia ruffled her feathers. Regnaryn immediately ran and hugged them.

"You must be Varlama. Aloysius, we meet again," Graeden said, bowing to the two. "I must thank you both for taking such good care of Regnaryn and for bringing her back to me. She has told me of your time together. You have obviously taught her much about her magic and powers over the last few months."

The pair nodded.

"I am glad to finally meet the young man I have heard so much about," Varlama said.

"And, I am surprised you two spoke at all," Aloysius said playfully. "It is indeed good to see you again. I take it you have not made the mistake of calling any other chetoga ferrets, have you?"

Aloysius asked.

Graeden blushed. "No, sir. I will never make that mistake again."

Aloysius nodded. "That is good to hear, boy."

"Enough teasing," Trebeh said to the chetoga.

"You two must be starving," Varlama said.

The couple nodded.

"I kept some stew aside for when you decided to join us. Let me get it," Varlama added.

"In the meantime, young lady, visit with your mother. She, too has missed you."

"Now, Aloysius," Trebeh replied, "leave her be. I understand. If I had been separated from Ayirak, I would do the same."

"For over a day, Trebeh?" Phrynia asked sarcastically. "I am not so sure you two could handle that at your age."

"Alright, perhaps not that long," Trebeh answered as everyone laughed.

# CHAPTER FIFTY-THREE

THE NEXT MORNING the group set out for Reissem Grove. As they approached the ridge that led to the Grove, they felt then heard screams of terror.

Phrynia took flight as she shouted into their minds, *:Hurry! The children!:*

The group ran to the top of the ridge. In the clearing outside of Reissem Grove, a group of children and adults were under attack by dozens of flying beasts.

Phrynia joined the other drageals to fight from the air, while her companions raced forward.

"We must do something now, we will never get to them by foot in time," Trebeh screamed.

"I cannot shield them from this distance," Varlama replied.

"I can," Regnaryn said calmly, glaring at the attackers with hate-filled eyes.

*:Go! Take the creatures down. I will protect our people,:* Regnaryn thought to the others as she stood alone.

In the next instant, the group, still running toward their friends, watched as the monsters' attacks, both physical and fiery breath, bounced away from their victims. Even more amazing, the assaults by the Grove folk reached their intended targets.

Trebeh, Varlama and Aloysius arrived, and they unleashed magical attacks at the creatures. A weaponless Graeden, felt of little use just throwing rocks, but his attacks, fueled by his anger, gained a force and precision he could not have imagined.

Too soon, the beasts recognized the lone figure on the ridge as the one foiling their onslaught. Several broke ranks and headed toward Regnaryn. Graeden screamed to her ears and mind, but she did not hear. He knew she had forsaken her own shieldings to protect the others. He feared the beasts sensed that, as well.

Graeden ran towards Regnaryn, shouting and throwing rocks at the approaching beasts. Neither action stopped them. Still, he refused to give up. His fury and rage took over. He turned toward the beasts and unleashed a barrage of fireballs from his empty hands, felling them before they could get close enough to attack his beloved.

The others gasped in awe as Jucara's prediction unfolded before them, then quickly turned back to the battle at hand.

Finally, the last of the beasts fell. Regnaryn released the shielding and dropped to her knees, exhausted. A voice suddenly boomed from nowhere and everywhere. Everyone stopped, readying themselves for another attack.

"You have not defeated me," the voice roared. "Your father tried and you know what befell him. Your end will be much worse. Twice you have slaughtered my servants. Next time we meet, your kith and kin will perish and you will watch as I feast upon the flesh and bones of this rabble you cherish and protect. I will then wrench your power from you and take it as my own."

The voice departed as quickly as it had appeared. Regnaryn immediately recognized the voice from her nightmares, the one she now knew to be the Master. But this time she felt anger, not terror.

### 

As much as the Grove folk wanted to dwell on the meaning of both the attack and the voice's words, they dared not, lest another attack was forthcoming. Instead, they gathered the dead and injured and returned them to the protection of Reissem Grove. At the same time, the most powerful of the residents, Regnaryn, Ayirak, Phrynia and others, as well as Varlama, Aloysius and Ellyss, put aside both their grief and anger to restructure the Grove's shieldings. All knew the current shieldings would not prevail if the Master and his minions decided to unleash another strike.

Graeden stood alone, stunned and confused by his own actions. The sound of woeful yowling that tore at his heart wrested him from his thoughts. He turned and saw Immic standing over the source of the keening. It was Neshya, who knelt beside several bodies. Graeden ran to his friends. The true horror of the day struck as he realized most of the dead were children and littles. When he reached Neshya, the tragedy took an even deeper turn at the realization the young yekcal was leaning over the bodies of his sisters, Nelluc and Katalanar.

Graeden touched Neshya's shoulder, shocked to feel the wet blood that quickly covered his fingers. He looked at Immic and saw he, too, was bleeding and his wing was broken.

"Nesh. Imm. You are both injured. We must get you help."

Immic shook his head. "I have tried, but he refuses to leave them."

*:Trebeh, I need your help,:* Graeden called.

Within the next instant, Trebeh appeared. By the tears streaming down her face, Graeden was sure she already knew of the loss of her daughters. But rather than go to them, Trebeh touched Immic and Neshya's arms. She did not say anything that Graeden heard, but he was sure she had spoken to the minds of the young yekcal and drageal, because they immediately came to his side.

"Graeden, take them to the healers. There is nothing they can do here," she said, her voice cracking just a little.

Graeden nodded and led his two wounded friends away.

"How did this happen?" Graeden asked as they slowly walked down the path.

Neshya shook his head and began his doleful wailing anew.

"The twins and the other littles were so excited when they heard you and Regnaryn were close by, they ran beyond the Grove's borders," Immic began, trying hard to keep his voice steady. "Nelluc and some of the others followed. We, I, never thought they would be in danger. But suddenly Nelluc mindcalled that..."

Neshya looked at the others and broke into tears. "I should have been there. This is my fault."

"And mine as well," Immic added, hanging his head.

"Stop it, both of you. Neither of you are to blame for this. Nor is it the fault of anyone in the Grove." Graeden stopped and looked at his friends. "If anyone here is to blame, it is me. I led that monster here. He followed me from the time he captured me at the inn. I have been nothing but a source of pain and sorrow since my arrival. And now, look what has happened."

"No, if we are not to blame then neither are you," Immic said.

Neshya slowly lifted his head, "You did not lead him here. He had already been in Regnaryn's dreams for months before you encountered him."

The three friends continued in silence until they reached the healers. Each had heard the others' statements, but mere words failed to absolve the young men from the guilt each felt.

### 

Sorrow filled the hearts of all in Reissem Grove. They mourned the dead, blood kin or not, and grieved at the realization that the idyllic world they had lived in these past twenty-three years would never again be the same.

The loss of innocence was made even clearer as plans were drawn to assess, train and hone the skills, magical or otherwise, of the youngest to the eldest. Should another attack occur, all vowed to be ready.

# CHAPTER FIFTY-FOUR

"YOU NEED TO VISIT your parents," Graeden said to Regnaryn the day after the burial ceremony of her siblings.

She shook her head. "How can I face them or anyone else? I not only caused the death of their children, I changed this place for evermore." Tears streamed down her cheeks, and she turned away from him. "Had I not returned, none of this would have happened. My sisters and the others would be alive, and no one would be suffering. It is my fault, all of it."

"You say you are to blame. Neshya says it is his fault. As does Immic and all the others. Your mother and the other seers curse themselves for not foreseeing the event. Ask anyone, from the elders to the children, and each of them will tell you they should have been there quicker. Their attacks should have been stronger. They should have done this, or should have done that. If this, then that. But if everyone, including you and I, look deep within, each of us knows we are not the ones at fault. The only one to blame is that monster," Graeden said.

He wrapped his arms around her. "And think of this, if the Master merely wanted to take your power, he would have taken you, taken us, on the road. No, he did this to make you suffer. To fill you with guilt and doubt. You cannot allow that to happen."

"I do not understand."

"I think after what happened with the gawara, he fears you are more powerful than he ever expected. And that thought both excites and terrifies him. I believe he is actually beginning to worry that, if you are at your best, there will be no way he can defeat you. So, he tries to chip away at your confidence and resolve. You must remain strong, and you must not allow his mind games to affect you. If you do, even a little, you will not be able to defeat him."

"I understand," she said, "but..."

He softly kissed her her forehead. "I know, the words do nothing to ease the pain he has caused. Just know I will always be here for you as will the rest of the family and everyone in the Grove. No one blames you. That fact is something you must believe. We are all here to help you in whatever way we can."

She said nothing for several moments, then turned to him. "What did he mean about my father?"

"I am not sure." He thought a moment. "In your dreams, he accused you of causing the illness, did he not?"

She nodded.

"So he has knowledge of the incident, and he is trying to use it against you."

"He is said to be adept at mind control."

"Yes, I have seen it first hand," Graeden replied.

"Is this another of his ploys? Is he just playing with me, or is there something more?"

Graeden shook his head. "I do not know. We need to learn more about him in order to find that out."

She agreed. "I fear that will be easier said than done."

Graeden nodded. "But, my love, that is a task for another day. Today..."

She looked up at him, and he gently kissed her. And for the first time since the attack, she allowed a slight smile to cross her face.

"I am ready to see my parents now."

#########

# Also by Dot Caffrey

## The World of Drejon Series
### The Power Trilogy
AWAKENED: Book One
CURSED: Book Two
CONQUEST: Book Three

# BONUS CHAPTER
# CURSED
## THE POWER TRILOGY
## BOOK 2

## A WORLD OF DREJON NOVEL
# DOT CAFFREY

# CHAPTER ONE

FROM A DISTANCE, the castle looked like every other she had been summoned to. The Seer approached, and the prickle down her back reminded her, things are not always as they appear. She stopped to enjoy the warmth of the sun – a sun she knew she would never again see. For a brief moment, she questioned herself for accepting this commission then shook her head and smirked. She of all people knew, one could not escape fate. Still, she hoped her plan might alter it, at least a little.

She squared her shoulders, took a deep breath and passed through the gate.

In the courtyard, an aura of evil permeated the very air she breathed. She pitied those without the Sight, unable to understand the fear and anxiety they constantly felt.

She paused at the castle steps. The evil now palpable. The Seer shivered and tried to imagine coming face to face with the King of Aelden. A ruler that despite his relative youth, was already renowned for his cruelty.

At the top of the stairs, a massive hulk of a man, clad in the same somber gray and black livery the messenger had worn, blocked her path. The guard, like everyone else in this place, looked grizzled and world weary. She presented the King's summons. The guard inspected both it and her, as if he did not believe this person could possess such a thing. Or, was she just imagining that degree of intelligence behind his dull eyes? He shook his head and barked at his subordinate. The second man jumped at the summons and led her through a massive door.

The Seer followed the guard through the maze of corridors meant to confuse and frighten. The man stopped. He pointed a shaking finger toward the large black door that stood before him.

She advanced and saw the source of his fear. The door was covered by a mass of hissing black snakes. *Childish illusion*, she thought and wondered how powerful this young King truly was, if he felt the need to employ such tactics. Or, was this a ploy to lull her into a sense of false security?

The guardsman nodded to the door, cringing as he watched her reach through the hissing snakes and turn the knob. The door was barely open before she felt the guard's boot press against the small of her back and impel her inside. The door slammed behind her.

The Seer peered into almost complete darkness. When her eyes adjusted, she saw a dim light at the far end of the room.

She strode across the room, easily sidestepping the low benches and tables purposely placed in her path. The room exploded with light revealing the young king seated on the throne.

*More games,* she thought and bowed her head ever so slightly.

The King was not prepared for the what stood before him – dull, mousy brown hair falling in strings across nondescript facial features, clothes just this side of tattered and, most surprisingly, youth.

Her appearance was a long-standing illusion, never penetrated over these last seventy plus years.

"I have come as directed," she said, showing neither reverence nor fear.

"I sent for a seer not a street urchin," he growled.

She did not respond.

"You? You are the great seer I have heard so much about?" He quickly masked his surprise. "You look nothing more than a common street whore, one even the lowliest brothel would turn away."

She ignored his flimsy effort to rile her. "And you appear kind and gentle." She gazed at his long curly blond hair, cherubic face and large blue eyes that gave him a look of pure innocence. "Looks can be deceiving."

He jumped up. "How dare you speak to me so?"

She smiled.

"You will address me as King, or you will not live long enough to regret your impertinence!"

She watched as he tried to regain his composure.

"King? You? Ha! A child who murders his father and eventually the true heir as well, is king in name alone."

"I could have your head for such accusations."

"Ah, but they are not accusations, they are truths."

He drew in a breath. No one, dared speak to him with such insolence.

She continued, "How may I be of service to you?"

"You know what I want. Even if you were not a seer, my messenger gave you the details of my request," he sneered.

She nodded. "Ah, yes. Your message. 'Tell me of my brother and how to get all the power in the world.' Such broad requests, so childish and ordinary. Nothing more than drivel."

"Do not toy with me. You accepted the commission, therefore, you are bound by the rules of your Guild to divulge all that you see lest your so-called gift be wrested from you, in what I have been told is a deliciously painful manner."

"Yes, it is true, I am bound to do as you have stated."

She strolled to the fireplace on the side of the room and stood with her back to him.

"Stop this foolishness, woman, and tell me what you see."

"You succeeded in killing your brother and, there is no way to possess all the power in the world. I have now fulfilled my oath."

She walked toward the door.

"That is neither answer nor fulfillment of the contract," he shouted. "Tell me the details I paid for, or I will make you suffer far worse than any oath-breaking could."

She turned to face him and laughed. "At last, the viper appears."

"Enough," he commanded. "Tell me how my brother met his fate."

"If that is your wish."

He grumbled.

"My, my dear boy," she began, knowing her irreverence would further irritate him. "You have indeed led a most despicable life, have you not? Even in the womb, you were causing your poor mother such problems."

The young King jumped from his seat. "I know my past. That is not what I have brought you here to discuss. Get to why you were summoned."

He glared and settled back onto his throne.

"Without the past, one can speak of neither the present nor future," her coy smile deliberately meant to further antagonize him. "Shall I continue or are you dismissing me from the contract?"

*So, that is her game, trying to provoke me,* he thought.

"No, you are not dismissed. Continue with your prattle if you must, but do so quickly and get to what I paid to hear or I will make sure you do not see the next sunrise."

She pondered, already knowing there would be no tomorrow for her. But, his future was unclear. She could not see him beyond this day. Would he, too, perish with her? It was times like this, she wished the Sight was more exact in what it revealed. Perhaps, if she could incite his rage to the point that both of them would succumb to his wrath, she could save the world from this monster. The Seer cleared her throat and began. She spoke of his childhood, of the merits of his father and brother, as well as the cruelty he inflicted upon those around him.

His ire grew as she chastised him for his wrongdoings.

"You are in no position to speak to me so." He snorted and waved his hand for her to go on.

"You must have thought yourself quite crafty, murdering your father and pointing the finger at your brother, the true and honorable heir to the throne. How much did it eat away at your insides, when the one you thought dim-witted slipped through your fingers time and time again," she snickered.

The King leapt from his seat, "His escape was only temporary and he suffered more in the end, did he not?"

She nodded, sickened at the pride he displayed in his cruel victory.

"He and many others. But, did your victory over him come too late? Has your fate been changed, not only by those you destroyed, but by those you did not?"

He flew across the room and seized her by the throat. He lifted her until her feet dangled inches from the ground.

"Do not try my patience any further, woman, tell me what I want to know, all that you have seen, or I will snuff out your sorry life right here and now."

He snarled and tightened his grip around her delicate throat.

She smiled, unaffected by his actions, and whispered, "If that is your wish. But, your anger will not change what is to come."

# About the Author

I was born and raised in New York, mostly on Long Island not "The City". After high school, I moved to California and then did a three-year stint in the Navy before going to college and getting a Microbiology/Medical Technologist degree.

According to my Dad, I've been a storyteller from the time I began talking (which was at a very young age). But, it wasn't until a few years ago that I decided to take my passion for writing and my love for all things magical or mythical seriously and set out to write fantasy novels.

When I'm not at my day job or writing, I enjoy creating and wearing costumes (cosplay), playing video games (though, I'm not very good at it) and watching NHL hockey and assorted other things many of which are merely time wasters. Of course, hanging out with my friends and my cats also pleasantly fills my time.

I invite you to join my mailing list by visiting my website at http://dotcaffrey.com.

You can also "Like" me on Facebook http://facebook.com/DotCaffreyFantasyAuthor

30921496R00200

Made in the USA
San Bernardino, CA
01 April 2019